Liquid Quiver

Tonya S Murray

Prologue

Early spring, 1883

As I break the soil with this pitchfork in my hands, the warm sun beats down on my back. I feel it burn my skin as I work in our garden. There is much to do, to sow; the beans must be planted, as too, the corn. Pausing for a moment to wipe the sweat from my brow, I look out toward my vast surroundings. The first signs of spring's arrival are starting to show. Wildflowers are beginning to reveal their faces; tufts of grass are getting greener by the day. Birds are busy singing while they gather materials to nest their young. The scent of lavender and sage wafts through the air—such a pleasant scent. You reminded me on the day we argued about coming to this place how I would enjoy this wonder of nature.

I do remember. It seems so long ago, that day, how silly it was to be so angry. You were only thinking of me. About getting out of that large city and going someplace more quiet and peaceful. I realized you were right. There's no one around for miles, and if you listen carefully, the babbling of the creek and its occupants seem to play their own symphony.

Breaking from my trance, I tell myself to continue. I take my place between the rows and once again resume my task.

After working for another hour or so, I pull the gift I gave you from my pocket. I glance at the timepiece; it's well past noon. With my middle protesting, I set my rake down and turn toward the house, our home. I still see you standing on the porch we painted together. As I walk forward and climb the steps, I walk past your memory. I open the screen door, and upon entering, time seems to stand still. I look to my left, at the kitchen table; your plate and cup sit there, awaiting your arrival, covered in dust and webs, never giving up their vigil.

I head to the washroom, where I pour water from the pitcher into the basin. I dab the washcloth into the cool liquid and wash the grit from my face. Orange petals scent the soap of my choice. How wonderful it feels to rinse away the earth's dust from my skin. When I am done, I walk slowly to the fire and stoke it to warm my meal. Putting the cast-iron pot on the hook, I persuade it to hang over the fire.

I go to the cupboard and reach myself a bowl. I love the pattern you picked, delicate tulips lining the rims of each one and laced with a gold border. Smiling to myself, I think of the day you brought them home from town. Worrying so, you had the team walk as if they were on eggshells. Each piece made it without a scratch. You always thought of me.

I shut the oak cupboard and open the matching drawer by my hip to reach a spoon. All the way from New York these came; I had begged you to place an order at the mercantile. How well you kept your secret. They arrived by my birthday. I take the utensils and place them next to yours. Moving to the fire, I grab a hot pad and check my stew: almost done.

As I stand up, my back aches from my morning chores. Milking the cow, feeding the team, and tending the chickens seems like a lot of work. But I perform these daily tasks with a smile on my face because I know it was your favorite time of day.

Once more I go to the fire. As I dig my portion from the black oven, I breathe in the scent of potatoes and beef. Then I shuffle to the table, where it feels so good to sit down and take the weight off my tired legs.

After unwrapping the biscuits from the gingham cloth, I blanket each one with a bit of cream butter I made just the other day. You would be so proud of me; Mrs. Wells came over for a whole day to show me how to make it just so. I thank her when I go to town to buy supplies. Selling the extra vegetables and butter does not bring much, but I make do. Having taught myself to sew, well, that helps, too. I never have needed many fancy things, but I am proud to have the few in my possession. My best dress I only wear on Sundays and our anniversaries.

I take the last of my biscuit and soak up the remaining juices from my stew. Feeling full, I draw a deep breath. I sit there and ponder the things still needing to be done.

Sighing heavily, I get to my feet and place my dish and spoon in the basin to be washed later. I put my work bonnet on my head and tie the frail ribbon under my chin. It needs to be mended when there's time; for now it will have to wait. As I head back outside to the garden, the sky is much darker than before. The clouds in the distance look to bear the threat of rain. I pick up my rake and go to work. Only a few more rows to tend and then I would be through.

I dredge along, despite the blisters starting to form on my hands. The gentle breeze causes stray hairs to whip my face. On the last row, the breeze picks up; it's much faster than before. I continue to cut the sod, which blows at my face, scattering particles in my eyes and mouth. The hem of my skirt is now pressed firmly to my legs. My poor bonnet sits sideways, trying to block my view.

I look behind me. The clouds are at my back, and the wildflowers and sage covering the prairie are now bending to the wind's will. No longer are the birds singing; they have already sought shelter from the beast at bay. My skin feels the pinpricks of the tiny drops starting to fall from the sky. Hurrying, I throw my rake to the ground. As I turn to rush toward our home, a loud clap of thunder surrounds me, soon followed by flashing light so bright the cattle scatter in the field. Drops now falling are so large they feel as if they are small pebbles being thrown from above.

Changing my path, I run to the barn instead. It is closer and just as comfortable. I tug hard on the big heavy door, and when it gives I hurry inside, shutting it behind me. The horses greet me softly glad to be out of the storm. I shake my skirt to repel the droplets; my shoes are soaked clear through. Taking my tattered bonnet from my head, I reason there's no use in mending it now; I will have to make a new one. A few strides in front of me are an oil lamp and the tin box where I find a match to light it with.

With the lamp leading the way, I find the small tack room. I sift through the shelves, taking several horse blankets to make my place to lie more fitting. Then I walk past the big geldings and pick a stall with fresh bedding, thanking myself for getting that chore done. After hanging the lamp on the nail, I lay the first blanket down. The second I fold to make a hasty pillow; the third I will use for cover. Satisfied with my efforts, I unlace my shoes and kick them off with gratitude.

All the while, the storm outside is taking over. Rain pounds on the barn roof with an unbridled intensity, as howling winds challenge the strong walls. There is no fear in my thoughts; when you built this barn, you made sure it could withstand the elements. My bed is dry, and the flame in my lamp burns strong and true.

Lying here, I smile again; you always think of me. I close my eyes, feeling a great relief to have an excuse to be done early for the day, then think of tomorrow and what it may bring. The storm outside provides a great musical background to slumber in. Between the timing of the thunder and the sound of raindrops quenching the parched earth, I am weary. As I fall asleep, I am awakened by you calling my name.

I open my eyes, and my heart begins to race. I throw back the blanket and, not minding that I am barefoot, run to the barn door. It easily gives way to my small stature. Peering out, I hear you call to me again. I look past the house to a small hill where you stand under the century-old oak tree. You are just as handsome as the day we met. The rain being more timid than before and the thunder and lightning mostly past, I run to you, as fast as I can move my feet through the sticky mud, telling myself to hurry faster so you do not leave. The distance seems much farther than before, and I yell for you to wait. You smile back and reply, "I will always wait for you forever." I close in on you, stopping just a few inches in front of you. I stare. You always did have the power to take my breath away. I am entranced by your very beauty: the color of your light eyes against your dark hair, the way your mouth curves when you smile, your strong hands that held me at night when I first heard the unfamiliar sounds of the prairie.

I move closer and cup your face in my hands. How wonderful you feel. In turn you encircle my waist with your arms and bring me closer to you. The warmth of your body against mine soothes the emptiness I feel. Speaking with soft words, I tell you how I have missed you, telling you of all the changes around our home. I lift my head and rise up on tiptoe to kiss your lips. Eternities have passed, or so it seems, since I have been able to do so.

Not wanting to miss a second of this time with you, I move my arms to embrace you around your neck. Lightning flashes all around us, a bright second in the few moments we get to share. As you move your hands to my hips, I press against you with a growing need. A soft sigh escapes your lips. You gently tug at the ribbon that holds the dress to my body. With a learned skill, you conquer it easily, and the dress falls to the ground. I too am working at the buttons on your shirt. I apologize to you for my fumbling; it's just these blisters really do hurt.

I then work on your trousers, which seem much simpler. I help you with my corset, and once more you make simple work of it. Gently you lay me down under the oak tree on a patch of grass surrounded by wildflowers. I can feel the earth's coolness at my back contrasted by the warmth of your body above me.

As you place a kiss on my forehead, then a second on my chin, I wait patiently for your lips to reach mine. Doing so pays off. As you place your lips on mine, I open my mouth to allow your tongue to enter at will; it meets mine with lustful greed. I run my fingertips slowly down your side, around to the small of your back, and then wrap my legs around your waist, trapping you against me. As I arch my body against yours, I feel you want me, too, with the heat that throbs in your very core.

Each flash of lightning exposes our sleek and damp flesh for an instant, making the water droplets seem like tiny crystals covering our bodies. How long it's been since I have held you like this, and how long is it going to be until I am able to live this again? Such a toxic addiction you are, the way you feel, taste, and love, and it runs rampant through my veins.

Not wanting to ever forget this moment, I memorize every sensation my body feels from your touch, the sighs that escape your lips, and how you whisper my name, only for me to hear. As we continue this ballet, as only lovers can, steam rises from between our bodies from the heat generated by the friction of skin on skin.

My heart is pounding in my ears with the anticipation of you and me becoming one. As you place a kiss on my ear, I feel your labored breathing on my cheek. You trail your tongue down my neck and stop with a gentle kiss at my shoulder, then rise to look me in the eye. Patiently I wait to listen to what you have to say.

"I have waited so long to tell you that I love you and how much I miss you," you tell me.

With tears in my eyes, I reply, "I love you, too. You mean everything to me. I miss you."

I close my eyes as you inch closer to kiss me. At the same moment, an ear-deafening clap of thunder rattles the ground and startles me so that my eyes open in a split second.

My eyes are blinking rapidly; my heart sinks. I am still nestled in my bed of straw, and the flame in my lamp has gone out. My shoes are right where I left them. With a heavy sigh, I turn my face against my pillow and let the tears come. They match the slow and steady pace of the rain. I cry myself to sleep.

When I hear the chickens cluck about and the birds singing and the soft nicker of the horses, I open my eyes slowly. They feel swollen, due to the emotions the night before. Realizing that today is Sunday, I roll back my blanket and gather my shoes. I must get ready.

After folding the blankets and putting them back on their shelf, I leave the barn and head to our home. As I walk to the porch, the cool mud oozes between my toes. Once inside I start a fire to warm the water for my bath. I drag the heavy wooden tub into the front room and fill it. Then I slip in, grateful to have the warm water caress my aching muscles.

After I get out, I look at my timepiece. If I do not hurry, I am going to be late. I get my Sunday dress on and finish by putting on my bonnet. In the looking glass, peering back, I look the same as every Sunday since you left. In my finest black dress that I purchased in town and the bonnet I made, complete with matching black veil, I am ready. I turn to walk out of our room, and there under the chair are your boots. I smile. I pause at our dresser to grab a ribbon. Walking through the kitchen, I see your plate and cup right where I placed them on that very day. Small reminders of you that keep me company each passing day.

I step out on our porch and walk down the steps, but I do not go to the barn. Instead I walk past our home and turn to my left, heading toward the century-old oak tree. On the way I pick a little sage and a bit of lavender; a sunflower or two will do just fine. I place these with the tulip I saved all year, and then gently I tie the ribbon around their stems. Only a few more strides until I get to see you again. I stop in front of a patch of grass under the old oak tree and begin to tell you how much I have missed you, that you mean everything to me, and I know you love me too. I also tell you that I learned to make cream butter.

Only inches away from you now, I kneel with my head down and eyes closed, clenching the bouquet. I tell you, *"It's Sunday. Do you remember what took place on Sunday? That's right we got married on that day in May of 1878. What a glorious day that was. I had a bouquet of wildflowers and tulips; you picked each one, because you knew they were my favorite. You were in your best shirt. I know you didn't mean to leave me here all alone; the accident was no one's fault. I just miss you and wanted to say I love you."*

When I open my eyes and look ahead, I place the bouquet at the bottom of the wooden cross that looks back at me. It reads, "Sam Wells, devoted son and husband. Died in the flood of 1881. To my love, I will wait for you forever at the steps of heaven."

CHAPTER ONE

Dawn

Monday morning is cool and damp. Sunrise came too early. After drinking my coffee and eating a piece of bread, I go to hitch up the team, doing chores along the way. Then I place the mended shirts and pants into the buckboard. Hopefully, I have a bit of credit left at the mercantile. Patiently I wait for my garden to grow the vegetables that I can sell for supplies. I have saved extra potatoes, though I'm grateful they are still bland when eaten every day. As well, I am not lacking in beans.

Keeping a mental tally on my goods seems to occupy most of my thoughts. There is so much to do: fences to mend due to the weather; some of the wooden posts have seen better days. As I pour milk from the pail into the pitcher, I close my eyes. How much longer can I keep up this pace? Am I going to make it from this spring into winter? Sighing, I tell myself to quit worrying; it will always work out. I may never have a moment's rest and it's tough, but this is my home now. Even though it gets lonely out here, I cannot afford to live in town. Where am I to go if I do not make it here?

After a few more minutes, I walk the pail over to the water pump, dodging the puddles as I go. In the tack room inside the barn, I reach for the harnesses. I dread doing this part alone. Thankfully the geldings, Otis and Jed, know the routine. After what seems like a lifetime, they are hitched and ready to go. I make sure I have a spare coat, then I climb into the wagon and take my seat.

Gathering the reins, I cluck to the horses, and with a jolt we are on our way. There is a soft breeze, and the sun peeks through the clouds at times, warming my face. It is really a beautiful day. The birds are out and rabbits are scurrying about. The five-mile journey to Munroe Junction never seems to take as long come spring. Just thinking about this past winter sends a cold chill up my spine. The neighbors across the way saw to it that my firewood was plenty. Such nice folks they are; I must repay them in some way. Maybe a pie or two will be sufficient. That, of course, depends on if I have enough credit. If so, then pies they shall have.

I pull the team up to the mercantile, set the brake on the wagon, and wrap the reins so they do not fall. Taking the mended shirts and pants, I walk in. The tiny bell alerts the storekeeper of my presence. A familiar face greets me as I walk in.

The gentleman behind the counter says with a soft but handsome grin, "How are you today, Ms. Wells? What a fine spring day." Cole Miller's father left him the business after he passed from sickness. How terrible it must have been to lose your only existing parent and your wife in the same year.

"I am well today, Mr. Miller, and it is a beautiful day. I came today to pick up a few supplies and to drop off the mending for this week."

"Do you have a list? I could gather this for you and credit your account toward the mending you have brought in."

"That would be wonderful. I do have a few more things to tend to, and I can be back in about thirty minutes," I assure him with a smile.

"I should have everything you need in a crate for you and have it loaded into your buckboard, if you'd like." He nods his head in approval.

"I would be delighted if you would be so kind, Mr. Miller. My wagon is right outside." I point out the window.

Since I work by myself all day, I appreciate any help that is so tenderly given. I turn and walk toward the door. Along the way, I pause and eye a bolt of fabric. I think how nice it would be to have a new dress and matching bonnet. Due to the recent storm, I had to discard my old one.

My mind wanders back to my dream. Closing my eyes to hold back the tears, I straighten my frame and take a deep breath. On opening them, I clear my mind and walk out of the store.

Back in the sunshine, I turn to walk toward the house at the end of the street. As I approach the door, I hear a small voice saying, "Come in."

I turn the knob and enter. Mrs. Wells is sitting at the table, working on her needlepoint.

"Come in, come in, my dear Tessa. How have you been doing?" Her voice sounds so small for a woman of such great strength.

"I have been doing all right; I apologize for not coming by sooner," I reply, hoping my despair does not show on my features.

With a look of wisdom, she continues her assessment of me while I stand in front of her. "My dear, judging by your hands, I would say you have been planting again. By your dress, I would also say you have been in the field." She winks and smiles.

I wish I would have chosen my other dress to wear. I looked them over and decided this one was the best out of the small selection I have. I curse myself in my mind, hoping she cannot hear my thoughts. I can almost kick myself.

"Now, dear, do not fret about it. Times are tough, especially for those who live alone. I could not do as you do," she says with a look of sincerity.

"You are correct, I have been planting." If she only knew that I have been pulling weeds by hand because the plow is broken...and I must admit my garden tool does not get me too far.

"I figured as much, you being who you are, hell-bent on taking care of that place all by yourself," she says with a stern look on her face. "Do you have time for a cup of tea? I could use some female company."

"No, ma'am, I must decline. I best get back and pick up my supplies from the mercantile. I assured Mr. Miller I would be back within the half hour."

She stands and walks over to me, embracing me in a hug, and reminds me that if I need anything, to please stop by. Thanking her, I turn to walk back through the door.

On the street I do not see many people I recognize. Are all these people new to the area? I really must come to town more often. It has been ages since I have come to just visit, and I have turned down many invitations to do so.

As I climb the wood steps to his store, Cole Miller kindly greets me at the door. "Tessa, back so soon? I have gathered all your supplies and put them in your wagon. I have also covered it with burlap just in case the weather turns bad again."

"Thank you kindly, Mr. Miller, I—"

He interrupts me, hurriedly spouts out, "Please call me Cole."

Stuttering, I finally reply, "Oh, well then, Mr. Cole, I do appreciate your kindness." Almost blushing, I have to turn away. I hear him let out a soft giggle that I think is almost giddy. Of course, it is probably just my imagination.

I say with one quick burst, as if I were short of breath, "I must bid you a good day, Mr. Miller…er, I mean Cole. I still have a lot to do when I return home."

"Good day, Ms. Wells. I hope to see you soon. Before winter at least," he says as he follows me to the door. There it is again, that boyish laugh.

Making quick time, I hurry to my wagon and gather the reins once more, looking over my shoulder to check my supplies. There they are, covered just like he said. Releasing the brake, I almost yell to the geldings as I point them toward home. The entire way back, I replay the day's events in my mind, especially the time spent at Miller's store: how odd he acted, also that I didn't see little Emma here today; I wonder where his daughter was.

After a while, I decide to let it pass with no regard. There are plenty of other things to worry about. The sun is out in full now, and most of the clouds have disappeared. The scent of wet earth still hangs in the air.

When we reach home, I pull the team and wagon up by the porch. "Whoa, boys, that will do," I say, assuring the geldings that their job is almost over. I set the brake for a second time and tend to the reins, then climb into the back of the wagon to push the crate to the back. I've learned it is much easier to unload that way. After jumping down off the back, I turn to remove the burlap.

As I stand on tiptoe, reaching into the crate, I feel something unfamiliar inside. I look around, hoping to find something I can use for a step. A block of wood comes into view. I go get it, rolling it to rest at the back of the wagon. I stand on it to see what's inside. I am taken aback by what I find.

There in the crate is the bolt of fabric I admired today at Miller's store. Instantly my mind starts to race with thoughts of why and what it was doing there among my things. Doing the math in my head, I add up the cost of what I purchased and come to the conclusion that I did not have the means to pay for the fabric. It would have taken weeks of mending for me to make such an expensive purchase.

Stunned, I reach for the fabric and take it into my hands, running my fingertips along the whole length. It feels so soft and smells wonderfully new. Blushing, I pause and think how nice a new dress would be. But

4

where would I wear it? I ask myself, laughing at the thought of wearing it in the field for plowing.

My heart sinks in an instant, and I decide to take the fabric back. I do not want to feel as if I have taken advantage of Mr. Miller. Shaking my head, I tell myself that would be the honest thing to do, to take it back. No matter how terribly bad I wanted to keep it. Mr. Miller, or Cole, couldn't possibly afford to just let this go unpaid for.

I take the fabric and walk straight for the house with the full intention of keeping it as clean as possible. I don't want it ruined by all the dust out here. I place it in my wardrobe, treating it with the utmost care; I now know it is safe. I have other things I need to bring in and put away—no more getting mushy over fabric; I have plenty to get done. Back at the crate, my heart and mind are still racing at the thought of that cursed bolt of fabric.

"What was he thinking?" I yell into the open prairie. "What was I thinking? I must be out of my mind! There is no way I could ever accept that. Something so, so…ugh!" With my temper flaring and my sack of flour almost squeezed in two from my rant, I realize it is doing me no good to take my emotions out on inanimate objects. Besides, I need all the flour to make the pies for my kind neighbors.

I fill my arms with the flour, tea, coffee, and sugar; I am going to have to make another trip—there is still the lard and the mending that was dropped off last week. I take my supplies inside and put each item in its proper place on the shelves. I go back out and lug in the heavy bucket of lard, having tucked the mending under my arm. All that's left is to put Otis and Jed away.

Heading back out a third time, I feel as if the day will never end. After taking the harnesses off and brushing them down, I put the horses in their stall. They eagerly munch at the hay I put in the manger. By the time I get everything done, the majority of my day will be spent.

Before I finish my chores, I step inside the house and grab a piece of bread and salt pork. Striding out the door with my small bounty, I give myself just a few more things to do before I can sit down for the evening. On second thought, it may be better to just go to bed.

Back in the barn, I hear the tinkering of a bell. "Yes, Maddie, I know you are hungry, too." The face covered with black and white looks at me over the stall gate, mooing in agreement. After I dig her portion of the oat hay out of the loft and milk her, I remind her that she will see me bright and early with the stool and pail.

After making sure that all is secure in the barn, I latch the door shut behind me. Feeling confident after making my rounds, I turn back to the house. I pull my timepiece from the pocket of my coat; the face reads five forty-five. Shaking my head, I wonder where the day went.

Once inside I collapse into a chair, knowing full well that I should stoke the fire. Even though it's spring, the prairie nights can still be a bit chilly. Finally I talk myself into getting up, and I move toward the fireplace where I stir the hot embers with the iron poker. I place a few bits of kindling onto the coals, waiting for it to catch, then reach for a couple of bigger logs. After I stack two or three on the fire, it doesn't seem to take long for the house to warm up.

If I weren't so tired, I would drag my tub into the room to take a bath. Instead I choose to only wash my face and hands; a bath will just have to wait until tomorrow. I get water from the pail, pour some into the heavy kettle, and then swing it over the fire. It should only take a few minutes. Not feeling too hungry, I slice another portion of bread and pork. I pour the hot water into the basin and then set the kettle on the stove to cool.

In the bedroom I sit on my bed and reach down to take off my shoes and then my dress. I slip into my gown and robe, and tightening the sash, I look into the mirror. Staring at my reflection, I think what a horrid sight I must be. My curly hair has come loose from its braid and looks frightening. It's a miracle I didn't get plumb laughed at in town today. Frustrated, I try to tame it, but it's no use; I give up. Besides it is bedtime anyway. I walk back to the basin to wash my face and hands, getting a washcloth as I pass the linen dresser. I dip the cloth in the water, then rub it on the soap and wash my face. After patting my face dry and wringing out the washcloth, I decide to sit by the fire and read my book.

My timepiece now reads six fifty-two. After closing it, I set it on the table and reach for the matches. Even with the fire roaring, I must light a lamp to see the pages. I place it on the table and get my book, trying to remember the last time I read from it. I blow on the book and watch the dust motes gently fall to the floor.

"Perhaps I will take a day and do my housework after chores," I tell myself quietly, thinking that it may be a good thing I do not have much company. How embarrassing that would be, knowing that I used to keep it much nicer in here. I make a mental checklist of inside chores that need to be done tomorrow. Dusting may be the first thing on that list.

I gather myself and return to the chair, moving it a bit closer to the fire before I finally sit down. What a day it has been: the trip to town and having to unload my supplies. That also reminds me that I have to make an additional trip to return the fabric. Not wanting to continue thinking of it, I open my book.

I open it to the marker I placed between the pages some time ago. Because it's been so long since I have read it, starting over may be my best option. I focus my eyes on the print that covers the page and begin to read.

"Come Darcy," said he, "I must have you dance. I hate seeing you standing about yourself in this stupid manner. You better dance."

"I certainly shall not. You know how I detest it, unless I am particularly acquainted with my partner. At such an assembly as this, it would be insupportable. Your sisters are engaged, and there is not another woman in the room whom it would not be a punishment to me to stand up with."

Stopping there, I say out loud, "What a fool—a selfish one at that!" My dislike for this Mr. Darcy coming out through my words, I continue reading about this pompous ass. When I reach the part where he tells of his distaste of Elizabeth, I shut the book and place it on my side table. Yawning, I close my eyes and lean my head on the back of the chair. The fire feels amazingly good as it warms my legs and feet. Sitting in the silence, I hear the sounds from outside: the crickets chirping, the owls hooting, and the occasional coyote howling.

Those are the sounds I feared the most long ago, when we first came here. My weary mind drifts off to the time when we arrived, the bare land and all the unfamiliar surroundings. It looks so different now with all the work we have done. Sighing, I tell myself to just relax. I think of the list I have prepared for tomorrow, and a giggle escapes my lips. The scene with the dust earlier made me just shake my head and think of the many things I have been slacking on.

Letting my eyes close, I try to focus on the warmth of the fire and the sound of the crackling wood as it's being consumed by the flames. I take a deep breath and relax, remembering the short passage I read and wondering what is to happen next. Maybe I will find another time to read. Maybe.

I feel a chill on my legs and awake to find the fire has died down. Leaning forward, I churn the embers and stack four or so pieces of wood on the glowing coals. Then I grab my lamp and head to bed. The small mattress is cold, so I pull up the quilt and extra blanket at the foot of my bed. After extinguishing the flame in my lamp, I close my eyes and try to sleep.

Chapter Two
Exhaustion

After tossing and turning all night, I wake in the morning to feel as if there is no sleep to be found.

Sitting on my wooden stool in the barn, I hear Maddie chewing on her breakfast. With my forehead resting on her flank, my eyes are closed. I let myself doze off, then suddenly feel something prickly slap me in the face. Startled at first, I realize it is just her tail.

"Thanks, girl, I needed that," I say, patting her side.

When finished, I take the pail of milk to the house and pour it into the pitcher. This routine, which takes place every day, is wearing on my nerves—the same thing over and over again. Although my list is waiting, I am thinking of putting it off for a few hours and instead saddling Kate, the mare I received in a trade.

An excellent idea! Considering I have not given myself much thought or time lately, a little fun could be just what I need. I quicken my pace and rush through the rest of my chores. Even I surprise myself with the excitement I now feel in my chest. I run to my room and change into more appropriate clothing to ride in. Back in the tack room in the barn, I grab a halter and lead and almost skip to the pasture. I am still in disbelief I talked myself into such a thing. This will be so refreshing!

I catch the small mare easily and lead her out through the gate, then tie her to the rail. I jog back to the barn for the saddle and blankets and back again for the headstall. I am in such a hurry! I throw the blankets up on her back, making sure they are square, and then hoist up the heavy saddle. I tighten the cinch and check my work, then remove the halter and put the headstall in its place, and lastly fasten the throat latch buckle.

"There now, see what I have accomplished?" I say proudly, with enthusiasm.

The small buckskin horse turns and stares at me with a questioning look. I am almost positive she is asking why.

"Oh, it's not that bad," I reassure her as I put the reins around her neck. "Besides we will not be gone for long—just around the farm, OK?"

I reach for the saddle horn and place my foot in the stirrup, easing myself into the seat. With my right foot now in place, I nudge Kate forward with slight pressure from my heels. She plods ahead at a ridiculously slow pace. I get the feeling I could make better time walking.

"Just enjoy yourself for once—you need something like this to lift your spirits," I scold myself out loud.

As I take a deep breath, the mare turns her ears back, listening to me talk to myself.

"You must think I am crazy, don't you?" I ask her. "Sometimes it just gets so lonely with no one to talk to, well I hope you don't mind." I realize my babbling means absolutely nothing at this point.

I close my eyes and think of how quiet it is out here. The only sound I hear is the sound of my horse's hooves thumping on the soft earth, which brings back memories of riding with my pa when I was young. He was the one who taught me how to saddle my own horse and also how to care for them. After all, being a blacksmith, he had a gentle way with horses.

I open my eyes, chuckling at the memory of when Mama yelled at Pa when he let me race my horse against a boy, Tate Wilson, and his horse.

"Eli Tucker Jackson, that girl has no business racing horses!" Ma yelled at the top of her lungs.

Olivia Rose Jackson was not only my mama but the town's only schoolteacher. She wanted me to have a proper feminine upbringing. Being their only child, I think I am perhaps a little bit of both Ma and Pa. Reading, writing, and arithmetic have been a part of my life since I was five. Mama instilled in me a love for books and for putting my thoughts on paper, both of which I truly enjoy. I never did like the arithmetic; it just wasn't as interesting.

Pa was the one who gave me the sense of adventure, a taste for freedom. I didn't just go riding with him, he took me fishing in the pond and let me accompany him to the livery. There I got the chance to brush the stabled horses, as well as grain them. I watched him as he nailed each shoe on carefully with skilled precision; he was truly a master of his trade. It always seemed to upset Mama when Pa and I came home and I had soil and soot on my face. My hair was full of knots, and she had to work extra hard come bath time to scrub my face clean.

If I didn't have so much to take care of here and money weren't so hard to come by, I would get on the train and travel to see them for a visit.

"Who am I kidding? I rarely make it into town for the same reason," I whisper to the wind.

Once again the mare is the silent partner in my conversation. Feeling as though we have gone far enough and that I must get back to do my chores inside the house, and against my better judgment, I decide to let the mare stretch her legs and run home. I take my seat and turn her around, then bend slightly forward and squeeze hard with my heels.

I yell, "Go, Kate!" encouraging her.

With that she lunges ahead and steals her freedom, running as fast as her legs can carry us. Sagebrush and trees start to blur as we pass. I hear her sucking the air deep into her lungs as she approaches her top speed. The wind deafens me as it rushes over my face; I feel the goose bumps prick on my skin. The pure rush of adrenaline is running just as fast as the mare that's eating up the ground under me. Tears are now streaming down my face. How exciting! It has been ages since I have done this. If Tate Wilson were here now to race, I would have beaten him for sure.

With home fast approaching, I gently pick up my reins and slow the mare down to a trot, then to a walk, so she has a bit of time to cool off before we arrive. She is breathing rapidly but looks to have had as much fun as I did. I rub her neck and give her my gratitude.

After making sure the mare is cooled down, I step off and repeat the previous process, only in reverse. With the halter and lead now in place, I loop the slack over the rail. While I loosen the cinch, I explain to Kate that having a great morning like this one tempts me to have even more. Sliding the saddle and blankets off her back, I walk them into the barn and put them away in the tack room.

Walking back from the barn, I tote a curry comb and a stiff brush to clean her up and a pail of grain to feed her. She perks her ears as she looks at me, and I know I have her full attention when she nickers softly as I walk in her direction.

How many times I have wondered how an animal spoiled to having her own grass pasture could gobble up grain in a matter of seconds. After tending to her, I walk her back and put her away. I leave the halter on the wood gate, considering the thought that she and I may be doing that again real soon. Now it's time for housework and a few pies.

Chapter Three
The Invitation

A couple of hours later, a small portion of the house is tidy again. The dust is gone, only to return at a later time. After putting on my apron and washing up, I gather all the ingredients to make the pies. I start with the crusts. I am in a wonderful mood; the ride really did me some good. I measure the flour into the bowl, then add the salt. Next I take a fork and mix the two together. Then it is time to add the lard and cut it in. The water soon follows.

After sprinkling the tabletop with a bit of flour, I plop the dough down and begin to roll it out, adding flour when needed. I hum a tune as I shape the mass into a flattened circle. When I finish that task, I begin again on a second crust.

I lay the bottom crust into the shallow pan and press it gently, then trim the edges and add a bit of sugar and cinnamon. Wiping the excess from my hands onto my apron, I walk to the stove and check it. I use a hot-pad holder to open the door, checking to make sure there is plenty of heat to bake the pies. I decide it will be ready in a few more minutes and return to the table.

Grasping the jar of apples by the lid, I twist as best as I can. The stubborn lid doesn't give an inch. Trying again even harder, it still does not budge.

"Just my luck," I spew into my empty surroundings. Looking about the room, I search for a tool of some sort.

"Got it!" I exclaim. There on the mantle is a pair of pliers used to build fence. Maybe those will work. I put the jar on the table and open the pliers, placing the metal teeth on the lid's ring. I try with all my might, but I get nowhere. Frustrated, I try again; again nothing happens. Despite all my efforts, all I have accomplished is to bend the ring on the jar. I take a deep breath to try and calm down, and I say through clenched teeth, "You best open up or so help me!"

I put the pliers on a different part of the ring and heave with all my will and strength, and again nothing happens.

"That's it! You will come open—so be it!" I scream in frustration.

I bear down on the jar with so much determination, my arms start to shake, and I can feel my face getting hot. Today is not the day to mess with Tessa Wells!

My teeth are closed tight and my brow is furrowed. Giving it my last-ditch effort and every bit of strength, I scream at that cursed jar in complete madness, "Dammit, dammit, dammit!"

At that moment the lid pops off with such force, it knocks me off balance and into my table. Trying to catch myself, I stick my hand into the middle of the soft doughy crust I just made. I fall backward then and reach to steady myself. But I grab the tablecloth instead. I crash to the floor, still holding the open jar of apples squeezed tightly in the nook of my arm, lying flat on my back in the middle of the floor.

The cloth now covers the middle of my body. Flour is everywhere: in my hair, on my face, and down my shirtwaist. The pie pan that held my crust only moments ago, now sits to the left of me, on the floor. As for the apples, they, too, are in my hair. The front of my shirtwaist is soaked with the juice from the jar of fruit. Feeling defeated, I turn to stare at the ceiling and sigh, "Damn."

I hear a knock at my door and freeze where I lie. Who on earth could that be? I wait a whole minute, then hear the knock again.

"Oh no!" I whisper. Maybe if I lie still as could be, they will go away.

"Tessa, are you in there?" a voice says through the door. "Emma and I were riding by and thought we would check and see how you were doing."

I mull over the sound of that voice, then recognize it. It wasn't just any man; it was Cole Miller. The only one I knew who had eyes like that and features capable of making a woman stare. With the information my brain just processed, a feeling of panic washes over me. What am I to do?

"Just a minute, I will be right there!" I call back from my side of the door. *Heavens to Betsy, what am I to do?* I think. Sitting up off the floor, the apples fall to my lap. I roll up the tablecloth and shove it under the table.

"Tessa, are you sure everything's all right?" he asks again.

"Yes, one more minute please," I reply. Goodness, hang on a second. Rushing furiously, I try to make myself look decent, then I decide to give up. It is no use; there is too much of a mess. My nerves are already shot. I might as well answer the door. Practically running to get there, I step into something mushy. I pay no mind, reach for the knob, and pull the door open.

"Cole? How are you doing? Emma, I am glad to see you as well," I say as if nothing at all was out of place. Cole's face wears a look of shock. I try not to break my concentration; I am playing my part well. The giggling of a five-year-old seems to bring him back from his confused state.

"Emma! Do not laugh at Ms. Wells. That is rude and unkind," he scolds the little girl. When he looks back at me, his eyes reveal that he is having a terrible time keeping his laughter at bay.

"Are we interrupting something? It looks to me like you have had a disagreement with a pie, and it won," he says with humor.

"Well, Mr. Miller, if you would have shown up about ten minutes before, you may have been able to assist me. Seeing as how you are obviously late, I took it upon myself to quarrel with the jar of fruit. As you can see, I do not need help."

"Ms. Tessa, I could help you make a pie if you would like. My mama taught me how before she was taken by the angels to heaven," Emma informs me in her tiny voice.

"Emma, I'm sure Ms. Wells has everything under control—maybe another time," Cole tells his daughter.

"But Pa, aren't we at least going to ask her? We rode out here all this way."

I look back at Cole; I am also curious as to what Emma is talking about.

"Now, Emma, Ms. Wells looks entirely too busy right now," he tells her.

"But Pa, I want her to come with us!" the little girl says as she stomps her foot. Having never seen her throw a tantrum, I decide she must be serious.

"What is she talking about, Cole?" I ask with great interest. "If the two of you rode all this way, I would dislike the idea of you leaving before stating your intentions for coming."

Before he can gather his words, Emma beats him to it. "My pa woke me up early to come here and ask you if you, Ms. Tessa, would come with us to the spring social in town. Everyone will be there," she adds.

With a feeling of pure disbelief, I answer, "I don't know what to say, it's been so long. I…I have nothing to wear." I stumble through my words.

Emma now has her bottom lip stuck out and a frown on her face. Feeling terrible, I make a quick decision to take the little girl up on her offer.

"On second thought, Emma, I would love to come; it will be an honor to meet you there."

She smiles and looks at Cole with a crooked brow and asks, "But Pa, weren't we going to pick Ms. Tessa up?"

To which he replies as he glances my way, "Sure we can—that is if she will be so kind to let us escort her to town."

"That would be great," I say. "What time will I be seeing the two of you again?"

"How about eleven o'clock?" Emma answers.

"Wonderful, I will be ready then," I tell her. That puts a smile back on her face.

"Thank you, Ms. Tessa. My pa has wanted to ask you for a long time," she confesses.

Blushing, I smile at her. Judging by how warm my face is at the moment, I am surprised the apples that still cling to my hair are not half baked by now.

Looking down at Emma, Cole takes her hand and says, "Well then, come on, Emma Mae, we must get on our way. Ms. Wells looks as if she has had quite a morning. We should let her get back to her pies." He picks up his daughter.

Emma has the same features as her father. The dark eyes and hair and her porcelain face almost make her look like the dolls out of the fancy books I've seen.

"Good-bye, Ms. Tessa, see you soon." She smiles as she waves.

"Bye, Emma, and you, too, Cole. Thank you for the visit. Oh and Emma, I would most enjoy the day when you come by to show me the proper way to make a pie," I tell her.

The Invitation

She smiles a wide grin back in my direction. Cole places her on his bay gelding, then mounts and takes his place behind her. Tipping his hat, he turns his horse toward home.

I shut the door and laugh out loud. I have to wonder what a sight I am. On top of it all, now I am going to the social in town. Oh, the things I get myself into.

A couple to three hours later, I have cleaned up, and two pies are cooling on the table. With a bath out of the way and the treats done, I am able to do the evening chores. After putting my sweater and shoes on, I get to the chores.

Once back inside, I go to my room and investigate what I am to wear this Saturday for the social. I open my trunk and take out the few dresses I own.

"Terrible, just terrible!" I exclaim.

Frustrated that I do not have anything decent to wear, my thoughts turn to the bolt of fabric. I really shouldn't use it; returning it is still the best thing to do. I open my wardrobe and take the fabric out. I unfold it a time or two so I can examine the beautiful pattern. Then I see something pinned to it that I hadn't noticed before.

It is a small scrap of paper folded in half. After removing the pin out and releasing the paper, I open it to see what it says:

Dear Tessa, I watched you the day you had come into my store. It touched me the way you longed for it, so I placed it into your things at no charge. Please accept this, not as charity, but rather as an invitation.

If you would like, Emma and myself are asking you to accompany us to the spring social, we would be delighted.

Your Friends,
Cole and Emma Mae Miller

Liquid Quiver

How did I not see this note before? There is no way I can return the fabric now. This leaves me no option but to sew a new dress. Excitement fills my thoughts—how wonderful! I get a new dress!

I rush to my trunk and retrieve my sewing basket and scissors. Then I light my lamp and go to the fireplace, where I make a hasty fire by tossing logs, one after another, onto the half-burned pieces still in there. Then I run to get my things from my room and gently place them on the table. There are butterflies in the pit of my stomach from the excitement. I best get started now if I am to be finished by Saturday.

After cutting the right amount of fabric for my dress, there is plenty left over to make a matching bonnet. In my basket is a bit of lace left over from a previous project that I can use as well. This will be the finest dress I have made yet. I turn to the stove and put a kettle of water on top to heat. I usually do not drink coffee at this hour, but it sounds good at the moment. After finding some ribbon for my bonnet, I am satisfied that all the materials are in place.

I get my coffee and add a bit of sugar and cream. Then I set to work. The pattern on the fabric is a wonderful cream-colored background with little pink roses. At the bottom, I will sew a lace hem, and at the wrists of my dress, I will sew lace cuffs. I have the prefect buttons for the back of the neck: three, to be exact. The ribbon I have is a lovely shade of pink that matches the pattern well. I'll use a bit for the bonnet, the remainder to lace up the back of the dress.

In the basket is another roll of white eyelet lace I plan on using to line the cutout portion on the bust. This will be grand! Working on the dress gives me a zest to live again; it has been lifetimes since I traveled to town for just fun. The best part is I do not have to hitch up the team—such a tedious task, and besides I would get all soiled doing so.

I will bathe in my lavender soap for the occasion, and Mother's string of pearls will complete my wardrobe. Refilling my cup, I set to work a second time. A few more minutes of work and I better call it a night. With this much excitement, I am sure to be worn out come morning.

* * *

The Invitation

After just a little more than two days' worth of sewing, I am finished. When I put the last button in place, my dress looks exquisite. Carefully I check my work for any loose or stray ends. Stepping back, I admire my creation. With only a finger sore from a few pinpricks, I feel I fared well. Since it is well into the day, I may allow myself a short nap; I want to be well rested for the big day tomorrow.

Yawning, I take my dress, neatly fold it, and place it in my trunk. Then I put all my sewing materials off to the side. I glance outside; everything seems to be doing fine. I let my hair down from its bindings, lie on the bed, and close my eyes.

I can smell the fried chicken and the warm bread rolls at the social. There are salads galore. The tables are lined up one after the other. People on both sides are getting their portions and filling their plates. Pies of apple, peach, and meringue look scrumptious. There are straw bales for those who wish to sit and enjoy watching the couples dancing.

Everything is decorated with spring flowers and beautiful ribbons in shades of lavender, mint, and cream. Children play while the adults visit and catch up on the happenings of the prior winter.

"Tessa, would you like to dance with me?" Cole asks as he extends his hand.

I look around to see if anyone is watching, then accept. A small quartet provides the entertainment. Mr. Webster, an older gentleman who helps at the hotel, is playing the banjo. Middle-aged Mr. Davis, who runs the post office, is strumming the guitar. Ms. Gustav and Mr. Rigatti are quite the pair: he plays the accordion and she the violin. Though they will never admit it out loud, the affection between them shows. Both being from other countries, I believe they share things in common.

As we reach the stage built by the townsmen, Cole embraces me gently while we await the next song. A waltz is chosen, and he begins to guide me about the dance floor with a masculine grace. I feel as if we are floating and are the only ones hearing the music. His eyes are looking into mine with such intensity I almost feel them burn right through me. Trying to look away, I realize I am in a trance-like state. It is just he and I, no one else.

Liquid Quiver

As the dance goes on, I see a figure fast approaching. A woman's figure, I can almost make out her face. As she comes into view, sudden panic sweeps over me.

"What do you think you're doing?" Her voice is harsh and cold. "To betray my own son this way, you Jezebel of a woman!" she yells for all to hear. "How dare you!" she spits out like a venomous snake. With that, she raises her hand to place a blow on the side of my face.

"No, please!" I shout as I wake up from my nap. Sweat sits on my brow, and tears run down my face. With my chest heaving and my hands shaking, I realize it was a dream. I blot my forehead with my sleeve and take a moment to gather my wits. Never before have I considered what someone may think of me for not going to the social alone.

Even though it has been two long years since losing Sam, I would never taint his memory that way.

"What will she think? Will she even be there?" I whisper to the empty room. Fear now ruling my thoughts, I almost feel like crying. What am I to do? I look out my window; it is almost dark outside. I better tend to the chores; it's getting late.

When I come back from outside, I do not care if I even have supper. After stoking the fire, I go right to bed. It is only a bit after seven, but the extra rest will be greatly appreciated. Finished with my nightly routine, I finally settle in. My thoughts take over, telling me not to dwell on it, that everything will turn out just fine. As I drift off to sleep, I wonder if I should break my word and not go to the social. But after imagining what Emma's face might look like, I decide against it.

CHAPTER FOUR

Patience

With the coyotes yapping and the owls hooting, sleep is hard to find. When I finally doze off, I don't dream anything at all.

Opening my eyes, I realize it is still dark out. I wonder what time it is getting to be. I rise and put on my wrap, then strike a match to light my lamp on the nightstand. The warm light fills the room, and I search for my timepiece. I focus in the dim light; it reads four thirty. I rub my eyes, wondering if it is showing the correct time. It's never been a minute off, so I decide that I am the one who is wrong.

"It is way too early to be up. Oh well, if I were to go back to sleep, I may not get up in time to have everything done before the spring social," I admit.

I take my lamp and proceed to the front of the house. The fire is completely out. I set the lamp on the mantle and select a few pieces of kindling to use to rebuild the fire. I pull a match out of the tin, strike it, and attempt to light the small sticks.

Testing my will, the fire is slow to burn. I crumple up a sheet of newsprint and place it at the bottom of the wood. After the flames consume it, they go on to the larger logs. It seems like forever, but eventually a fire breaks out. Crouched in front of the fireplace shivering, I put even more logs on the inferno.

I get my kettle and refill it with water. I am looking forward to the first cup of coffee. A little while later, the scent of coffee fills the room. Sitting in my chair, sipping the hot brew from the mug in my hand, I watch the fire. In just a short while, I will tend to chores and then bathe to get ready. The coffee tastes delightful, and I enjoy the crackle of the fire and the warmth it gives.

Liquid Quiver

My thoughts turn to the dream. Will she really think I would be that crude? Worried, I change my thinking in a hurry. After not going to the social for two years now, I think it's time to once again enjoy life with friends. To get out a little more when time allows.

The horseback ride really lifted my spirits. I have decided I need more of that. As Mama used to say when I ended up cooped up in the house and under her feet, "Get out and blow the stink off you." I hated that saying, and she used it more than I cared for.

I get my chore clothes on and head out to get them done as soon as possible. The chickens are still in their coop with it being so dark out. None of the animals expects breakfast this early; Maddie doesn't even greet me at her stall gate. She is lying on the bed of straw and only glances at me to let me know she knows I am there. I hurry through the chores.

Entering the house after I complete the chores, I throw my shoes to the side and head to the back of the house where my tub is kept. It's dark and cool, almost dungeon-like. When I open the door, it squeaks from lack of use. I stand alone in the doorway. This room is two to three times bigger than the other room. Its massive fireplace can consume unlimited amounts of wood. Most of the furniture occupies this space. Everything is covered with sheets; it looks like ghosts live here.

The bookshelves that were my grandma's are here, along with her books. My piano, hope chest, and jewelry boxes are here as well. In the small boxes, the jewelry that has been worn by the women before me is kept safe within the tiny wooden walls. Maybe this year I will bring every-thing back out and to life, uncover the furnishings and release them from their dormant state.

I locate my wooden tub, grab the end, and drag it through the doorway into the other room. I begin to heat water on the stove and over the fire. After filling the tub, I sprinkle soap shavings into the water. Then I step in and let the hot water soak away my worries. After washing my hair and face, I get a small brush and get under my nails. It would not be proper to attend such a gathering with dirty hands. I will also pay attention to my feet. Everything must be in order and look proper.

Butterflies are filling the pit of my stomach, and my hands are getting shaky. I stand up to rinse off and wring out my long hair, silently thanking myself for building a hot fire. I wrap myself in a towel and use a second for my hair, then step out. The tub of water will have to be dealt with later. I move to the fire to dry off a bit. My biggest task will be to tame my hair; it is going to take a lot of hairpins.

The sun is now shining through the windows, and I hear nature talking outside: what a gorgeous morning. After getting another cup of coffee, I go to my room. With my comb I work the tangles out of my tresses. I apply a little lavender oil afterward to give my hair a bit of shine, and the scent has a calming effect. Then I tie it back with a small piece of ribbon to dry. I want to get started on getting dressed.

With my bloomers and camisole on, I sit in front of my mirror. I dab a little bit of lotion from a small jar and rub it on my cheeks. From a second jar, I take some lotion and place it under my chin, smoothing it over my shoulders and down my neck onto my chest. The scent is lavender, of course; how I love that scent, even though it took me a while to get used to it. Then I get to work on coloring my eyelids. I choose a shade that is a warm earthy tone to match my green eyes. Using a pressed powder, I blot my face. A fair pink lip stain is best, I think; I do not want to look like one of the girls down at the saloon—I just want to look like me, only better.

As for my hair, I part it in the middle and braid it back on each side to the nape of my neck, leaving the length to hang freely. I use a bit of ribbon to secure the braids. From my closet I get the white lace-up-style boots I wore the day Sam and I got married. Telling myself it's all right, I go sit on the edge of my bed.

Then I slip on my dress—a perfect fit. The sleeves look lovely with the added lace, and the rose pattern is glorious on the cream background. The bust is cut just enough to be feminine, but not ghastly. Reaching around to the back, I tighten the ribbon and make a nice bow. I finish by closing the buttons at the back of the neck. Then I pull on the boots.

After lacing each one, I stroll over to my mirror. To my surprise, I do not recognize the woman who peers back. I have not dressed in this fashion for years. I attach the ends of the necklace behind my neck. My shawl is the only thing I lack. I place it over my forearm and leave my room to sit by the fire.

I check my timepiece; it's only ten fifteen. Inhaling a deep breath to relax my nerves, I notice the butterflies are now even worse. I sit in the silence and begin to fidget. I open my timepiece again; it reads ten twenty-three.

"Gracious!" I say impatiently, leaning my head back against the chair.

To pass the time, I have a quiet conversation with myself. I reassure myself that my nerves will not get the best of me, and I give no time to worrying about my dream. Today is about fun. If I can't stop dwelling on the dream, my mind is sure to spin out of control to the point of sheer craziness.

Ten thirty-five. "My goodness! Can time move any more slowly?" I shout.

My impatience gets the better of me. I stand up, wrap my shawl around my shoulders, and move to the porch to enjoy a bit of the warm sunshine.

Ten forty-eight. No sign of Cole and Emma yet. Just as I start to scan the horizon, I spot movement. Sure enough, it is them, and he has the horses moving at a pretty good clip. Within a few minutes, they are only a few feet away from the porch.

"Good morning, Ms. Tessa, how are you? Do you like my dress?" Emma asks as she stands and bows.

"I sure do, Emma, it's beautiful," I assure her.

"Good morning as well, Tessa," Cole chimes in with a handsome grin. "You look wonderful this fine spring day. Are you ready?"

"Why, thank you, Cole, I am ready. As usual you look very handsome indeed," I reply, seeing him glance to the ground in a hurry.

He exits the buggy and walks around to help me get inside. His pants are freshly starched, topped with a dark blue shirt and a black jacket. The hat he wears is not the same hat as before. This one is more formal looking.

I think he is rather handsome, his dark hair contrasted by his deep blue shirt, his tanned skin making him even more attractive. I can't stop myself from staring.

After we're on our way, Emma asks curiously, "Ms. Tessa, are you going to dance today?" I was happy she piped in to break the thoughts swirling inside my head.

"I would like to, Emma. I think I remember how. It has been quite some time since I have done so."

"How can you forget how to dance? Seems silly," she retorts, her face looking quizzical.

"Sometimes when a person does not practice, they have a tendency to forget," I tell her.

"Are you going to dance with my pa? If so, you may have to wait, Ms. Tessa. He promised me the very first one."

"Oh, I don't mind, I'm sure you are a wonderful dance partner."

With her eyes gleaming and her cheeks plump from her smile, she points toward our destination.

When I glance in that direction, my stomach almost flutters away without me. Judging by the number of buggies, the whole town must be there. I wonder if my feelings of fright are due to the number of people—or the uncertainty of just one. After Cole stops the buggy, he gets down and secures the horses. He returns to first help Emma out, and then he turns to me.

Gathering my hem, I am able to step down when he offers his hand. I place mine into his; there is kind warmth to his touch. He holds my hand with a firm but gentle grip. I am taken aback by the comfort that washes over me.

"Are you two ladies ready to have some lunch?" he asks.

"Yes, Pa! Then you and me can dance!" Emma spouts out while giggling.

"It's 'you and I,' Emma. Don't you remember your studies?" he says.

"Aw, Pa, I do not like to study," she replies with a pout.

"Well, we can worry about that later. Shall we show Ms. Tessa a good time?" he says with honest enthusiasm.

At that very moment, Emma takes my hand into one of hers and then takes her father's with the other one. "Come on, come on. Hurry, everyone's waiting!" she demands as she rushes the two of us along.

Cole looks my way, and I glance back his way. It is then that I notice we are both laughing and smiling. The butterflies are gone now. Being with Cole and Emma brings a feeling of ease and comfort, almost as if I belong here.

As we approach the festivities, I am a little shaken by the surroundings. There are spring flowers for decoration. Ribbons of lavender, mint, and cream. There are also the straw bales—all so familiar, just like in my dream. I suddenly feel anxious, so much so that I am startled when Cole calls my name.

"Tessa, I'm so sorry, I didn't mean to scare you like that. Is everything all right?" he asks kindly.

"Yes, of course. I guess I am just a bit nervous. It has been some time since I have been to the social."

"All right then, if you are sure nothing is wrong, ready to eat?" he asks.

"I am more than ready to eat, starving practically." All the while I am hoping he cannot hear the uneasiness in my voice.

Walking toward the tables, I see food lined up on all sides. Cole hands me a plate and utensils, then does the same for Emma. I choose some chicken, potatoes, and a bit of salad. At the end is a basket of fresh rolls. Using my knife, I slice a bit of butter and put it on my plate. Then I stand to the side, waiting for Cole and Emma.

"Where shall we sit, Ms. Tessa?" Emma asks in her small voice.

"How about we let you pick it out?" I reply. Before I even finish, she is walking in the direction of her choice. Reaching a table that is covered with a wonderful spring print, Emma takes a seat and indicates Cole and I are to sit on either side of her. As we begin to eat, others start to come by and visit, to see how things have been going. The chicken is excellent. I haven't had fried chicken in so long, and it leaves me longing for another.

"Tessa Wells, what have you been up to? I haven't seen you in ages!" a woman's voice shouts from behind me.

Turning, I see my dearest friend, Maria Grayson. I stand up, rush to her, and hug her with deep sincerity.

"Maria, how have you been, and don't you look beautiful," I say with excitement.

"As do you, Tessa. I am all right. Been wondering if you still existed here. I was hoping you would come. Did you come all this way alone?" she asks.

"No, Cole and Emma Miller invited me along with them for today," I reply.

There it was—exactly what I expected—the look of shock all over Maria's face.

"Oh my, I...I don't know what to say," she stammers. "Tessa that's great." She embraces me so tight I can hardly breathe. "I will let you get back to your table then. I promise to see you before the day is through," she says with a wink before disappearing into the crowd of hungry people.

I once again take my seat and start on the salad on my plate. "I am very sorry to have gotten up so abruptly," I say apologetically. "I didn't mean to be rude."

"Tessa, please, no need for apologies. This is a day for fun, family, and friends," Cole says.

"Are you going to make Ms. Tessa a part of our family, Pa? I would really like that, then we wouldn't have to get up so early to make pies," the little girl says with such honesty that Cole has a difficult time with the bite of food he placed in his mouth. His face is even a bit flushed from the innocent notion of his young daughter.

"Now, Emma, such thoughts are sure to embarrass our guest," he manages to say.

"Who's our guest? Ms. Tessa? I thought she was our friend."

"Tessa is our friend. You must remember we asked her to come with us today. That makes her our guest."

Seeing that Cole was clearly struggling with keeping Emma's curiosity at bay, I decide to change the subject.

"Emma, how are your studies going? Do you like attending school?" I ask out of the blue. She takes a bite of food—and her time to answer.

"It's just Pa and me—Pa and I, I mean," she finally answers. "I don't like the arithmetic, but the reading is fine."

"Very good," I compliment her. She is very focused on the remaining food on her plate. Cole, with a grateful look on his face, and I get back to eating as well. I open the roll, spread a bit of butter on it, and take a bite. The butter tastes familiar, almost as if I could tell someone the exact ingredients used to make it. Then I realize she is here.

My heart starts to beat faster, and my ears begin to throb in rhythm with my pulse. Inside my head I am trying to tell myself to calm down, that things are going to be OK. As I finish the last bite on my plate, I remember my dream. But I clear my mind swiftly and put a smile on my face. Today is a perfect day, being surrounded by people. Some are friends and some are strangers; regardless, all I know is that I am not alone. There is the sound of laughter and voices and children playing.

"Pa, can we dance now?" Emma's voice breaks my concentration.

"Sure, are you ready then?" Cole replies.

Nodding her head, she turns to me and asks, "Can you excuse Papa and me for a minute, Ms. Tessa?"

"Of course. If the two of you don't mind, I may try to catch Maria while the two of you dance," I say.

"Please do," Cole responds. "I'm sure it has been ages since the two of you have been able to visit."

He escorts his daughter to the stage, then gently picks her up and starts to sway with her from side to side. You could hardly tell that she was a few feet shorter than her partner.

I glance about the crowd, trying to spot Maria. When I see her, I notice she is visiting with an older couple who I believe own the homestead next to her. Instead of interrupting, I decide to walk around the crowd and see if I recognize anyone else here. Most of the people I see when I come to town for my supplies. There's the banker and his wife, the cook from the hotel, and the postman, just to name a few. As I pass through, everyone introduces themselves and bids me good wishes for the day.

I eye the table where the punch sits and walk over to it. I ladle some into a small cup for myself. The cool liquid is rather refreshing. As I refill it, a female voice speaks to me.

"Good day, Tessa. I'm surprised to see you here. How are you?" the voice says warmly.

I turn around and answer, "Good day to you, Mrs. Wells. I admit that I am glad I came today. Faring well, you?" I ask, trying to stay calm.

"I am doing fine. Would you care to join me for a walk?" she asks.

"Yes, I can join you," I reply. My eyes search about for Cole and Emma. The two of them are still dancing. She must have noticed I was seeking something, as if I would have been missed. Her eyes search to see perhaps if anyone is missing me.

"Unless of course you are busy, Tessa. I do not wish to keep you away from your friends," she explains dryly. With that said, she and I begin to walk. She wraps her arm in mine. Patiently I wait to hear what she has to say, good or bad.

She begins, "Tessa, I am a bit worried about you. Being out there all alone, you need help."

I cut her short. "Wait, please, I do not wish to be a burden, I cannot move to town." I am trying to make her realize I am going to stand my ground, without being rude to her.

"No, I know you don't—that is not what I was implying. I see that you were sitting at the table with Mr. Miller and his spitfire daughter, Emma," she says.

Stopping her short and with no hesitation, I retort with what's on my mind. "It's not what you think! I would never disregard Sam's memory like that. I'm no Jezebel!" I'm almost screaming in her face.

As she stares back into my eyes with a blank expression, she is quiet for some time. Finally she says, "Maybe you do not know me as well as I thought. What would ever give you the idea that I brought you over here to tell you such a thing?"

With tears threatening my eyes, I offer my explanation. "I had this dream about coming today. It was so real—the food, the decorations, everything. Then there was you, I was so frightened that you would think ill of me for coming and that you may hate me for accepting Cole's offer." I feel awful and like I have done wrong, so I bury my face in my hands.

"Tessa Ann Wells, I love you like you were my own daughter. I brought you away from the crowd to tell you that I am so happy for you," she tells me.

As I pick my head up from my hands, I almost cannot believe what she said. I look into her eyes; they are filling with moisture. Suddenly I feel selfish—never giving her feelings a second thought where I was concerned.

"I had no idea, truly I didn't," I confess. "You must believe me."

She proceeds to explain her feelings about everything. "Tessa, it hurts me to see that you live your life in sadness. Let me take some of that weight you carry. When you and Sam married, and even though his death meant losing my only son and child, I have not lost you. Your strong will is amazing; I would have given up long ago."

As she tells me her most secret of thoughts, I begin to admire her even more. Here I thought her to be the opposite. It is my own fault I could not see the real woman behind the mask she wore. I didn't see any of it. After Sam's passing, I stopped seeing my friends and my family, sinking into a dark blackness that was cold and full of misery. Now I realize that I not only shut out the world but hid from it, too—all the while thinking I could make it without the people who care for me in my life.

All I can do is thank her for the honesty she gives me at that moment, for making me really think about what is important.

"Thank you," I say. "Not only have you helped me realize my life is worth living, I now know that being with friends and family really does matter. If it wasn't for you, I may have gone on living my life the same as I have been."

"I am so glad you have figured that part out. We have all missed you, Tessa. Missed seeing you and hearing you laugh. I know in my heart you loved Sam; however, he wouldn't want you to spend the rest of your life in sadness. It's time to move on, experience new things, and cherish every day you have here."

Her words are full of wisdom and take a deep hold in my mind. I feel as if a heavy burden has been lifted, a great weight cast from my shoulders. Embracing her tightly, I thank her from the bottom of my soul. When I release her, I see that she, too, is smiling. She looks at ease, younger even than before.

"Come now, Tessa, there is much to enjoy today. Let's get back so we are not missing our chance to have a good time," she says, giggling. Arm in arm, we walk back with a lightness in our steps.

Thank goodness I've finally escaped the entrapment of a lingering past. I feel so alive. The sun is brighter, the air crisper, now that I once again seem whole. I'm happy to be a part of life again.

Rejoining the festivities, I make an honest effort to tell everyone hello, even those I may not know. Then, feeling a tug at the hem of my dress, I turn and see Emma.

"Where were you, Ms. Tessa? I have been looking for you," she says.

"I was talking with a dear friend of mine. Are you all right?" I ask.

Just then Cole approaches and sees the two of us standing there. "There you are, Emma Mae. What have you been up to?" he inquires.

"I was looking for Ms. Tessa, Papa, to tell her it was her turn to dance if she wanted."

"Now, let's not make her feel like she has to. Remember, I think she has forgotten how," he says, looking my way with a sly smile.

"I believe you should be held to such an offer, Mr. Miller. Would you like to dance?" I say with a hint of mischief.

"Why yes, Ms. Wells, I would be honored," he quips back. I find Maria and quickly introduce her to Emma so she has a new friend to talk to while Cole and I dance.

As we approach the wooden floor, the quartet strikes a lively tune, one that makes your heart race and your head spin. The perfect choice for such a moment. As my partner in this dance spins me about, I think of all the things I have missed. Dancing, singing, and laughing. Most of all the joy of interacting with others, ones who care for me and I for them.

At this moment, I vow to never again stop living my life. Each day is a new gift to do something big or small.

When the music ends, Cole and I are laughing. We both are truly enjoying ourselves. I haven't laughed or felt so at ease in a very long time. Cole makes me feel as though no harm will ever come my way. I am safe in his presence.

"I could go for a bit of punch, how about you?" he asks, out of breath.

Nodding my head, I agree it's a good idea. We both seem to have danced ourselves weary.

When he arrives at the table, he first serves the punch to me and then himself. "Looks like Emma is enjoying your friend," he points out.

Through the crowd, I find the two of them at a table with plates bearing pie. It looks as if Maria is telling the five-year-old some kind of fairy tale. They are both giggling uncontrollably.

"Shall we get some pie and join them?" Cole asks.

"I do think that's a wonderful idea. Heaven knows what ridiculously spun tale Maria is reciting to her," I reply with a laugh.

After choosing our pie, we walk in their direction. Maria's voice grows louder as we get nearer. Her arms are posed as if she is wielding a sword; I try to listen in on her fantasy.

"Then she starts swinging the stick with all her might, screaming in fear!" I hear her say.

Not ever remembering a tale such as that, I make the mistake of asking, "Goodness, Maria, what kind of child's tale is that?"

Liquid Quiver

Before she has a chance to reply, Emma pipes in. "It's no child's tale, Ms. Tessa, it's about you!" she says while laughing so hard she can barely speak.

"What? I don't understand," I say, confused. I am starting to think I maybe should have thought twice about leaving Emma with my dearest friend, who has a vivid way of telling such tales.

To my surprise, Emma is the one who fills me in. "It's when you first came here from Boston, Ms. Tessa. Were you really afraid of a chicken?" she is finally able to say through her laughter.

Almost choking on my pie, I shoot Maria a look of irritation. She, as well as Emma, laughs twice as hard. I cannot believe she has chosen that memory to relive out loud in front of Cole.

He looks in my direction and says, "What's this I hear? Afraid of a chicken?" A wide grin spreads across his face. If he weren't so handsome, I might smack it right off.

Gathering my composure and trying to keep my irritation hidden, I decide I have to set them straight. "No, Maria didn't tell it correctly," I shoot back. With the three of them laughing, it is difficult not to laugh as well. "She does have the gift of storytelling," I say numbly.

With that said, I cannot fathom why, but Cole looks at Maria and in a smooth voice asks, "Maria, can you give us an encore of this tale?" Quickly I send a glance of pure evil her way.

"Why sure, I wouldn't mind telling it again." Her voice seeps with playfulness.

I then realize I am doomed to be the laughing stock of the table. I ready myself for her antics; she has always been good at exaggerating things. I roll my eyes and sigh as she starts.

"This is a tale about a young girl who moved from the bustling city, full of all things unknown to us. Little did this girl know that where she was going there were beasts! The beasts were covered in feathers. She met another girl, one who told her about harvesting the eggs of the fearsome creatures. She couldn't believe what she heard of the eggs; she had to see for herself. She asked her new friend where she could find the beast and its eggs." Maria's eyes are round as she retells her story.

"Agreeing to take her, both girls ended up at the entrance. The new girl's friend handed her a magic sword to protect herself from the beast.

She explained to her to grab the eggs and hurry to escape the beast with her life." At this point Emma's eyes are wide, and Cole is paying close attention.

"The new girl felt unsure of herself, but promised to be brave. Entering the cold and dark cave, the girl yells to her friend outside that she sees the eggs and will go for them." As Maria tells the story, her arms are flailing about.

"Just then, they heard a loud caw, caw! The girl was too slow, and the feathered giant came out of nowhere to attack. The girl raised her sword and swung it this way and that. It was no use! She charged the beast like Don Quixote and stabbed it right in the heart, saving both their lives. Then they went back to the friend's house and had eggs and bacon. The end." Maria finishes in one quick breath.

Cole and Emma burst out laughing; both have tears in their eyes. I am chuckling more at the way Maria tells her stories—truly a gift. When the commotion finally dies down, they all turn to me.

"What? You must realize that is not how it went," I say, shaking my head. "As I mentioned before, she has a way with words. This event has now turned into a conversation piece. Now it is my turn to tell my side. Shall I tell the story as it should be told?"

"There are two sides to this story?" Cole asks.

"As always. Of course I know the actual way it played out. It's much different than Maria's version," I tell him.

"Do tell. Now I'm even more interested in the turn of events. How did it play out?" he asks with a wry humor. In my book, one day that may just earn him a tongue-lashing.

I let the three of them finish their pie, waiting until I have everyone's full attention. Then I begin to tell the story—my way.

"There was this young woman who was indeed traveling to a new land. She was looking for adventure and excitement; so many new things awaited her. In her travels, she came across new people and animals galore. Some did frighten her, but she urged on, with her journey ending here at Munroe Junction. She was used to being alone and eating berries and stones."

"Stones, Ms. Tessa? That's icky," Emma says with a scrunched-up nose.

"Yes, stones. Then one day she was picking berries and met an old, wrinkled, and stinky crone," I chime in.

Liquid Quiver

At that moment, Maria shoots up an eyebrow and doesn't look amused.

I continue on with my story. "She told the fair maiden, that if she were to follow, she would take her to get some scrumptious eggs. The old crone informed her that she was too old now to do it alone. A deal was struck between the two, and it was decided they will share the bounty in equal parts. Agreeing, they set off on their journey." I stop for a bite of pie.

"How stinky was she?" Emma asks.

"So stinky, it was as if she never bathed," I reply.

"Ew, that's even ickier," Emma responds. All the while Cole and Maria have a look of wonder on their faces, so I push on.

"The maiden, who thought she may have finally found a friend, even if it were a stinky one, was happy. Little did she know it was a trap! The crone planned to capture the girl and steal her youth. She led her to the cave and told her the eggs were inside. Entering the cave, she went to work searching. Then a great beast with claws of steel came at the fair maiden, trying to eat her! The old crone left her to her doom. The beast attacked the maiden time and time again. She fended off the bird—and who has no feathers whatsoever. She threw stones and sticks but nothing worked! The young girl could hear the old woman laughing outside the cave. Finally the maiden grabbed the eggs and tucked them into her basket as the beast came from behind. She picked up a log and smacked the horrid creature and knocked it out. Running quickly from the cave, to the crone's disbelief, the maiden shoved her into the cave and blocked the entrance with boulders. That way the crone cannot hurt anyone else. Lastly the maiden went home and fried the eggs and had them with bacon. The end." I finish my story with a smile.

"That was quite a story, Ms. Tessa. I liked Maria's better," Emma says.

"Goodness, Tessa, that was a tall tale!" Maria says as she bursts out laughing. Cole also stares at me in disbelief. I know Maria told a much better one, but this way I am able to make her look like a villain.

CHAPTER FIVE

Dusk

As the four of us continue to visit, well-wishers stop at our table to chat and say a final good-bye for the evening. Sometime later, Emma falls fast asleep on Cole's lap. She did play hard with the other children, and she and her father danced countless times. Her dark curls cover her face, and she is hanging onto Dolly as Cole holds her. The two of them are quite the pair. I can't imagine raising a child alone. It would be difficult to answer some of the questions that arise. He does so well with her; in fact, when I see them together, they seem like the best of friends.

A couple of hours later, Maria confesses she must go but has had a wonderful time. It is then that Cole and I agree we should be going, too. After making sure we bid goodnight to all the neighbors and hugging our friends, I find Mrs. Wells and bid her a good evening. She is smiling widely as I walk away.

With Dolly in hand, I walk beside Cole as he carries Emma, who is still fast asleep. In the darkness, I hear him ask in a low voice, "Did you have a good time, Tessa?"

"Yes, Cole, I had a wonderful time, the most fun I do believe I have had in a long time," I say honestly.

"Me too," he replies in a low tone.

The rest of the way back to the buggy we walk in silence. Thinking of his last comment, I feel extremely happy. Just the way he said it, even in the dark, it sounded sincere, like he truly meant it. For some reason it makes me wonder if it has anything to do with the fact I came along. So much so, I find myself hoping it is true. For him to see the Tessa I was once—and now feel I am back to being—would be wonderful and exciting. Being with him and Emma today, and having the visit with Mrs. Wells, has brought me out of my shell just a bit.

When we reach the buggy, I tell him I am capable of getting in on my own, since he still holds Emma. After I settle into the seat, he places Emma next to me. As we get on our way, she moves to make herself more comfortable, with her head in my lap and her feet on the seat. There is a bit of a chill, so I take my shawl and cover her small body. While she slumbers, she holds her doll tightly in her arms. It looks rather torn and tattered; she must love it very much. It doesn't look store-bought, and I wonder who made it for her.

Arriving at the front of my home, we come to a stop. Cole turns to me and says, "We're home." Those few words shock me to my core. I look at Emma and carefully try to move without disturbing her, but I have to ask Cole for help. He holds her head off my lap while I slide from beneath her. Then he gently lays her head where I was sitting.

"Tessa, your shawl is still covering Emma. Do you want to take it?" he asks in a whisper.

"No, that will not be necessary; I can retrieve it another time," I say quietly. I gather my hem and move to step out of the buggy. He takes my hand to offer his help; little waves of electricity radiate from his hand to mine. I'm not sure what to make of it; all I know is I have a heightened sense of awareness whenever he is close by—almost as if I know where he is even when I can't see him. It alarms me to even think about it; to do so only confuses me that much more. My thoughts are so clouded when he is near, I almost tend to lose all coordination, like I will stumble on even ground.

"I will see you to your door, Tessa, then I must bit you good evening," he says kindly. That familiar tone of his is back, the one I could swear is laced with honey. Walking side by side, we approach the steps. We are both silent as we walk up them. Because of the sudden stillness, I can hear a slight ringing in my ears. It seems that even all the creatures that sing at this time of night are waiting in the shadows to see what happens.

As I reach my door, I am almost driven crazy with the thoughts racing in my mind due to the awkward silence. Does he regret asking me along? Did I bore him out of his wits? I certainly hope not—I think it was a wonderful day for us. I don't want to end the evening thinking I spoiled his time. I decide I should speak first, to clear the air.

"Thank you, to both you and Emma. I had a wonderful time. I confess it has been quite some time since I have attended. There isn't anyone else I would have wanted to go with; you two were the perfect escorts. I will not forget this day," I tell him with sincerity. As I stand on the porch in the moonlight, I can somewhat make out the features on his face.

The air around us is suddenly thin; I am having a hard time breathing. Even though there is a chill, it seems to be rather warm, as if summer is already here. When he looks down at me with his dark eyes, my stomach starts to flutter. I swallow hard; my mouth seems dry as well. After being in the silence for several long moments, I grow more and more nervous. The thought that there might be a bit of food stuck to my face comes to mind. I debate whether to speak again, but don't know what else to say. As I move my hand to my cheek to inspect for food, he captures my hand with his.

I freeze. I have to remember how to stand on my own two feet. He turns my hand over, and traces it with his finger, running it along the small scar I received while plowing, then in a slow swirling motion in my palm. When his eyes meet mine, it is as if they hold some sort of secret he can't tell.

"Tessa," he says at last, "I cannot even begin to tell you how happy I am that you agreed to accompany us today. I mean Emma and I are happy, I mean." He speaks with a crackle in his tone.

I think he is nervous, but I can't figure out why; he has never lost his composure before. Feeling a bit out of sorts myself, I struggle to find the right words in my head, and in a hurry I end up stuttering, "Th…thank you again, I do not know how to repay you. I wouldn't have gone; I certainly had nothing to wear. Then you asked and made sure I was able to make a new dress. I didn't see your note, because I was angry and foolish. I am in debt to you," I say.

Both of us seem to be searching to find the right thing to say, which I admitted to myself long ago, is nearly impossible when he is so close. He takes my hand, enfolds it in his, and places them both up to his chest. I can feel his heart beating, fast and hard. My own pulse is thumping in my ears, and I feel light-headed. Then he finally tells me what is on his mind.

Liquid Quiver

"There is no debt owed on your behalf; it has been paid in full today with your presence at the social. Seeing you smile and laugh warmed my heart. For a day I was able to see the real Tessa from before. Just knowing you kept and used the fabric for your dress, and if that alone brought you some happiness, then that is all I ever wanted." He whispers so low I almost don't hear him. He raises my hand to his lips and gently kisses the back of it, then bids me goodnight.

He walks down the steps of the porch and halfway down the path, then stops and looks back at me for only a moment. I smile at him, and then he turns and makes his way to the buggy.

I wait until he is well on his way before I enter the house. I almost can't believe what just took place, I think of it over and over. Standing inside with my back against the door, I think perhaps I am dreaming. Of course, I could have gone mad and just not know it.

I recite each word again, just to make sure I didn't imagine the whole thing. I pinch myself; given the pain I now feel in my arm, it's clear I am not dreaming. The way he kissed my hand—I certainly would have never fathomed it. Brushing the back of my hand against my cheek, I still feel the warmth that lingers from his touch.

I move across the room and start a fire. I decide to get into my night-clothes as the fire removes the chill from the room. In my room, I grab a blanket to sit in front of the fire to ponder the day's events. As I sit in my chair, a feeling of ease settles over me. A calmness I have never felt before. This is all new to me. While watching the glowing coals, I start the day over from memory, beginning from when Cole and Emma picked me up, then the fear I felt when we arrived at the social. How ridiculous I felt after my conversation with Mrs. Wells.

The dancing was a special treat. I haven't danced like that in ages, not since I was a young girl back in Boston. As I think of when we danced today, a warm feeling washes over me. With a smile on my face and my cheeks growing warm, it's as if I am a young naive schoolgirl again. A small chuckle escapes my lips. Cole is an extraordinary man, with his dark hair, his expressive eyes, and his hands. How wonderful they are, warm and caring. When he took mine into his, he was able to completely consume mine in his.

Dusk

Even though he has only held my hand, I find myself wondering what it would be like to have him embrace me fully. My insides quiver, and the tingling in my core increases. I even begin to wonder what it would be like for his lips to brush against mine. It's then that I realize the fire is too warm to sit by, and I have to move back. In the back of my mind, I almost feel ashamed at the explicit thoughts and notions I am having. However, the other half of me doesn't seem to mind that they linger there. Tired from the day's events, I decide to turn in for the night.

After stoking the fire, I take my lamp and go to my room, setting the lamp on the side table. I lift the glass shade and extinguish the flame and then lie down. Settling in, I wrap the heavy blanket and lie on my side. When I burrow the side of my face into the pillow, I am finally comfortable. Inhaling deeply and exhaling seems to soothe my nerves. As I lie motionless, a smile sits on my features, unwavering; it's stubborn and will not let up. I don't mind really, I decide as I close my eyes and fall fast asleep.

CHAPTER SIX
Renewal

Hearing the birds chatting outside, I slowly open my eyes. My room is filled with light. The dust motes look like small snowflakes as they drift through the rays. Wondering what time it is, I reach for my timepiece.

"Goodness!" I exclaim and sit up abruptly. To my surprise, it is nine fifteen. Startled that I have slept so long, I stand to get my wrap. I run to the other room, make a quick fire, and start some coffee. An overcoat hanging by the door will have to serve as my chore clothes this morning, since there is no one here to see. Besides I can have them done quickly.

I open the door, and the sunshine is warm as I slip on my shoes. Stepping out, I survey my surroundings. It is so beautiful. A bit of dew lies on the grass, and with the sun shining, it looks as if a blanket of stars covers the ground. The air is fresh and the trees are greener than the day before. I love this time of year—the drab of winter giving way to the colors of spring. As I go down the steps, I feel giddy and perhaps a bit silly.

Letting my new-found emotions take over, I skip to the barn with my arms swinging to and fro. My hair rises and falls with each step that takes me closer to the barn. I have never allowed it to fall freely before; it always gets so tangled. But the old Tessa is now gone—no more living in the darkness of sorrow or hiding behind the walls of my home. With my senses and spirit renewed, I am now back to being me. When I awoke this morning, I didn't have the same dampening mood as before. I woke to find myself excited to be alive and breathing the fresh air, the scent of the prairie.

Not only do I feel like my life is now worth living, I am going live it. I will no longer live in the back of my house. I will start to live in and appreciate the whole house, move all my things back to their rightful places.

Liquid Quiver

As I enter the barn, I am glad that only animals live in here—not those who have the gift of voice—because at this moment I am singing as loud as the barn can allow. Otis, Jed, and Maddie must know that I have changed for the better; With their mangers brimming with breakfast, all they seem to want to do is stare in my direction with curiosity.

I take my wire basket in one hand and bound out of the barn, toward the chickens. In my other hand, I have the bucket with the day's ration of grain. As I arrive outside their door, the chickens greet me with enthusiasm. Inside the coop I spread handfuls of grain over the ground; the remainder will go into the feeder. In the nesting shed, I gather a dozen or more eggs. Doing this part of my chores reminds me of Maria's story and how silly it was.

Thinking back on that day, I shake my head. I was nervous when I came here, and Maria was my first acquaintance. Indeed, coming from Boston, I had no idea why she handed me that stick. I picture her rolling with laughter while I stood toe-to-toe with a rooster hell-bent on taking my head off. That thing was a ghastly sight: feathers bloomed out of his head, and his wings were in fine shape. On the other hand, his poor body had no feathers at all! He looked as if he had been plucked for dinner, then got away at the last minute. I think he held a grudge against all humanity.

However, that day was the beginning of a wonderful friendship. I had just moved here from Boston, with Mama the new schoolteacher and Papa the blacksmith. Maria was the girl I sat by in school. Not long after we met, she invited me to dinner at her house, and we became fast friends; we were inseparable. She was there for me when my ma and pa went back to Boston after Sam and I married.

Even now she and I are the best of friends, I being the elder of us two. Seeing her at the social brought back a lot of memories. How radiant she looked with her amber-colored hair and green eyes. I used to wish I could trade my unruly curly hair for hers, which is straight and tidy. I tell myself that I should go see her—it's been too long.

With the last of the eggs, I exit the coop and take my goods into the house, where I place them on the table. I am glad to be done with the chores; now the real work begins. First I find a suitable crate; it is time to put the painful memories of the past to rest and tuck them away in the barn. I gather the boots from the floor of my room and put them in the crate. From my wardrobe's bottom drawer, I take out the two shirts and pair of pants that Sam had worn and lay them on the top of the boots in the crate. When I'm done, I take a piece of burlap and cover his things. The timepiece and his six-shot revolver are his only items that do not go into the crate.

I put the overcoat on again and take the crate to the barn, where I put it on a shelf in the tack room. Feeling at ease, I walk back to the house.

I start by opening all the doors to welcome in fresh air and allow everything to awaken from its dormant state. There are four bedrooms total, the biggest of them being my room. I moved all my things in there after Sam's passing. He wanted to have a large family, so there are plenty of rooms to go around. Beyond the kitchen is a large sitting room with a nook to sit in and a large window that looks out over all our land. The floors are all made of hardwood, which needs a good polishing.

Moving from room to room, I tear off all the burlap I had nailed over the windows. My eyes are not used to so much light in these rooms, but it feels wonderful to have it. The sunshine streaming through allows me to see the ornate woodwork all around. It has been so long since I've seen it, I've almost forgotten what it looks like. The wooden walls are in a rich hue of red. It is going to be a chore to move everything by myself, but in time I think I will be able to get it done.

After welcoming the sunshine into every room, I set to work. There is no need really to dress formally for the day, since I'm the only one here. I find my broom and start to remove the cobwebs from all the corners of the house. The largest room holds all the furnishings; it will be saved for last so I can first clean where they are to go. Once that room is empty, I can live in there again. My trunks and bed are stored in that room, and soon I will be able to enjoy them again. My spirits are high, and I'm excited to live my life to the fullest, to appreciate the things around me.

A few hours later, the prep work is finally finished, and I am ready to move the furnishings out into the open, where they belong. In the large room, I start with the dining table and chairs. I dust and clean all of them before placing them in their spot. The table is beautiful and able to serve six; it's made of oak and very sturdy. I bring two other chairs to put in the room as well, just in case there are more people than I expect. I find the cloth to cover the table, but on second thought, decide to let its splendor shine openly.

Working on the living area, I move in the four upholstered chairs that go along with the two side tables, which match the rose pattern perfectly. The two side tables have roses engraved on the four corners and are made of mahogany. In one of the trunks, I find deep-green curtains that complement the chairs. Then, to finish the room, I hang a wreath made of willow.

The beds in the rooms Sam spent many nights building all by himself. He made the bed in our room first, then worked on the ones in the three smaller rooms. When I find the linens, I will wash and hang them to dry.

Everything is coming together, just as I had hoped. The items I have moved so far make it feel as if it is all new. I am going to fix up every room as it should be and then have Maria and others over for dinner. A visit would even be fine; coffee and cake sounds ideal.

CHAPTER SEVEN
Awakening

As I sit in the chair with my mug of coffee, I cannot believe it's taken all week to get my tasks accomplished. I now sit in the corner on the bench-style seat in my breakfast nook. I have forgotten how large this house really is. Seeming almost unfamiliar and dreamlike, what was once part of my everyday life now surrounds me again. I smile with satisfaction. I am proud of what I've accomplished.

All the rooms are complete with freshly washed linens on the beds. The rugs are clean, as well; it has been ages since I have cleaned them. All the wooden floors and furniture are bright, due to the vigorous polishing they just received.

The burlap that used to cover the windows has been replaced by curtains with bright-colored sunflowers on a cream background. Only the curtains in the sitting room are done to match the rose pattern that adorns the two chairs and the chaise lounge. The iron cooking stove proved to be quite the chore; it hasn't been used since that day.

There was talk in town when Sam and I built such a home as this. I wanted to bring a bit of Boston here. A grin touches my lips as I think back on the days we spent building it; I didn't think we would ever be finished.

Sitting here now, my eyes grow weary, and I am still a bit sore from all the work. I get to my feet, cross the sitting area, and enter the kitchen, where I put my mug on the counter so I can retire for the evening. I enter my room through the French doors and walk across the room to my bed. The large bed is comfortable and soft. After sleeping on the smaller bed for so long, I now wonder how I did it. I dress down to my night shirt and pull the coverlet and blanket down so I can crawl in. The linens are cool to the touch, but I don't mind at all. After covering myself and getting comfortable, I close my eyes and quickly drift off to sleep.

I awaken to find my room bright with morning sun. After pushing the blankets back and getting out of bed, I walk to the kitchen to start some water for coffee. My spirits are bright. I am looking forward to having Maria over, or perhaps Mrs. Wells. Whoever decides to take me up on my offer, it is sure to be grand. There will be plenty to eat and fun to be had. Secretly I think about asking Cole and Emma to attend, as well, and wonder if he would accept. I do admit it would be an interesting notion.

The thought of seeing him again makes my stomach turn flips. It seems whenever I am in his presence, I have to be extra careful. It's as if my body and brain are not on the same page. Concentrating deeply on such ordinary tasks as walking is truly difficult. I never felt so flustered and uncoordinated before. I'm not even sure why he makes me feel as if I'm fumbling. I make up my mind that if he takes me up on my invitation to come and visit, I will try harder and pay attention to what I am doing. I nod in agreement with myself.

The next morning after my bath, I go to work in the garden wearing a pair of pants and a worn shirt. Even though improper, I don't want to chance my hem dragging in the mud. It has been raining steadily for most of the morning; pulling the weeds will thankfully be easy.

As I work I think of what I have in mind for the get-together here at the house, mainly what to prepare for dinner and then dessert. Checking my cellar earlier this morning, I counted plenty of canned vegetables and fruit and a plethora of potatoes. The only meat I have is a bit of salted pork—not enough to feed everyone I intend to invite.

Then a thought suddenly comes to me: I could serve up a nice chicken dinner with vegetables and maybe a pie. I look at my coop. Judging by the number of birds it contains, it has been quite some time since I have cooked chicken.

With dinner taken care of, I think back to the last time I made a pie. My cheeks grow warm; what a fool I made of myself that day. Just then I pull a weed with more force than I intended, and mud splatters up in my face. Sighing heavily, I decide it is time to go inside—besides, now I am soaked clean through from the rain.

Awakening

After changing into some dry clothes, I make a mental note of all the things I have to do tomorrow in town. First I shall take the mending in and have my account credited, next visit Mrs. Wells and invite her and Mr. Wells to dinner. Last I must find Maria; if she isn't in town, I may have to go to her, hoping she is not going to be busy. Maria's company is greatly needed, even if only for my sake.

At the oven I check my biscuits. It's a simple supper that, with eggs, is at the moment all I need. When finished, I take my dishes to the basin and peer out the window. The sky is still gray, and clouds loom overhead. I hope the weather has different plans for the morning.

The next morning, I finish my chores and then lead Kate to the rail and tie her rope around the thick post. The rain has stopped for now. It was beating down so hard last night, I was sure I would wake to find it had washed the farm completely away. Taking Kate to town is more suitable for the weather, and with all the mud, I don't want to take a chance of getting the wagon stuck.

After gathering my things, I settle into the saddle, squeeze the mare with my heels, and ask her to walk on. The ride is quiet, with a soft breeze blowing. It is still cloudy but doesn't look as if rain is a threat. As I closely approach town, my insides grow heavy and my palms clammy. Suddenly I am short of breath. Not wanting to turn home and run, I urge the mare into a trot straight into town.

"Whoa, Kate," I say when we are in front of the store. I dismount, loop her rope over the rail, and retrieve the mending from the saddlebags. I don't need much today, just sugar, coffee, and fencing staples. Walking up the wood-plank steps, I hear the familiar tinkering of the bell that announces my arrival. Shortly after, I see Cole. He rushes to help me carry the mending.

"Good morning," he says with a wide grin. "How are you this fine day?"

"I am doing very well this morning. And you?" I reply, smiling back.

"Near perfect, now that you have arrived," he answers.

That one statement alone makes my face feel as if it were burning and has an effect on my middle, as if I ate butterflies for breakfast.

"Oh come now, Cole, you must get many people that come each day whom you are glad to see," I say with a bit of sarcasm.

"Of course," he says. "However, there is only one Tessa."

My face must be showing my feeling of disbelief.

"You have brought in quite a bit of mending for the week," he says.

"Yes, it seems that word has gotten out that I offer the service. I don't mind it, I earn a bit of extra credit that way."

"And what is it you need today?" he asks.

"Not too much, only sugar, coffee, and fencing staples."

"Is your wagon out front? If so, I could gather your things and walk them right out," he tells me.

"No, no," I say hurriedly. "I have an errand to run, so please take your time."

With that, I turn and almost run out. Where did all the air go? I couldn't breathe in there, was close to feeling faint. The cool breeze now washes my face, and I inhale deeply as if it were my last breath. Cole must be thinking I am half crazy. Not wanting to think about it, I shrug it off.

Upon arriving at Mrs. Wells's home, I knock, and even to my ears, it sounds louder than I mean it to be. When I enter the large house, I find Mrs. Wells in the sitting room, visiting with a friend.

"Hello, Tessa. Come in, my dear," she says.

"Thank you, Mrs. Wells. I see you have a visitor. I will not take too much of your time."

"Nonsense, you may stay as long as you please," she replies.

"Actually, I just stopped by to see if you and Mr. Wells would perhaps join me for dinner? At my home, of course." I spit it out in one gush of air. As I stand before her, I wring my fingers together to ease my nerves. It seems like forever before she speaks.

"Certainly! Oh, my goodness, Tessa, we wouldn't miss it for anything," she says with enthusiasm. She leaves her chair so quickly that before I know it, her arms are wrapped tightly around me. I believe she may squeeze me right in two.

"I am so happy that you are doing things again. I was getting worried about you," she says.

"Trust me, you have nothing to be worried about. I worked all week fixing up the house. It looks grand; I cannot wait for you to see it."

"Oh, Tessa, I can't wait to see it. When would you like us to come?" she inquires.

"Would Saturday work for you? Say four o'clock?" I ask.

"Excellent! That will do fine," she says.

"Great, then it is all set." I smile. "I cannot wait to see you and finally get to visit."

"Then Saturday it is," she replies.

"I best be going. I have a few things to get finished before supper. Good-bye, Mrs. Wells." I also bid her guest a good day before exiting the room. As I walk back down the hallway to the door, I hear the two older women chatting the whole way out.

Outside once again, I turn to walk back toward the mercantile. I reassure myself that I am quite able to keep my composure in front of Cole— at least that's what I repeat in my mind the whole way there.

By the time I return, I am even more of a wreck. My pep talk apparently wasn't as reassuring as I thought. When I go inside, Cole is helping a patron. I walk to the area that holds the canned goods and pretend I am interested in the apples. Every couple of seconds, I glance his way to see if he has noticed that I returned.

When he is finished with his patron, I see him coming my way. Looking intently at the glass jar in my hands, I try to calm myself, but so far it's not working. My mind races at the thought of what to say first, before asking him to supper.

Just then I hear his voice. "Careful, those apples could be quite dangerous," he says in a playful tone.

Confused, I cock my head to one side and ponder his words. "What? How on earth can this simple jar of apples be so dangerous?" I say.

"The way I hear it, the unsuspecting victim has no idea that once the jar is opened, they become overwhelming and attack without mercy! In your hair, on your face, and make a mess of your kitchen!" he replies with the biggest grin on his face I have ever seen.

Thinking back, I quickly dart my eyes to the floor in embarrassment. My mind is blank. As my thoughts return, I look at his face and inform him I can handle almost anything, even a wicked jar of apples.

"As well, Mr. Miller, you should have come around a bit earlier that day. Then you could have witnessed what fury I did unleash on the unwilling jar of fruit. Too bad that you were late." I speak calmly, trying not to falter.

49

Liquid Quiver

"No, ma'am, I wasn't any help at all. But you are mistaken; I believe I arrived at the proper time," he replies smoothly, raising an eyebrow. "At the moment of my seeing you, I do recall that you looked rather perfect. Even with the apples in your hair and the flour on your face," he adds proudly.

It is times like this when I wish I could be invisible. Perfect was far from what I looked like then, or so I thought. Horrid maybe, but nowhere near perfect like he mentioned.

I put the jar back on the shelf and decide to get on with it. It is now or never; I know that neither of us has all day. Taking one long breath, I make a quick wish that this goes as planned.

"Cole, there is something I would like to ask you. I hope you don't mind, I do not wish for you to think ill of me for being so forward," I manage to blurt out in one fell swoop.

"What do you have on your mind? Do you need help plowing? I noticed on your list you bought staples. Help with your fence maybe?" he asks with concern.

"No, I thank you for your offer. I was just wondering if perhaps you and Emma would like to come to dinner, say Saturday?" I blurt out. "Of course if you are worried that some may speculate, there will be others attending."

Being hopeful, I try to read the look on his face. The feeling it projects is apparent: he is going to decline.

"I am sorry, Tessa, there is another obligation I must see to on Saturday," he replies.

With my heart now at my feet, rejection hits, and I am lost for words. Then the manners my mama taught me when I was young come to mind.

"Maybe some other time. I am sure I will be holding dinner again soon. That may be a better time for you to join," I say with a smile. With that I bid him a good day and inform him I must find Maria. As I turn to walk out, my mind is screaming for me to run as fast as possible instead.

"Tessa, wait," I hear him call from behind me.

Not wanting to look him in the eyes, I hurry down the steps to find Kate waiting patiently. Fumbling, I make sure the cinch is tight, then reach for the rope and undo it from the rail. In one swift motion, I mount and turn the mare toward the other end of town. Before we go, I stop and look back in Cole's direction, to find him still standing there in front of the store.

"There are no hard feelings, Cole. I just didn't know you were busy. I am sure we will meet again soon," I explain.

With that, I kick Kate into action and hightail it out of there as fast as I can. After passing Mrs. Wells's home, the bank, and the saloon, we are soon on our way to Maria's. The ride is quiet and refreshing; there are more birds out today than before.

The scene in town has left me feeling more confused and even a little angry. I am not even sure why I thought it was a good idea. I did overreact a bit; I couldn't help it, my emotions took over and seemed to have full control. Quickly I decide to not do that again, ever.

At Maria's, I see no one about. Just my luck; the day I choose to invite friends and family to dinner, the one person I need most is not at home. When I reach the hitching rail, I decide to look around. The wagon is by the barn, and the horses are in the pasture. After dismounting, I tie Kate to the rail. At Maria's front door, I peer in but see no movement inside. I walk back down the steps and head toward the barn. Before I reach it, I see Maria come from the back of the barn.

"Maria!" I shout.

"Tessa? What are you doing here?" she asks.

"I came to see you and ask if you would come to dinner," I reply. If she declines as well, I don't know for sure what I will do. "That's if you are not busy, of course. I couldn't find you so I thought about looking in the barn," I tell her.

Maria stops short, waiting for me to come to her, and when I get there, she gives me a hug.

"Of course I was in the barn," she says. "Would you like to come see what has been taking up most of my time this morning?"

"Sure, I have time. What's in there?" I ask.

"You will see," she replies with a smile. As we walk through the smaller door on the side of the barn, the scent of fresh straw and manure overtake my sense of smell; it is an earthy and comforting aroma, much like the barn at home. Together we walk past the many stalls that line the barn, stopping at a stall near the end. I look over the wooden gate. Inside stands a mare with her tail facing Maria and I. She has bits of straw in her mane and tail, and the backs of her legs are damp.

Bending down to see the surprise, I squint my eyes. It is then I realize there are eight legs instead of four. Out of nowhere, the foal comes from its hiding spot. With huge eyes it stares at Maria and me, seeming very curious as to what we are. The newborn even shows itself fully without the protection of its mother.

"It's a girl, isn't she beautiful?" Maria asks.

"Yes, indeed she is," I say.

The foal has a sorrel coat and a mane and tail to match. A wide blaze runs down her face, and one hind leg has a white mark just above her hoof. Her legs seem too spindly to be able to hold her frame. She ventures over to learn more about us and doesn't act afraid when we touch her muzzle.

"She is so wonderful and cute," I say.

"So what's this I hear about you having a dinner?" Maria asks.

"Yes, Saturday at four o'clock, if you can make it, of course."

"That sounds great; it has been a while since I have been to visit you. Do I need to bring anything?" she inquires.

"No, that won't be necessary. Just your company will do," I tell her.

With that she and I saunter out of the barn. She asks if I would like some tea. I agree since it is only a bit after noon, and something to drink before the ride home sounds delicious.

Maria and I visit, talking about all the projects we have planned for spring around the house and in the fields. Maria only employs one ranch hand, Flint, who is extremely nice and respects her to the greatest lengths. Maria helps with the horses every chance she gets. I think secretly she has a crush on Flint, though knowing her, I suspect she would rather deny it than admit it's true.

Flint Anderson came to Maria, looking for work, about two years ago. She was a bit hesitant to hire him on, but he proved to be a wise invest-ment. Not only does he know about livestock, but he knows quite a bit about planting and harvesting. He is handsome enough, for sure, with dark hair that holds a curl or two, blue eyes, and a muscular frame from all the hard work around the ranch.

Even though Maria helps out when she is able, Flint is a gentleman and only lets her do what he thinks is easiest. I knew from the very first day that he was sweet on her. Neither of the two know how to tell the other, or maybe they are too afraid. So they just keep it to themselves; maybe when the time is right, it will be known.

The first winter after Flint arrived, he was rather late one morning. Maria saddled up her horse and went looking for him. It was a good thing, because she found him down in a draw. Earlier that morning the snow had been blowing something fierce, and he and his horse had lost their way and went down a steep embankment. He was half frozen when Maria found him. She was able to get both man and beast back to the ranch. Not wanting that to happen again, he now lives in the bunkhouse across the way from the house. He works for his room and board and a monthly paycheck, which comes from the cattle he works and the corn they grow.

I sip my tea and sway in the rocking chair on Maria's porch. "You know, Maria, I wouldn't mind if you were to bring Flint along to dinner," I say, looking at her only through the corner of my eye. As she takes her time to answer, I know she is thinking of something witty to respond with. I continue to sip my tea as I wait for her to come up with something to say.

"Tessa Ann, what would ever give you the notion to come up with such a thing?" she finally asks.

Laughing on the inside, I turn to her, but before I can speak, she does so first, with a hint of mischief in her eye.

"I will make you a deal: you ask Cole Miller, then I will ask Flint," she says firmly. I am sure she sees the irritation creep into my face.

"No deal, Maria. I already asked if he and Emma could attend. He told me he had other obligations to see to." Looking confused, she lets my words sink in.

"What do you mean? Did he flat refuse you? Just like that?"

"Goodness, Maria, he said no! Maybe not outright, but it was still a no!" I reply in frustration.

"Wow, Tessa, tear my head off," she says.

"I'm sorry, Maria, it's just that I really thought he may want to come. I shouldn't have gotten so hopeful." After a pause I add, "Oh, well, it will still be grand. I am looking forward to preparing a meal for everyone."

"Well, I am glad you came today, Tessa, not just because you invited me to dinner. I have missed your company greatly."

Liquid Quiver

"I hate to say it, Maria, but I must be going. I have missed you, too. Let's not make it a habit of not seeing each other. Saturday cannot come soon enough."

"No, it won't. I better go too; I have to check on the foal."

We both stand, and she walks with me the short distance to Kate. After we exchange good-byes, I mount and ride back toward town. Halfway there, I am tempted to go all the way around so I don't run into Cole. I am a bit embarrassed about my actions earlier. I acted selfishly and unkindly. Wishing I could go back and change it didn't make it any better. I would have to travel a few extra miles around town to not be seen, which would put me returning home later than I want. I decide to tough it out and ride right through—it can't be that bad.

As I get closer to town, I hear all the noises of a growing city: the horses whinnying and the sounds of men hammering away at the nails that hold the lumber together for the new schoolhouse and the town's first boutique. As I enter the town, I feel regret for the first time. I should stop and apologize to Cole, but at this point I just want to get home.

The town seems much busier than it was this morning. From my coat pocket, I pull out the timepiece. Three thirty. No wonder there are so many people; usually I have my errands tended to before now and have returned home.

I have never liked it when the stagecoach arrives in town this time of the day. The men look harsh and filthy, and they also run the horses aimlessly through the narrow streets. Those animals are exhausted and covered in a thick lather; I'm curious how they survive the trip.

With so many people about today, I am having a hard time navigating Kate through the massive crowd. One thing I've always thought is that too many people in a small space can only mean disaster.

It was then I heard it, faintly at first and growing louder by the second. Searching for a spot for Kate and me to take refuge, I dismount and lead her to a place in front of the bank, which is on the opposite side of the street from the saloon. Like magic, people start to dissipate with the sound of the heavy hooves approaching. It is almost like a heed or warning of the oncoming danger.

Across the way, a man who has had too much to drink is stumbling to his horse. I watch as he works to free the reins from the rail. He curses at his mount to stand still, but the poor thing is only trying to get out of his way. Seeing enough, I turn away. The sound of the stage is getting closer. My ears perk up at the screams now coming from the drunken man. Looking over, I see him kicking dirt under the boardwalk. Shaking my head in disbelief, I continue to watch.

Just before I turn away, I spot a flash of movement where the man was kicking dirt only a few minutes ago. Straining my eyes to see what is hiding under there, I catch a glimpse of white. The man crouches down, trying to reach whatever it is. On further inspection, I can see it's a small dog.

In a hell-bent fashion, the stage is now coming into town. I can even hear the chains clinking together and the men yelling for the horses to run faster. Looking away from the stage to the man across the way, I judge the distance against when the stage will pass by, doubting myself, for the instant I took to decide was too long. Then out of nowhere I hear a gunshot. I twist my neck in the direction of the saloon. The man has a pistol in his hand. I watch him cock the hammer back to fire another round.

Before he is able to shoot again, the frightened dog runs from his hiding spot and directly into the path of the stage. Fear for the animal now consumes me; watching closely, I silently urge it to run, to get out of there as fast as it can. But frozen in its tracks, the dog cowers down and waits.

Glancing about, I realize no one has noticed that the small creature even exists; they are all too busy with their own affairs. Time is running out; if I don't do something, it will end poorly for the dog. A blow from a stage will end its life for sure. My heart is pounding, knowing I have only a few moments to react. I drop Kate's reins and run. I feel like everything is in slow motion; the half-dried mud of the street is tiring me out quickly.

When I finally reach the dog, I scoop it into my arms. Only when I look for the rumbling hell-on-wheels do I get frightened. Its close, too close. A voice in my head is screaming at me to run, but my legs don't move. I then realize that the dog and I may both die on this very street. I tighten my grip on the dog and run as fast as I can. My legs feel as if they are made of lead. I struggle to make them run faster. Every instinct I have tells me I am in grave danger.

Suddenly I receive a blow and get thrown to the ground with such force, I would have thought I got hit by a train. I keep the dog close to my body as I fall. The next thing I know, I can taste the mud in my mouth and feel its coolness on my face. Fearing for my life and the life in my hands, I try to get up. A sharp pain in my side prevents me from doing so, and my head is throbbing. As I lie on the street, I can feel the pounding of the horse's hooves in the ground as they continue on.

I blink my eyes, trying to rid them of the dirt. The small dog wriggles to get free from under my body. I roll onto my side, feeling terrible. Peering down into my arms, I see the ball of matted hair that is mostly gray with white mixed in. It is so matted, I can't tell which end is looking at me: the head or the rear.

"Tessa, is that you?" a voice asks.

Groaning in response, I recognize who is speaking: the town's doctor, Emery Johnson.

"Gracious, my dear, don't move. Let me take a look at you," he says with sympathy. "Can you tell me, Tessa, where it is you are hurt?"

"All over," I say.

"Can you move at all?" he asks.

"Yes, Dr. Johnson, I think I am fine. Only got the wind knocked out of me."

"Let's get you back to my office so I can examine you further," he says.

"No, I am fine. I just need to get home."

As he helps me to my feet, I suddenly feel dizzy and light-headed. Doc Johnson helps me along, guiding me by the sides of my arms toward his office. I still hold the dog in my arms.

"Who do you have there?" he asks.

"I'm not sure. I saw a drunk shoot at him, then he ran out in front of the stage," I explain.

His office smells of fresh linen and antiseptic. He helps me to one of the exam tables. "OK, Tessa, can you tell me anything that happened after you got the dog?" he asks.

"I remember getting up to run, and I only made it a couple of steps, and then I felt like I got hit by a train," I tell him.

"Good, at least you still have your memory," he says.

As he continues to examine my wounds, he lifts my right arm, and I wince in pain. Seeing my discomfort, he then checks my side.

"Well, Tessa, you do not seem to have any broken bones. However, you are badly bruised and beaten up. My conclusion is you had a run-in with the lead horse pulling that stage," he says. "I'm going to clean you up, then I will take a look at your dog and see if he needs any tending to as well."

By the time he finishes cleaning my face of the dirt and mud, I know that I have suffered more damage than I thought. I try to not let it show that the antiseptic burns some, but I think he can tell it does.

When the doctor is through with me, he takes a look at the dog as I hold it in my arms. After carefully examining every inch, he tells me the pup only gained a few scratches and scrapes. Declaring him underweight and in need of some food was about the gist of his injuries.

"A good bath and some vittles is just what he needs," he says with a smile. "As for you, young lady, take it easy for a few days. Mind that you will be sore. Getting hit by a horse is no laughing matter," he says in a serious tone.

"Thank you, Dr. Johnson. I do not know how I can repay you," I tell him honestly.

"Do not worry, my dear, it wasn't anything too serious. Just a few bandages and antiseptic. I do have a fondness for your butter; think of me the next time you make some?" he says kindly.

"Yes, I will deliver it to you the next time I make some." I smile back.

As I get off the table, I realize my body is already becoming sore and stiff. Doc Johnson shows me to the door and wishes me a good day. Now I have the task of finding Kate. I only hope the mare is close. I do not feel like walking all over town looking for her.

As I trudge down the boardwalk, it seems to take forever to get anywhere. The pup is sleeping peacefully; I wish I could be home doing the same. I see a wooden barrel and decide to sit and rest for a minute. Peering down the way I came, I can still see the sign above Doc Johnson's place. I sigh loudly; it tells me I have not come very far and still have a ways to go. Completely exhausted and bone tired, I close my eyes for a moment.

CHAPTER EIGHT
Cole

When I glance out the store window, a wandering horse catches my eye. Furrowing my brow, I realize it is a horse I have seen before.

"Mason, watch the store for me, would you? There is something I need to tend to," I tell the young man.

"Sure, Cole, I'll be here," he replies. Mason Barlow is a great deal of help. He was the second eldest of the siblings and until he can continue his studies as a student when the new schoolhouse is finished, he helps out at the store to aid his family.

I take off my apron and set it on the counter, then rush outside to the mare. She doesn't seem skittish, as she aimlessly walks about. I go up to her; she is easy to catch.

"Where's Tessa, Kate?" I ask. I look around but do not see her. I take Kate to the rail in front of the store and tie her there, then start to walk up this side of the street. My mind is racing with thoughts about what could have happened. The idea of Kate bucking Tessa off, leaving her lying somewhere hurt, crosses my mind. I quickly disregard the notion; that mare has no such ambition. Besides, it makes me sick to think of such a thing.

Every business I come to, I duck my head inside and call her name. With no answer coming from any of them, worry and frustration are seeping in. I recall how upset she was this morning; I should have just told her what was going on. The event this morning has weighed heavily on my mind the entire day.

How do you explain that your daughter's high-class, snobbish aunt, who has never had any interest in Emma or in coming here, wants to take her? That wicked woman believes this is no place to raise a child, and especially a female one. She will be arriving on Saturday to see if she can charm Emma into going with her.

Over my dead body is Emma going with that vulture. I plan on stuffing her and her fancy fluff back on the train as soon as it comes to a stop.

"Tessa! Where are you?" I yell as I walk down the street.

I'm almost on the verge of going crazy; a lot crosses a man's mind when he's at his wits end trying to find the woman he cares for. I never took into account how much I looked forward to seeing her come in most every Monday—until now.

As my eyes scour the town, I feel as if something is working against me. There is no sign of her anywhere; she isn't at the post office or the bank. My legs are carrying me faster and faster, and my chest is tight. I run frantically, my footsteps echoing on each of the wood planks I pass over.

I come to a sudden stop. I see her, or at least I think it's Tessa. Her eyes are closed, and she sits on a barrel not too far from the hotel or Dr. Johnson's place. She looks far different than she did this morning; her shoes are caked in mud, and so is the length of her hair.

Approaching slowly so I don't startle her, I see what seems to be a cat resting on her lap. Tessa's face has cuts and scrapes, and her right cheek is bruised. Inching forward, I whisper her name. She doesn't respond, so I try again, and still I get nothing. I am almost tempted to shake her vigorously just to be sure she is still alive.

As I raise my hand to nudge her shoulder, the ball of hair that had sat in silence on her lap suddenly comes to life, startling me. I jump back; it's a dog, and it's baring it's teeth and growling with full intent to bite. It's then that Tessa springs into action and wraps her arms around the thing.

"What? What is going on?" Tessa says in confusion.

"It's me, Cole," I say, trying to calm her. "What on earth, Tessa? What happened to you?"

She closes her eyes and tells me the story of the dog and the stagecoach.

"And you flung yourself in front of it?" I ask her in disbelief.

"Yes, Cole," she says, frustration in her tone.

Honestly, I am relieved to find her alive and doing all right, even if she is battered and bruised. Not even a team of horses could knock her orneriness out of her. I am secretly amazed.

"I am going to help you back to the store, Tessa. I have Kate there," I say.

"Oh good, I need to get home," she says.

"You are not riding home all by yourself; I will get my wagon and take you."

"Now wait just one minute, I——"

I cut her off short, the irritation showing in my voice. "No! You haven't a choice. I am taking you home and that's the end of it!" I growl back. I know this is the only time I will come out ahead when facing Tessa. I feel a bit sheepish, knowing I have the upper hand because she doesn't feel good, and we both know it.

Helping Tessa into the wagon isn't easy. Her entire body is stiff and sore, and I don't want her to suffer any more than she has to.

"I am going in to tell Mason what is going on. Do not even think about taking the reins and seeing yourself home," I say sternly. The look she shoots me should burn me to a crisp where I stand. After informing Mason of what is going on, I tell him to close the store at the end of the day. He is a smart young man, and I know he can handle it himself.

I climb into the seat next to Tessa, take the reins, and start in the direction of her home. Kate is following behind the wagon, content to be on the way. It is hard for me to not feel for Tessa; she is ragged and beat to a pulp. I can see the bruises on her face, along with the scratches. All in all, she is still beautiful to me. There isn't a female alive who would have done what she did for that dog, and if there is, I have never met her.

Glancing in her direction, I see that she is half-asleep, her head bobbing around, and that thing snuggled up next to her is napping as well. Shaking my head, I think back to when I tried to wake her. It was funny how that dog protected her, even though she had only found him a short time before.

"Tessa, if you would like, you may rest your head on my shoulder," I tell her softly. She doesn't hesitate; I feel the weight of her ease against me. How could I let this happen to her? I know it's impossible for me to know what she is doing every minute of the day, but I feel responsible anyway.

Wanting to be sure she is comfortable, and not getting jarred, I keep the team at a gentle walk. Finally we arrive at her house, and I set the brake on the wagon.

Liquid Quiver

"Tessa, Tessa," I whisper to her. "We are here."

Moaning, she stirs slowly and sits up. I hurry out of my seat and rush to her side to help her get down. Her face strains with each movement. I want so badly to ease her pain. Once her feet are on the ground, she struggles to keep upright.

"Tessa, I am going to carry you in," I tell her. I scoop her up, and she wraps her arms around my neck. It feels wonderful to have her so close, yet I am feeling guilty about the circumstances that make her do so.

When we reach the front door, I use my left hand to turn the knob while supporting the lower half of Tessa's body. As I walk across the threshold, the smells of polishing wax and clean air greet me. With my heel, I shut the door. I see the lounge and decide that is good enough for now.

I gently lay her down on the lounge. She has fallen asleep again. I cover her up with the quilt on the back of a chair next to the lounge. With her shoes still caked in mud, I get on one knee to unlace them. Once I have removed them, I tug on the blanket to cover her feet.

Just then I hear a faint scratching noise coming from the door. I walk to it softly and open it. The small dog runs to where Tessa lies and jumps up to be with her. I close the door, thinking the dog feels comfortable with Tessa and now believes he owns the place.

When the two are settled in, I decide to put Kate back in her pasture and tend to the chores. The whole time I think I should stay for a while, to make sure she is going to be all right. By now the store is closed and Mason should be headed home for the night and I must pick up Emma from Mrs. Lacy before it gets too late. I walk Kate to her pasture, open the gate, and lead her through. After I undo the halter, she trots off to find some grass.

I get the tack and head to the barn to put it away. The animals inside know it's feeding time. I take the pitchfork and dish out everyone's dinner. I take two feed buckets and place a bit of grain in each one to take to my team. It should hold them over until I get them home. After I feed the chickens, the chores are done, and I head back to the house.

I peer into the room where Tessa lies, and I can see the rise and fall of her chest as she breathes. I start a fire to warm the room. It isn't chilled; I just feel better doing so. Once the fire is going strong, I put on a few extra logs to be sure it lasts for the night. Then I find a chair, place it next to where she sleeps, and take a seat to relax. Enjoying the quiet, I sigh heavily.

Thinking of the dog, I smile. I am still amused at the whole thing. He lies there with her just as comfortable as he can be. An instant bond was struck between the two; he is just as good for her as she is for him. I let out a soft chuckle. What an unlikely duo: a half-starved mutt who gets rescued by a woman with a large soft spot for anything in need of care. Truth of the matter, he will have a great life now that he has found her.

I think how lucky anything or anyone would be to find her. I now sit in her presence, and I cannot begin to tell her how I feel for her. I've longed for the right time, but have yet to find it. Whenever I get brave enough to tell her, I end up backing out. I'm not sure why; all I know is I am unsure of what she feels for me, or even if she feels anything. Being a widower with a small child, I don't know how she would feel about taking on such responsibility. Emma and Tessa get along well enough; I wonder what she thinks.

Watching Tessa sleep is a rare treat for me. I am hoping that the longer I sit here, the better chance I have for the picture of her lying there to be permanently etched into my memory. I bend forward and adjust the blanket to better cover her shoulders. In return, a warning in the form of a growl comes from the dog.

"Easy, I am not going to hurt her. Not now, not ever," I tell the animal. "You should feel so lucky—if she wouldn't have saved your butt, you would have been left to an uncertain fate."

As time passes, I look at my watch; two thirty in the morning came faster than I thought. I get up from my chair and stoke the fire again. I better get my team home and put away. Tessa and the mutt are doing fine. Although I can't tell which of them is snoring, it is a sure sign they are getting some much-needed rest.

After finding a piece of scratch paper and a pencil, I scribble a quick note to let her know I will be back, just in case she awakens. I put it on the table next to where she is sleeping. With a sudden impulse, I softly place a kiss on her forehead. Then I show myself to the door and walk out, closing it quietly behind me.

CHAPTER NINE
Recovery

"Shh, Emma, take care to not drop the plates when you take them to the table," Cole whispers.

"OK, Papa, I will be careful," Emma replies.

Hearing the two voices, I wonder what they are up to. Am I at home? Maybe I am dreaming. Lying still, I open my eyes and turn my head the direction of their speech. Though my memory is a bit foggy, I am quickly reminded of what happened the day before as my whole body protests in pain.

The scene being played out in my own kitchen is comforting. Cole is fixing to make breakfast, and Emma is helping by setting the table. The dog is bounding around her feet and yipping at her to play.

"Tigg, I can't play right now, I am helping Papa," she tells her new friend.

"All right, Emma, here are the forks." Cole hands her the utensils, and Emma takes them to the table as well. Watching them makes me smile. Cole glances my way, and he smiles too.

"Good morning, Tessa. How do you feel?" he asks.

"Sore and tired. Much better now that I know the two of you are here," I reply with a smile. My head is aching and my limbs are stiff. I turn to better observe the activity in the kitchen.

As Emma sets the forks on the table, the puppy follows her closely.

"Looks like you have a new friend," I say.

"I hope you don't mind, but I named him Tigg. He has been very nice to me," she says, giggling. "And he really likes to eat." Crinkling her nose, she also informs me of his dislike of taking a bath.

Liquid Quiver

"Tessa, it's almost noon. I hope eggs, biscuits, and bacon are OK," Cole says.

"Goodness yes, I haven't had anyone cook me breakfast in some time. This is really a treat."

Sitting up makes me a bit woozy. When it passes, I stand to move toward the table. Feeling weak and feeble, I shuffle in my socked feet across the floor.

Cole comes rushing to my aid. Taking my hand, he helps me to a chair.

"I'm OK, really," I tell him. He just smiles and pulls my chair out to help me sit down.

"The table looks wonderful, Emma; you did an amazing job." I compliment her efforts. Smiling, she sits in the chair next to me. The dog takes a place under her chair, hopeful he will catch a few crumbs.

"Papa and I did the chores, Ms. Tessa. Then we gathered the eggs for our lunch," she says with pride.

"I must thank the both of you for doing them. I am sorry I wasn't of any help," I say.

"Well, I was a bit mad when Papa woke me up so early, but after he said you had been hurt, I ended up not being mad at all," she blurts out in all honesty.

"Oh, I see. When did he come and get you?" I ask.

"I'm not sure really. All I know is he put away the team, and it was awfully dark when we left," she says while yawning.

I try to remember what time he brought me home. It was later in the afternoon, and I fell asleep somewhere between town and home. I must ask him when I get the chance. I begin to wonder what time it was when he did leave and why he would wake poor Emma up so early.

The food he is preparing smells good; my stomach growls as I breathe in the aroma drifting from the kitchen. Emma and I continue to chat about the things she wants to do today. Her plans far exceeded the hours left in the day, so we pick a couple that sound fun.

"All right ladies, breakfast—or I guess it would be called brunch—is ready," Cole says to us.

"Do you need any help?" I ask.

"Nope, you just sit right there and relax. I got it." Walking our way, he carries three plates dished up and ready to serve. He sets Emma's down first, then mine. He puts his plate on the table and sits on the opposite side of Emma and me.

The food smells delicious. I can't remember exactly when I last ate. I reach for my napkin, and Emma asks if she can say grace.

"Of course you can," Cole answers. After clearing her throat, she folds her hands, placing her elbows on the table, and closes her eyes. I bow my head and wait for her words.

"Dear God, thank you for my papa, because he takes care of me. Thank you for Mrs. Lacy, who takes care of me when he is at work. Thank you for this food and for Ms. Tessa doing just fine. Thank you for the puppy. Amen."

I think her prayer is perfect and very well said. I take my fork and begin to eat; Cole and Emma do the same.

The three of us chat about what to do today. Cole volunteers to fix the plow. Emma and I decide to work in the garden pulling weeds. I hope I can keep up with her.

After cleaning the kitchen and washing the dishes, we go outside to see what we can get accomplished. In the garden, the weeds have gotten tall and thick—evidence that the weeding hasn't been done for some time.

"Don't worry, Ms. Tessa, we can do it," Emma says enthusiastically.

"You think so, Emma? I hope we can, too," I say in return. We take our wicker baskets into the fenced area, then kneel down and begin to pull weeds.

Being around Emma is truly an experience. Not only does she have an honest way of thinking, she also seems to shed light on all things around her. Just when you think life has you down, her warm personality makes it easy to forget your troubles. Looking over my shoulder, I can see Cole working on the horse-drawn plow. At that moment, I feel helpless. My body still hurts from the day before, and I am weary. Even though I am grateful for his help and Emma's company, I feel as if I am a burden.

I have been used to doing everything alone and don't know what to think of their generosity. How will I thank them both? I glance at Emma, who is pulling weeds while humming.

"You are doing a great job, Emma," I tell her. Smiling at me, her eyes are bright and her cheeks plump.

"I used to help my mama pull weeds in our garden. She is the one who taught me how."

"I think she would be very proud of you. I know I am," I say.

"Thank you, Ms. Tessa. You see, you have to get it by the root. If you don't, it will grow back even quicker," she tells me. Grabbing one by the stem close to the dirt, she shows me how it's done. With a swift jerk, the weed pops out of the ground. "See? Just like that," she says.

"Very nicely done!" I say, grinning. As she giggles, I begin again to pull at the invasive plants.

"Did you know, Ms. Tessa, that I am going to be six years old?" she asks.

"No, I didn't know that. What day is your birthday?" I ask.

"June twentieth," she replies.

"Oh my, that is coming up, isn't it?" I say.

"Yep, it sure is. Sometimes my papa gets sad," she says in a low voice.

I'm confused, wondering why she would think he is saddened by her birthday. I'm not sure I should ask, so I stay silent and mull it over for a while. I figure if she wants to tell me anything more, then I will let her, in her own time. I'm not going to pry or make her feel like she has to tell me anything she doesn't want to.

"What do you think we should plant in the garden?" I ask.

"Oh you know. Potatoes, corn and squash, some beans, too, I think," she says.

"I was thinking about carrots, too, and maybe tomatoes," I add.

"That sounds yummy," she says. "Are you going to plant cabbage?"

"Maybe," I say, lifting my eyebrows.

"Yuck!" She pinches her nose closed with her fingers. Laughing at the look on her face makes my sides hurt, but I can't help it. Then she begins to laugh as well.

After a bit, we both decide it's a good time for a much-needed break and something cold to drink. We leave our baskets where they lie to await our return.

We go inside and wash our hands and get a cold glass of water each. Sitting at the table, I realize I am more tired than I thought. My limbs feel heavy, as do my eyelids.

"Ms. Tessa, do we have to go back outside and pull weeds some more?" Emma asks as she yawns.

"Honestly, Emma, I do not think I have the energy," I tell her.

"Me either. Papa got me up in the dark, and I feel tired, too." She yawns again.

"What do you say we take a nap?" I ask.

"Sure, Ms. Tessa, I would like that. Can I bring the puppy?"

"That would be fine. I will get us a blanket."

As she gathers the dog, I walk to the linen closet and get a large blanket for the two of us. I cannot wait to rest my tired body. Both the puppy and the girl, with Dolly in her arms, come bounding toward me at a rapid pace. I go into my room, the two of them following. I reason that my bed has plenty of space for the three of us, with room to spare.

"Wow, Ms. Tessa, your bed sure is big, and it looks fluffy, too," Emma says. Smiling, I help her and then the dog up onto the bed. Once the three of us are settled, I take in a deep breath and close my eyes. I can feel Emma stirring to get more comfortable. When she stills, it's then I feel the dog plop down beside her. "Shh, Dolly, it's nap time," she says quietly.

Before I drift off to sleep, I hear her sigh, and then she is perfectly motionless. When I awaken, something heavy is lying across my stomach. With my hand, I try to feel what it could be. The room is dark, so I figure it is early in the evening. On further inspection, I find that it's Emma's leg that is resting on my midsection.

"How on earth can anyone sleep sideways?" I ask myself quietly. Gently patting my way around, I conclude that the little girl is lying on her back, her arms are out from her sides, and one leg is thrown over my body. I chuckle softly when I come across the ball of hair wedged between us.

Suddenly I think of Cole and wonder where he is. Ever so slowly, I inch my way out from under Emma. As I walk into the dining area, I can hear the fire crackling. I scan the room but cannot find him. I go to the door, where I happen to look down and see his boots. Glancing behind me, I see a form on the lounge.

Quietly I sneak over to him. His body is a bit too long for the lounge, so he has his legs bent at the knee. One hand rests under his head and the other is curled up against his body. I feel almost as if I am intruding. I find it hard not to stare; he seems even more handsome when he sleeps. His tanned skin looks bronze in the light from the fire. The darkness of his hair even seems to shine in the dim light.

The shirt he wears is undone halfway, giving me a glimpse of what is hidden underneath. Soon I realize that the small patch of skin showing through the front of his shirt is the same tone as his face. In an instant, my face warms at the thoughts that flash through my mind. Not only is he handsome in the face, the build of his frame is very masculine. His arms are strong; he is tall, but not too tall. Judging by the patch of flesh exposed by his open shirt, it occurs to me that he must be masculine everywhere.

Moving in closer to his face, I try to memorize every line and curve. As I stare at his closed lids, I even notice that his lashes are so long they leave small shadows under his eyes. Placing my hand gently on the side of his head near his temple, I slowly caress down his cheek and then along his jawline, finishing at the point of his chin. He twitches for a second but doesn't awaken.

Smiling, I decide to get him a blanket just in case it gets chilly when the fire gives out. I cover up his lower body, leaving the upper half just the way it is. After a few more moments, I go back to my bed. There is Emma, still sleeping sideways, and the dog is in the same place as when I left. Being crafty and quiet, I am soon nestled comfortably back into my bed.

When I open my eyes, I see a small pair of feet next to my face. Lifting my head, I see Emma's head down by my knees. The small dog is lying up against my backside. Placing my head back on the pillow, I giggle at the sight the three of us must make.

I hear a noise coming from the kitchen, so I slowly get out of bed and retrieve my wrap. In the kitchen, I see that Cole is setting the table again for breakfast.

"Good morning," I whisper to him.

"Good morning back," he says with a grin.

"You know, you could have woken me so I could have helped you," I tell him.

"I know. I just thought you could use the rest," he replies.

"I must thank you then, it was much appreciated."

"No need. How are you feeling today?"

"Much better. I am still a bit sore, but not as stiff. My face isn't hurting as much either."

"Emma and I should probably head home today. I need to check on the store, and you would like some alone time, I'm sure. Since we have been here, you haven't had much of that."

"Actually," I say truthfully, "I have enjoyed both yours and Emma's company. For once it was nice to not be alone." A warm smile crosses his face, and his eyes are softer than before.

"I can assure you, Tessa, that the two of us have greatly enjoyed being here, too," he says, staring back at me. I feel myself blushing and can't help but smile back. Then the two of us hear soft footsteps coming into the kitchen. Emma is rubbing the sleep from her eyes.

"Papa, what time is it?" she asks.

"It's eight in the morning, sweetie," he tells her. "We should eat some breakfast, and while you two girls relax afterward, I will tend to the chores. Then we best be going."

"Aw, I don't want to go just yet. What about you, Ms. Tessa? Who will be here to make sure she is OK? What about the puppy?" she asks, her lip trembling.

The sight of her makes my heart melt. There she stands, her dark hair a mess and one of her stockings missing, her doll tucked under one arm. If it were up to me, I would give her anything she wanted.

Cole says as he walks to her and kneels down, "Tessa would like to take a bath, I'm sure. She hasn't had one since Monday. Must I remind you that you, as well, haven't had one either. I think she will do just fine until tonight, when we come again to do the chores."

"But Papa, I'm not dirty—look! Ms. Tessa said I was a big help too."

"Of course you were, sweetie, but Tessa won't be able to clean up if we are here. How about we come back later to check on her?" he says, trying to calm her.

"Oh all right," she spits out.

"Emma Mae, there is no back talking," he says sternly.

She turns on her heels and goes to the basin to wash up for breakfast. After she finishes, she marches to the table to take her seat. Her chin is now protruding, and her face is tense. I wash my hands after Emma and help Cole tend to the plates. He has made biscuits and gravy, one of my favorites.

Liquid Quiver

Once we are all sitting, Emma again says grace. She pokes and prods at the food on her plate. She appears to still be upset about the earlier incident. When everyone is done eating, Cole heads outside to do the chores, while Emma and I do the dishes. I help her gather her things and then I brush her hair.

"Do not worry, Emma; we will see each other soon," I reassure her.

"I know, Ms. Tessa, it just seems so far away."

Cole comes up the steps, knocking gently before he comes in. "Are you ready, Emma? I have the bay all saddled up."

"Yes, Papa, I am ready," she says quietly. Slowly she walks toward him, looking back at me a time or two.

"Good-bye, Ms. Tessa, see you in a while." she says in a small voice.

"Good-bye, Emma. It won't be long, I promise." I wave to her. Once they are both mounted and on their way, I shut the door. A hot bath does sound good.

I wait for the water to get hotter than I normally do; I figure a long soak will do my body a lot of good. After I fill the tub, I undress and get in. The steam is rising and it smells of rose oil. I sit for quite some time and think of all that has happened in the last few days.

First, I think of the day I got hit by the stagecoach, then of the time I spent with Cole and Emma. The house didn't seem to be as empty; it had a sense of ease, and I really did like having Emma here to talk to. This time I even felt that I could function properly when Cole was around.

I recall the night I watched him while he slept, the way his hand was tucked beneath his head and the peacefulness on his face as he slumbered. Not to mention how handsome he was. Closing my eyes, I bring back the memory, and after playing it out several times over, I decide to get washed up and get something done.

I douse the cloth in hot water to wash my face, being very careful to mind the scrapes and bruises. I am amazed to find my face is still rather tender to the touch. I lift my legs out of the water, one after the other; they are mottled with purple and green.

"Gracious!" I say out loud. This is the first time I have looked over the damage from the horse. It's then I wonder that if my legs look this terrible, what does my face look like?

Recovery

"Oh heavens," I groan aloud. "Is there ever going to be a time I don't look horrible in front of Cole?"

After stepping out of my bath, I dry off in front of the fire. I choose a dress from my trunk to wear; it isn't flashy, but it is much nicer than the other one. I had forgotten how many dresses I do own, since I hid them all away in my trunk. I may just burn the ones from before.

After the tub is emptied, I put it back where it belongs. My hair is now confined by a ribbon tied at the back of my neck. I apply a loose powder to my face, hoping it will cover some of the bruising.

In my kitchen, I busy myself making a stew and a loaf of fresh bread. If Emma and Cole are due back this evening, I want to be sure I at least make them a good dinner. A while later the bread is cooling on the counter, and the stew is simmering. Thanks to the extra help the past couple of days, there really isn't much tidying to do. When I feel caught up, I sit down for a while. Putting my feet up does feel wonderful. It is fairly nice outside, and I crack a couple of windows to let some fresh air in.

Nature sure is chatty outside: all the creatures and the birds carrying on their conversations. The house smells good from the stew. I surprise myself when the bread comes out as good as it does. It has been a long time since I have made some.

I find myself growing more excited by the minute for Emma and Cole to return; the past few days have been fun and exciting with them here. It makes me think I could live it every day. Except the part where I got hurt—I don't ever want to do that again. I know that deep down inside, my feelings for Cole are getting stronger. It is more than his handsome face. It is the way he looks after Emma with his nurturing but stern ways that makes him even more intriguing than before.

Lately the idea of how I would do as a mother has crossed my mind, even though I have no children of my own. I'm not at all trying to impress Cole by showing a false feeling of fondness toward Emma. My feelings are genuine, and my heart loves her as if she were my own child. I also know I can never take the place of her real mother. Not that I want to—I just want her to know that I am here for her whenever she needs.

Many times I have wondered if Cole thought I was suitable. I don't even know if he feels for me the way I am starting to feel for him. I can't recall when my feelings for him started. Maybe they were there all along and are just now starting to surface. All I know is that I am completely comfortable with the notion.

I am truly excited for them to return, as if it is meant to be. I don't want to get my hopes up too high, just in case I am wishing for something I am never to have. For now I am blessed to have them in my life, to enjoy the everyday things life can bring.

Wanting to get a bit of sunshine, I grab an overcoat and shoes. I check on the stew before going outside; it is simmering nicely. By the time they arrive, it should be done. The afternoon sun is peeking out from behind a cloud. I pass up a chair on the porch, figuring I will walk around the farm to stretch my legs.

As I go along, I check on all the livestock. They are content to be lazy for the day. In the next few weeks, I will need to ask Maria and Flint if they can help me drive the fifteen head of yearling calves to the market. The beef prices this year should be good. I will use the extra money for dry goods and supplies. I hope the grass comes in quick before I run out of oat hay; that will be far from now, but I like to plan ahead.

Walking out back behind the barn, I see the plow Cole worked on. I notice it looks recently used. Hurrying to the field, I am shocked to see that the whole thing has been worked. Cole completed in just a day a task that would have taken me at least two or three. No wonder he fell asleep; he completely exhausted himself. Walking on, I make a loop around the barn and end up back by the garden.

The sound of hooves catches my attention, and I turn in that direction. I see a rider on a roan horse approaching. I walk to the porch to see who it can be. As they get closer, I recognize the rider as Mason Barlow. He stops in front of the rail, dismounts, and ties up the gelding.

"Good afternoon, ma'am. Cole sent me out to tend to your chores," he says.

"Oh, is everything all right, Mason?" I ask.

"It's a matter of a personal affair, ma'am. I think I heard something about a visitor arriving," he says.

An alarm sounds in the back of my mind as I spin with ideas on who this visitor could be. Cole didn't mention anything about it. Not that I need to know everything—I just find it odd.

"OK, Mason, I can take care of the chickens if you will feed the live-stock in the barn. Then I will milk Maddie."

"Yes, ma'am. I will get to it right away," he calls back, tipping his hat. He turns on his heels and heads straight for the barn. I can barely keep up as I go to fetch the grain for the chickens.

Before he leaves, I gather the stew and the loaf of bread and package them up for Cole, Emma, and himself.

"Thank you, ma'am, I sure do appreciate it. I haven't been home yet— Cole asked me to come here right away," he says with a smile.

"It was the least I could do for you, since you helped me," I reply. He tips his hat as he bids me goodnight, then turns his horse toward town.

As I walk back to the house, I find that I keep thinking about the visitor. I want to know who it is, but I am fearful of seeming rude if I were to ask.

I continue to ponder a way to give myself a reason to go into town and maybe bump into this visitor. An idea strikes me. Remembering back to Monday, I do believe I brought home a dog. However, I didn't make it home with my supplies.

CHAPTER TEN
Dinner with Friends

After rushing through my chores, I saddle Kate, tie on the saddlebags, and am ready to go. I quickly undo the neck rope and mount up. Not knowing who I may face today prompted me to wear one of my better shirtwaists that is a nice cream color. I paired it with a broom skirt a shade darker than the blue that hangs in the sky. My face still shows a bit of purple and green from the bruises, so I used powder for cover. As for my hair, a simple braid lies down the middle of my back.

The whole way into town, my mind flips through all the possibilities of who had arrived for an impromptu visit. Was it a friend? A relative maybe? I start to feel foolish; I know it doesn't concern me, but it drives me crazy anyhow.

In town everything seems normal; I'm not even sure why I thought it wouldn't be. It isn't like the queen was coming for a royal visit. Last night left me plenty of time to figure out how to approach the situation. I have it all planned out: if by some chance I see Cole, I will say I came to town to confirm the attendance of Mrs. Wells at dinner on Saturday.

"Yes, that should be reason enough," I say to myself.

Eying a spot on a rail close to the store, I turn Kate in that direction. I tie her up, loosen the cinch just a bit, and take the saddlebags. Inside the store, I don't see Cole anywhere. Mason is tending the counter and peers over and offers me a grin.

"Good morning, Ms. Wells, how are you?" he says.

"I am fine, Mason, thank you," I reply.

"Is there anything I can help you with?" he asks.

"No, no. I am just browsing," I say, fully knowing that I never have the time or extra funds to do so. I almost feel bad for lying.

"The stew you gave me sure hit the spot. Thank you again," he says kindly.

"It was the least I could do." As we talk, my eyes scan the room. I'm not sure who or what I am looking for; I only hope I'm not being too obvious.

"Are you sure there isn't anything I can help you with?" he asks again with a quizzical look.

I whip my head back in his direction, feeling as if I were caught at something. "No, I just forgot my list and may have to browse to recall what I had written down," I say sheepishly.

"All right, Ms. Wells, just holler if you need anything," he says.

With that I wander throughout the store, picking up odd items and pretending to be interested in them. I make a few turns about the room and begin to think I won't see Cole or his mysterious guest.

"Ms. Wells, I have noticed you have been here for an hour now," the boy's voice rings out. "Did you remember anything from your list?"

"I'm afraid not," I reply. "However, Mason, I did have a few supplies that I do not remember receiving the day I got hit."

"Yes, your items are here behind the counter," he says. I am embarrassed as I walk up to the counter to fetch my things. My facade is over.

"Thank you, Mason. When you see Cole, please tell him I am sorry to have missed him on my visit into town."

"Oh, if that's who you were waiting for, you should have said something," he says.

"Nonsense, I wasn't waiting on him. Just figured that since I had come into town, I would bid him a good morning," I say as if I hadn't a care in the world.

"Then I guess you have no interest in knowing he is at the hotel having brunch. With a girl," he adds. I'm not sure he is being devious, but I am shocked, to say the least.

"Come now, what he is doing is none of my concern. For that matter, who he is having brunch with is also none of my business. Thank you for everything," I tell him as I gather my things.

"My pleasure, ma'am," he says with a smile. "Anytime."

"Good day, Mason," I say.

Not wanting to seem too eager, I slowly place my things in my saddlebags and secure the flaps. I then turn to walk out the door, fully knowing I should get back on my mare and go right home. I shouldn't be sticking my nose where it doesn't belong.

Before I enter the hotel, I check my reflection in its window; I am satisfied with myself. I look around the first room, where only a few guests are eating. Sauntering through, I go to the next room. I let my eyes dart around that room; there is no one that I recognize. I begin to think I am on a wild-goose chase. I decide to give up for now and go home.

I go back toward the door, reasoning that I have missed them and there is no use sitting around and waiting any longer. After latching the door behind me, I walk back in the direction I came. Now that my supplies are in hand, I have no excuse to go back into the store.

When I reach Kate, I throw the saddlebags onto her back and affix them for the ride home. The feeling of defeat is the only thing I have gained from my trip to town. Once in the saddle, I point Kate toward home. And for the time being, I don't mind her slow and steady pace.

Back home, I put her tack in the barn and take some grain as I walk out with the brushes in hand. Kate eats the grain greedily, as I work her coat over with quick strokes to remove any dirt from our ride.

Suddenly she picks her head up and pricks her ears forward. Spinning around to see what has caught her attention, I notice a buggy getting closer. Curiosity sends me forward to the edge of the grass to get a better glimpse of who may be coming down the road. Right away I know it is his buggy.

As it gets closer, I can see a woman sitting next to him. Her hair is a golden hue of yellow and is done in ringlets. The dress she wears is of the highest quality; it is emerald green and looks to be made out of silk. The dust that the horse kicks up blows on by me as they come to a stop. I also see that she has a lace parasol and matching gloves. Judging by her rigid and stiff stance, she has her corset laced too tight.

"Ms. Tessa! I'm here!" Emma says aloud.

"Emma. That is so way for a young lady to speak. One must contain their excitement and not be boisterous. It's rude," the woman spouts out in a high voice.

"Good morning, Emma. I am so glad to see you, too," I tell the young girl. Cole doesn't look at all amused by his passenger; it's almost as if he regrets being in the woman's presence. I can't blame him at all; I have a feeling about her that the two of us are not going to get along. She is harsh and rude, not to mention unforgiving.

"So this is the widow Emma speaks so much about," the woman says, turning her gaze from me to Cole. She raises her hand and orders him to help her out of the buggy.

I mull over her words as Cole helps her out. I know her type. I remember seeing women like her when I was young and lived in Boston. A "hoity-toity" was the word I used then; at this moment it is fitting for her. Now that I have her pegged, I know it will take a silver tongue to knock her down a notch. The big advantage is that I now know more about her than she does about me, and she only arrived ten minutes ago. Unlike her, I can disguise my comments with a smile on my face.

"Yes, I am the widow, and Emma and I do have a grand time together. By the way, no one here has ever spoken of you before. If they had, I must have not had much interest. I am Tessa Wells, and you, madame, are who?" I ask with a smile.

Before she answers, she lifts her parasol to shade her face, which is a ghostly white. Then she walks toward me with an icy stare and introduces herself.

"I am Roslyn Adams, Mrs. Adams to those whom are not close friends but rather acquaintances. You know, such as yourself." She looks me up and down.

"Do not worry, Roslyn," I say. Over her shoulder I can see Cole busy tending to the horse and buggy while Emma plays in the grass. "We would never be close friends, for you and I are very different. You see, I have dealt with hoity-toity before. In this part of the country, you will not last," I tell her in our own private conversation.

"I will have you know widow, I always get what I want, and you will not stand in my way. You are nothing but a thorn in my side. I heard rumors about you, trying to sneak your way into my sister's place. Ha! A simpleton such as you will never be welcome. Stay in your place; it is you who does not belong," she says through clenched teeth.

I keep my calm as we both look each other squarely in the eyes. Before I can reply, Emma is at our side.

"Ms. Tessa, this is my auntie Roslyn. Papa said I met her before, but I don't remember," she says.

Turning my attention to Emma, I ask if she is thirsty and would like to come in for a cool cup of water. After going inside and giving Emma some water, I go to the screen door to look outside. Cole and Roslyn seem to be having a heated discussion. I try to listen in but can't hear what they are saying.

"It's not that she doesn't like you, Ms. Tessa. She hardly likes anyone at all," Emma says from her seat. I walk to the table to join her.

"I'm sorry, Emma. Let's not worry ourselves over her. How was your morning?" I ask.

"No fun at all. Mrs. Roslyn was very strict with me at breakfast. She kept telling me to sit up straight and to act like a lady."

Knowing this upsets me even more; this woman is a product of an overbearing finishing school. "Emma, have you told your pa?" I ask.

"Well, not really. He was pretty mad last night. I heard them talking very loudly. She was telling him this was no place for me and she wants me to go with her to become a lady."

Having this new information made me leery of this so-called proper woman. I wouldn't put it past her to do everything in her power to carry out her venomous plan.

"What am I going to do, Ms. Tessa? I don't want to leave my papa or my home." Tears are welling in her eyes.

"Don't you worry, Emma, I wouldn't let anything happen to you, and I know your papa isn't going to let you out of his sight." I open my arms and give her a hug; she squeezes me back tightly.

"Thank you, Ms. Tessa." At that moment I feel very protective of her; she is really concerned that her poisonous aunt is going to take her away. All I know is that she isn't going to take the child anywhere; I will risk what little I have to see to it.

A knock at the door catches my attention.

"Come in," I say.

"Emma, sweetie, are you in here?" Cole asks.

"Yes, Papa, I am in here with Ms. Tessa. Are we having to leave now?" she asks.

He walks in and sees her embraced by my arms as she sits in my lap. The look on his face is one of sympathy.

Liquid Quiver

"Cole, you and I need to talk," I say seriously. Then I turn to Emma. "Emma, why don't you sit here for a minute while your pa and I talk in the kitchen?"

"All right, I will be right here," she says.

Smiling I head straight for the other room as Cole follows. When we are finally alone, I decide to tell him everything.

"Cole Miller! Your little girl is scared to death that her aunt will make her leave everything she knows. I realize that not having any children of my own makes this none of my business. But I care dearly for that little girl, and I will let nothing of that sort happen." I can feel the heat in my face.

For what seems like an eternity, Cole doesn't speak.

"Well? Aren't you going to say anything?" I ask.

He places a finger to his lips, and the only thing I hear is "Shh."

Completely confused, I open my mouth to say something. He moves in swiftly before I can speak and places his lips on mine.

I close my eyes, feeling his lips soft and warm on mine. He is gentle, but I can tell he is holding back, just on the verge of letting go of his inhibitions. His hands cup my face while I hold his shirt at both sides of his waist. Moving backward as he moves forward, I am stopped by my counter at my back.

As he meshes his body to mine, the very thought of where this could lead overwhelms me. His muscular stature seems to consume my smaller frame. Moving my hands down to rest on his hips, I hear only a soft sigh. I slowly pull him even closer to me.

With his entire length against me, I feel the hardness at his groin that throbs at my middle, just above my navel. Our kisses grow more feverish and intense. Sucking on his bottom lip, I hope to tempt his mouth to open so my tongue can explore the wetness within.

Just as he parts his mouth, he shoves away from me abruptly and backs off. We stand and look at each other as we both struggle for air, our faces hot with emotion.

"I want this to be right, Tessa. I will never be sorry that I kissed you; I just can't let this happen right now," he says while gasping for air.

Feeling dizzy and even more bewildered, I stand frozen in time. Then I say, trying to sound convincing, "I understand, Cole. There is no need to explain. I also know that I overstepped my boundary on the subject of Emma. I know you will do everything right by her."

"I never thought you would have doubted me, Tessa." he replies dryly.

The expression on his face has an edge to it, as if he is caught somewhere between confusion and anger. I never meant to make him think I doubted his abilities with Emma; now I wish I could take back what I said.

"I better get back to Roslyn and Emma," he says.

"Yes, that would be ideal. I am sure the three of you have plenty to do today," I say quietly.

Back in the dining area, Emma is holding the puppy, which has finally woken from his nap. "Thank you for taking good care of the puppy, Ms. Tessa," she says as she looks at me.

"You're welcome," I reply.

I glance at Cole; the chiseled look on his face is still there. As he walks to the door, his footsteps are heavy and echo throughout the house. Turning around, he calls for his daughter.

"Coming, Papa. Good-bye, Ms. Tessa; maybe I can come back soon," she says, putting the dog on the floor.

"You sure will, but not if I see you first," I tell her with a half-hearted smile.

I follow the two of them out into the grass; Mrs. Adams is waiting by the buggy. I can only guess she is going to demand help to get in. She squints at me as I walk toward the buggy. It's as if she is threatening me in silence. Holding my gaze on hers the entire way, I only look down to help Emma into her seat.

Mrs. Adams holds out her hand to Cole—almost as if it is his duty to help her in. Once seated, she fusses with the hem of her dress. I have to hold back a laugh; watching her amuses me. Wearing a corset too tightly not only makes one dizzy and short of breath, but it also makes bending at the waist next to impossible.

The struggle with her garment goes on for a good five minutes. Not only do the other two passengers seem short of patience, the horse is shuffling its feet in anticipation as well. She finally gives up and leaves a bit of her hem hanging out of the vehicle.

"Well then, I bid the three of you a good afternoon. Good-bye Cole, Emma, and it was indeed a pleasure to meet you, Roslyn," I say with kindness dripping from my voice.

Her head snaps so quickly in my direction, I am surprised it doesn't break clean off. Her eyes meet mine in an instant.

"Yes indeed, Tessa. The pleasure was mine. In fact I think you and I can become close friends. Perhaps you can join us this Saturday for lunch—my treat of course. Judging by your meager surroundings, I would not mind," she says with poison on her lips.

"I must decline your kind offer, not that I would mind feasting on a meal paid for by someone of such a high status as yourself. I'd just rather eat dirt is all. Besides I am hosting a dinner for friends and will be preparing for it instead," I reply with a smile.

"Eww, Ms. Tessa, you wouldn't really eat dirt would you?" Emma blurts out. Cole lets out a half cough, half choking sound and then proceeds to hush his daughter. His sister-in-law looks at Cole, then at me, and I can tell she is up to something.

"Pity the three of us weren't invited," she says. "I would just enjoy a wonderfully home-cooked meal. After all the traveling all this way from Boston, the food on the train is bland at best."

"Ms. Tessa, I didn't know you were having a dinner at your house. Can I come?" Emma asks. That's when I know the bitch has used her niece to get what she wants. How low would this woman stoop?

"I do not mind, Emma, if you would like to attend. Maria will be there. I would say that you, Roslyn, could attend as well; however, I wouldn't want you to miss your lunch date," I say to her.

"Consider two more to make it on Saturday, my friend Tessa. I shall cancel my plans for the entire afternoon; that way I can look my best. What time shall dinner be served?" she asks.

"Four o'clock is when you may arrive, dinner will be served shortly afterward. I look forward to having you present," I reply.

"Done. Shall I bring anything?" she inquires.

"No, just you're most pleasant and respectful self, if you find her by then," I snap back. "Good day, Roslyn."

As I turn on my heels, I hear a snort, which makes me smile. I don't know if it was her who made the noise in disgust or Cole in disbelief, but it doesn't matter because I'm not going to turn back to find out. If it was her, then I am satisfied I have gotten under her skin.

As the buggy leaves, I go to put Kate away. Taking a quick glance over my shoulder, all I see is the dirt drifting in their wake. Then and there I vow to make sure Roslyn is held to her place. There is no way in hell she is going to defeat me.

I walk the mare to the gate, open it, and lead her through. I undo her halter, then exit and close the gate behind me. Standing there alone, I think of the things to come in the next few days. I need to prepare for the dinner and face a woman whose trickery has gone unmatched for far too long. Reciting her words in my head, I determine that this time she will not get everything she wants, so help me. Because this widow is going to prove it.

CHAPTER ELEVEN
The Secret

The alley behind the businesses reeks of garbage and filth. My path is lit only by the dim lights casting a small glow through the windows of each building I pass.

I walk briskly until I reach the corners, and then I peer around to be sure I am unseen. I know better than to be out at such an hour, but this cannot wait any longer. The man in the barbershop said to ask for a man by the name of Pete. When I asked for a description, he told me that I would just know him when I see him.

Continuing on, I see rats scurrying in front of me. The air is unusually stagnant. With each breath I take, I want to gag, so I cover my mouth with the crook of my arm in the darkness. Behind the brothel, I see a man standing in the shadows. Approaching slowly, I am cautious, and somehow when I stop in front of him, I do know this is the man I am looking for.

"Pete?" I ask.

When he comes out of the shadows, I gasp in fright. His eyes are sunk into his skull so far, his sockets are mere black orbs. The beard that covers his face is dirty and shaggy. Not only do his shirt and pants have numerous holes and tears, I can't even make out the original color of the fabric. His boots and hat are just as horrid. Judging by the odor he gives off, he hasn't bathed in some time.

"Are you the one with the job?" he asks with gravel in his voice.

"Yes, I am. Only if it suits you."

"Listen, lady, if I'm get'n paid, then it suits me," he says.

"Fine," I snap.

"Well, let's hear it," he retorts.

Liquid Quiver

"First things first. You must do exactly as I tell you with no argument. Come Monday, about midmorning, I need a diversion. One big enough to catch everyone's attention," I explain.

"You mean like a bank robbery?" he says.

"No, definitely not that far—maybe more like a fire. Something along those lines," I reply.

"A fire, huh. That's all? What are you gonna do?" he asks.

"While you start the fire, I will wait until everyone rushes to help put it out. I will be at Miller's store. When no one is watching, I will take the child. I have to keep her away from that woman at all costs," I tell him.

He seems to take his time pondering my plan. I want him to hurry and decide. Being behind this place is making my stomach churn, and I am feeling ill. Not only can a person smell the sex in the air, you can hear the men and women sporting together in doing the deed. If I were to be found here, or perhaps even seen, my reputation would be jaded.

"What's in it for me?" he says, breaking into my thoughts.

"Twenty-five dollars."

"Make it thirty, and we have a deal," he spouts back.

"The job is for twenty-five, no more no less." I scowl.

In a matter of seconds, he has me pinned up against the wall. He is pressed into me so hard that I can't scream.

"All right, twenty-five it is. I will have to get my other five dollars outta you some other way. Why don't you pull your skirt up and let me have some fun," he demands.

I can smell the whiskey on his breath and the rot on his teeth. I remember that I have my Derringer in the garter around my thigh; I think about shooting him and being done with it. But then how would I explain what I was doing out at this hour or what I had been up to? Instead I will offer a deal he can't refuse.

"I will pay you double. That's fifty dollars. Half for the job and half for letting me go unharmed. Just think of the tokens and whiskey you could buy with that money. You could have any girl you please," I tell him smoothly.

As he thinks, he rubs a lock of my hair between his fingers.

"Deal. It's too bad, though. You and I may have had the best screw ever. I can almost picture it. You naked before me, them legs you got wrapped

around my middle. All that hair of yours down outta their bindings, covering your breasts, with just your nipples showing through. Yep, you would
look just like an angel with all your yellow hair around your face as you lay
on the bed. Yep, real pretty, I will let you think on it. If you change your
mind, you know where to find me," he says with a toothless grin.

From my coin purse, I take out the fifty dollars and drop it into his
palm.

"Thank you, fancy lady. You best be ready for that fire," he whispers.

With that, he is gone into the shadows. Standing here, I almost can't
believe what just happened in the last half hour. But now that the deal
is struck, I have to focus on the next step. First there is the dinner on
Saturday at the widow's house. If I am not to be a suspect, I must grin and
bear it to attend the damn thing.

I turn around and walk back the way I came, to get to my hotel.
If anyone were to find out that a relative of Alicia's has left her a large
inheritance, and now that she has passed, her daughter, Emma, is the
beneficiary—all the planning and work I have put into this would be for
nothing.

Taking Emma back to Boston with me will be proof that I own the
wretched child, which will declare that I am to inherit the money. I am
unclear how much money; however, some is always better than none.
Using the excuse to take her to Boston to become a lady was a good idea,
thanks to my creative thinking. Since my husband cast me out for being
greedy and I am only a half sister to Alicia, my life has been pure hell. The
money my husband gave me to leave is going quicker than I thought it
would. I'm not about to go back to the life I once knew.

Running away from home at a young age leaves a woman with really
no proper way to support herself. The only choice I had was to become
a whore. I was tired of starving and begging for food. After a few long
years, a man I came to love bought my way out of there when I accepted
his hand in marriage. He was a senator, and he made me feel special. I had
everything I could have ever asked for.

I wasn't greedy until I figured out where he really went all those
late nights I waited up for him. Cheap perfume and the scent of another
woman, mixed with cheaper whiskey, were hard to hide from someone
who was all too familiar with those things.

Liquid Quiver

I had changed for the better on our wedding day because I vowed to love only one man. He changed for the worse on our eighth anniversary, betraying me by loving many more than one. As I see it, we both changed. Soon, when I have my money, he will get what's coming to him. He'll see.

I turn the key and enter my room, closing the door behind me. I light a lamp, then change into my nightclothes. As I get into bed, I begin to think about the deal I made only a couple of hours ago with this so-called Pete. I feel a little guilty involving someone who is so young, but since I have never been close to Emma, it makes it easier.

Alicia had it all; being the younger of two girls, she was always cherished. I was from my mother's first husband; we fled after his drunken fits turned into sheer rage. When she met Alicia's father, he changed our life for the better. Everything was great; he cared for the both of us and treated me like his own.

But when Alicia was born, I became the second favorite, and while we were growing up, everyone could see I was different. I had my father's straight blond hair, and she had the dark curls of our mother. At an early age, I began to rebel and act out, even though my mother and stepfather always showed me how much they both loved me. I didn't listen. After I ran off, they continued to write, asking me to come back home, but I was too ashamed. In a way I blame myself for not going back to my family, but it's too late to place any blame now. I haven't talked to them in many years; I did make it to Mother's funeral, but I felt like an outcast.

Knowing that I won't let any harm come to Emma makes me feel at ease. It is a simple plan: when Pete starts the fire, I will take Emma and convince her to come along. All I have to do is make it back to Boston and show them I am the child's guardian. When I receive the money, then everything will be just fine.

The only hitch is that I don't know how much time I will have before Cole comes looking for her. Propping myself up on my elbow, I lift the glass shade and blow out the flame. I will have to work out the small details, but I am sure it will go according to plan.

Turning to lie on my side, I close my eyes. My first task is to make it through the dinner on Saturday. I never thought the widow would be in the picture; I thought I would have to deal only with Cole.

The Secret

Emma has a great deal of fondness for her and mentions her often. I suspect she is the reason Emma wants to stay here, besides the fact her father is here. There is no way to make the little girl believe anything of a lie about Tessa, no matter how hard I try. I will think of something; I have to get her to come along. Taking a deep breath, I close my eyes and go to sleep.

In the morning, I get dressed and go down to get something to eat. I sit at a table, and the waitress brings the coffee. I ask for a small breakfast of fruit and toast. Thinking of the events that took place last night, I almost wish them away, but what's done is done.

As I sip the hot brew, I think of my plan for today. I will take Emma on a picnic and try to show her all the advantages of coming with me: the beautiful city, all the dress shops, everything she could want. After finishing the last of my drink and the fruit, I dab the napkin to my lips, then place it on the table along with my money.

Outside, I walk down the boardwalk and into the store. Mason is at the counter while Cole is helping an elderly gentleman with flour and lard. Strolling around, I choose some items to bring on the picnic. First I get a wicker basket and place in it a loaf of homemade bread that's on the counter. I also get a jar of honey, along with some fresh butter. I check the label on the butter; it reads, "Made with care from the home of Mrs. Lily Wells." I wonder if she is any relation to the widow; if so, I must find out. I take the items to the counter and have Mason put them on my account.

"Looks like you may be going on a picnic, Mrs. Adams," he says.

"Yes, Mason, I was hoping to take Emma with me," I say. "Do you perhaps know where she is?"

"I think she is in the back of the store, playing with her doll."

"Thank you, Mason, you have been most helpful," I say with a smile.

I go to the back and find her doing just as Mason had said.

"Emma, would you like to go with me on a picnic? I have some bread and butter, along with some honey. If you would like, we can also stop in at the hotel and order up something to take along as well."

"But I'm playing with Dolly. Can she come, too?" she asks.

"Of course she can; we are just going on a short walk to the creek. I am sure she would like very much to come along," I say to entice her.

"OK, I have to tell my papa where I am going. Let me go find him," she says, then runs by me and through the doorway to find Cole.

As I wait patiently for both of them to return, I hope he doesn't decline her request.

"Papa said I could go with you if I wanted," Emma says when she returns.

Cole is with her. "Are you sure, Roslyn?" he asks. "Sometimes she can be a handful."

"Yes, I am sure—that is if you don't mind," I reply.

"Not at all. Emma, you be good for your aunt, do you understand?" he tells her. Rolling her eyes, she agrees with him. "All right, I will see you girls after a bit." Cole smiles and goes back to tending the store.

"Come, Emma, let's get on with our picnic. I already have a spot picked out," I say.

She follows along as we exit the mercantile and go toward the hotel. Once inside she orders fried chicken to go with the other items in our basket. Carrying our things, we start to walk to the edge of town on the journey to the creek that flows beyond the town limits. Turning past the last building, I see Pete. I pull my gaze away from him, but he smiles and waves.

"Who is that man?" the child asks.

"I do not know, maybe just a friendly passerby," I lie.

"He doesn't look friendly," she whispers.

"Don't worry, I am sure that he is no threat," I reassure her.

I look back over my shoulder, but he is gone. Relief washes over me. I don't want to have a run-in with that rat.

When we arrive at the creek, I spread a small throw on the ground so that the two of us can sit down. My thoughts are to start by telling her that the city is really beautiful, and she would really like it. I may even try to convince her that there are shops with all different kinds of candy and sweets.

"Emma, would you like to come with me to Boston? I think you could have a wonderful time," I say while I open the cloth that covers the chicken.

"I don't want to go without my pa, he would be all alone without me," she replies.

"I think he will be too busy with the store to be able to make the trip," I say. "There is Mason to help with the store, and Ms. Tessa. They will keep him company for sure." I try to sooth her.

After I dish out our plates, both of us quietly eat our food. It is obvious that getting her to go isn't going to be as easy as I thought.

"Where did you get your doll?" I inquire.

"My mama made it for me before she went to heaven," she says.

"You know, there is a shop full of dolls in Boston that look just like real girls. I could take you there if you would like," I lie again.

"Maybe I can come just for a visit, Aunt Roslyn. That way I can come back and see my pa," Emma states.

I never thought of asking her to come for a visit. If I remember correctly, the legal guardian must have custody of the child to receive the money. An idea comes to mind. I could ask if she can stay with me until the end of summer. At least that's what I would make them all believe. If I can make her think she is coming back, then it may be easier to make her go.

"Emma, are you in school yet?" I ask.

"No, there is a new schoolhouse being built in town, and they are looking for a new teacher."

"What do you think about going with me for a while to Boston, just until school begins again?" I say with hope.

"I don't know, Aunt Roslyn. What would my pa say?" she asks hesitantly.

"Well I could ask for you, but you would have to let him know how badly you want to go. I will pay for your train ticket, so your pa doesn't have to worry and it's no burden to him."

"Do you promise to take me to see all the dolls?" she asks with her wide eyes.

"Of course, but you have to make sure that you do your part to make your pa understand that you want to go," I reply.

"Oh, I will! I want to see all the pretty dolls!" she exclaims.

We continue to eat our meal. I tear the bread into pieces and spread a glaze of honey over the butter, all the while wishing I had thought of this idea sooner; then I wouldn't have had to waste my money on that filthy man.

Liquid Quiver

Now I have to be certain that the fire doesn't happen, though on second thought, if Emma changes her mind, it is still a good idea for a diversion. I don't have to buy another ticket because I already saw to that when I arrived. I am going to get what I want—either way, as they will see.

Chapter Twelve

Illusions

I wake up early to get dressed and complete my chores. There are plenty of things to get done today before the dinner. Besides the chores, I have to pick out a couple of plump hens for the feast. In the kitchen, I pour another cup of coffee, sweeten it with a bit of sugar, and add some cream. I decided yesterday that I will use my grandmother's china—not that mine isn't elegant enough, it's just that this is the kind of event that only happens once. My excitement is growing to see my best friend; she assured me that if possible she will arrive early to help calm my nerves.

After everything is taken care of, I have to feed the bounding ball of hair at my feet. He seems to have doubled in size since I brought him home. His height is the same; he's just chubbier in the middle.

It's nine twenty, and I set my brew on the counter and busy myself with tidying up. The house is in pristine condition, but I feel the need to tie up a few loose ends. When I finish, I grab my chore gloves and a cleaver. If I am to get washed up soon and get dinner fixed, I need to get all the preparations out of the way.

At the coop, I see a few choice hens that will do for dinner. I find it odd that they stand motionless as they cock their heads to the side, staring at me approaching. It's almost as if they know something is about to happen.

I hide the large knife at my side, down by my leg, as I go inside.

"Here, chick, chick, chick. Here, chicken," I call out.

That's when my plan goes straight to hell. The fowl suddenly explode into chaos, the animals hurling themselves through the air and squawking loudly. Feathers are falling to the ground, and the dust is getting thick from the flapping of their wings.

Liquid Quiver

Now that they are upset, I may not get any eggs for a week. Trying to be subtle and pick out a couple is now impossible. I stand still, thinking that if I don't move, they will calm down and this will be simpler. Bringing in the grain bucket would have done the trick; I chastise myself for not doing so.

An hour later I have two fresh hens, plucked and rinsed. I fix the pies and use the heat from the oven to help the fresh bread dough rise in the pan. With those things done, I decide to take a bath, to be washed up and ready if Maria comes early.

The gown I choose is navy blue, with a white lace trim. The skirt isn't as full as a full formal gown; it is sleeker and flares out from my hip. The bust also has a heart-shaped neckline that also has lace. It has been a while since I had to put on my own corset, so I hope my friend will be here to help.

After getting out of my tub, I dry off and wrap my hair in the cloth until I am ready to fix it. I want to look superb for my dinner guests. With Roslyn attending, it is out of the question for me to look one bit shabby. Excellence is what I am striving for; what she doesn't know is that I am familiar with entertaining as well.

Taking my time, I apply rose oil to my entire body; the changing season takes a toll on my skin, and I don't want it to appear rough. The oil will leave a light scent and make my skin soft and smooth. As I dab a bit of lotion on my face, I inspect it and see that most of the bruising is gone, and my normal olive tone is returning.

I check the time; it is five to two. The pup is asleep on my bed with all four paws in the air. I wish I was that calm at the moment. Hearing a soft rap at the door jolts me into action. I sprint to the nearest window but cannot see who may be at my door. Standing up against the wooden door, I wait and the rapping comes again.

"Hello? Tessa, are you in there?" a female voice asks.

I sigh in relief; it's only Maria.

"Yes, I'm here," I say. "Is Flint with you?"

"No, he will be along in a while. I came early to see if you needed any help."

I open the door to my dearest friend and don't feel a bit foolish to be standing there in my wrap.

"Come in, come in. I'm so glad that you came early, I need help with my corset." I laugh.

Closing the door behind her, she heads straight through the kitchen to put her sweet-potato pie on the counter. Then, when she follows me to my room, I fill her in on Roslyn.

"She said what!" Maria exclaims. "I can't believe she had the nerve."

"I know, talk about first impressions. I almost had to pick my jaw up off the ground," I tell my friend.

"Tessa, I swear you need to stop and eat at some point in your day. This is the second time I am going through to pull your laces on this thing," she scolds.

"Maria, really, I do stop and eat. It's not like I have a man here, like some women I know," I tease back.

Quick to reply and to cut my sarcasm short, she brings up Cole. I tell her what happened the other day with Emma and the scene in the kitchen.

"Tessa! How dare you hold out on me? I tell you, that man has a soft spot for you," she says earnestly.

"Oh, I don't know, Maria. He confuses the hell out of me. One minute he is open and I feel a connection, and the next, he's quiet and guarded."

"That's how they are—and they claim it's us women who are mysterious creatures." She giggles and shakes her head.

When she is through with my corset, I pull my stockings on. We chat and catch up. I then tell her about the accident as she pets the dog that is still lying on the bed.

Her eyes widen when I retell the part where I got hit, and when I have finish, she looks down at the hairball in her lap.

"Tessa Ann, what on earth were you thinking?" she asks.

"Well, I just couldn't stand there; no one else seemed to want to help him out," I reply.

I unwrap the towel and let my damp tresses fall down my back. I sit in a chair opposite Maria as I comb my hair. Taking a bit more of the oil, I smooth it through my hair and then bring my locks to one side over my shoulder. Parting the hair twice, I begin to twist one and then the other. Then Maria helps me twist the two around one another until we reach the ends.

Liquid Quiver

The style is more formal than that of a braid, but not too exquisite to overwhelm the dress. After I slip into the dress, my friend helps with the buttons that start at the small of my back and stop at the nape of my neck. While Maria gets more coffee for the two of us, I apply color to my face. I see her reflection in my mirror when she returns.

"Goodness, Tessa, you look wonderful. It has been quite some time since I have seen you dressed this way," she says.

"We both look wonderful," I say. "Tell me, Maria, what on earth is taking that man so long to court you? I think the two of you would make a lovely couple."

"Hush, Tessa, you nor I could ever know if he has such feelings for a woman like me," she quips.

"We'll see. Shall we start dinner? Everyone will be arriving soon," I say.

Taking our mugs, we both proceed to the kitchen and put on aprons to cover our dresses. Maria dices the potatoes into chunks, and I heat the oven and begin to dress the birds. While we work, we talk about things from the past and ideas for the future.

I place the birds in the large roasting pan; the potatoes will be added when the main course is nearly done. Maria has also brought some cob corn, and working together, we break them in half and put them on to boil. After applying lard to a large Dutch oven, I place the dough for the rolls inside. I cover it with the heavy lid and take it to the fire, making sure it doesn't sit too close so it will not burn.

Now that everything is prepared and beginning to cook, my nerves are starting to settle. Setting the table is the only thing left to do. From my china hutch, I gather my grandmother's plates and walk them to the table. Maria follows with the forks and spoons in one hand and the linen napkins in the other.

After the places are set, I take the two oil lamps that have hurricane shades and put them in the middle of the table, leaving room for the main dish to sit between them. On the outside of the lamps are matching candles that are the same color as the linen napkins. I strike a match and light each one; a warm glow hovers over the table.

The silver trim on the dinner plates seem to sparkle in the light. All the dinnerware sits atop my finest linens, which I laundered the day before.

Stepping back, Maria and I admire our work. We look at each other, and smiles touch both of our faces. I feel proud to be hosting a dinner again in my home; it is the company and laughter I am looking forward to the most.

Maria and I return to the kitchen once more to check on our dinner. The rolls are baked to a golden perfection, so I take them off the fire to cool. The birds are cooking nicely, and the room is starting to smell of all the seasonings and spices we used to prepare it. Maria finishes the potatoes by sprinkling on sage and rosemary, and I help her place them in the pans to cook as the chicken gets close to being done. It is getting close to four, and my excitement is building for all the guests to arrive.

"Maria, what do you say you and I sneak out to the cellar and pick out a bottle of wine to go with dinner?" I ask her with a grin.

"I'd say that's a great idea," she replies.

The two of us go out and around the house to the cellar. After a few moments, we emerge from the dark room. When we return to the house, I hold two bottles, while Maria holds a third. I wipe the dust off the glass bottles and retrieve a corkscrew from the drawer.

"Tessa, you must not have too much too soon, or you will be the first to call it a night," she warns with a snicker.

"Shush," I spout her way as if to laugh at her fair warning.

Back in the kitchen, she and I again check on the food and decide that a few more minutes will be sufficient for it to be ready. Handing her a wine glass, I pour some for her and then some for myself. At first it seems bitter; I can tell it has been a long time since I have enjoyed some.

I look at my timepiece; it is creeping closer to four, and I begin to wonder if the dinner guests are going to show. If by chance no one happens to attend, I would be content to eat and drink wine with Maria.

"I think the chicken should be done. Shall we set the table?" I ask.

"Yes, indeed, everyone should be coming soon," Maria agrees.

As I take the roasted birds, complete with potatoes, out of the oven, the heat grazes my face, along with the scent of sage and rosemary. Both birds have turned out perfect, if I do say so myself. I am hoping everyone will have a dinner to be remembered. I place the hot pans on the folded linen; the table is coming together with ease. Maria helps with the corn and pies, which now adorn the table next to the main dish.

From outside we hear the sound of a horse approaching. Almost knocking Maria to the floor, I run to the window to see who has shown up first.

"Tessa! What on earth has gotten into you?" Maria scolds.

"Whew, it's just Flint," I reply as my heart races.

"What? He's here?" Maria exclaims as she frantically checks her image on the back of a silver serving spoon.

While watching my best friend tend to the stray strands of hair, I laugh and wonder if I have ever done the same.

"Tessa Ann. How dare you laugh!" she retorts.

"You better hurry, Maria; he is tying up his gelding. Oh no, here he comes," I say in a teasing tone.

When I look back at her, her eyes are squinted tight, and I almost feel myself turning into stone. "Tessa, I swear," she says.

I rush to the door and eagerly pull it open. "Good evening, Flint, it's so nice to see you again," I say smoothly.

"And a good evening to you, as well. I brought some cornbread to go with dinner, I hope you don't mind," he says.

"No, of course not, it smells delicious," I say.

He walks into the room and looks about.

"Flint, you may take it over to the table if you would like," I say while shutting the door.

When Maria steps out from the kitchen and Flint sees her, his face softens, and he fumbles with his hat, which he holds in his hands. She cannot seem to remove the smile that is etched into her features. No matter how much the two of them deny it, they obviously have feelings for each other.

"Is there anything I can do for the two of you lovely ladies before the others arrive?" he asks as he looks at Maria.

"I think we have it all under control. Thank you, though, for the offer, Flint," she replies.

Smiling, he turns and goes to the chair next to the piano. Out of nowhere, the little dog leaps into his lap. He welcomes the pup and scratches him behind the ears.

"Dinner will be served shortly, Flint. I am waiting on a few more people," I tell him.

He nods his head, and I retreat back to the kitchen.

"Maria, where is everyone?" I ask under my breath.

"Calm down, Tessa. Help me with my apron, would you?" she says.

"I am calm!" I say as I work to untie her apron.

"Oh, look. Isn't that Mrs. Wells coming?"

Looking around Maria, I peer out the window.

"Yes, that is her. I recognize her buggy." I turn so she can help with my apron. All the while, I'm thinking that Cole isn't going to show. My hopes are dwindling and I am saddened by the thought.

"And I do believe Cole is right behind her in his buggy as well," Maria blurts out.

"Hurry up, get this apron off!" I exclaim through my teeth.

"Now who's giggling at whom?" Maria chimes in.

"For goodness sakes! Stop fooling around," I say, trying to reason with her.

As soon as I am free, I cross the kitchen in two strides, pick up the lid to a silver serving bowl, and check my hair and face.

"OK, Maria, here we go. We set the table correct? Are there enough chairs for everyone?" I ask impatiently. I go to the front door and look out to see my guests tending to their buggies.

"Maria, where are you?" I ask, running back to the kitchen. I find her filling our glasses again with wine.

"Here, take a sip. It will calm your nerves, Tessa," she says as she hands me the glass. I drink it down in one quick shot and return to my post at the door.

Hearing the footsteps coming up the wooden porch, I open the door for them to enter. Flint stands as they cross the threshold.

"Good evening, Mrs. Wells, Roslyn, Cole. And how are you, Emma?" I say kindly.

"I brought a pie, Ms. Tessa. Mrs. Lacy helped me a little," the young girl replies.

"Thank you, Emma, it looks heavenly."

"I, too, brought a little something. A cake with a butter-cream frosting," Mrs. Wells says.

"Thank you so much. I am grateful for all of you attending tonight," I say. I shut the door behind everyone, and Mrs. Wells and Emma take the baked goods to the kitchen.

"Hi, Maria. I am glad that you are here. Maybe later you can tell me another story," I hear Emma say with enthusiasm. The guests are admiring how good the table looks and the food placed on it.

"Tessa, you have a wonderful home," Roslyn says. "How lovely it is decorated and kept. It reminds me of the home I used to live in." Her remarks almost seem genuine, as if she really cared. I have already planned to keep my guard up because I still hold feelings of uneasiness toward her.

"Why thank you, Roslyn. I am glad you approve of my meager surroundings. I hope the dinner Maria and I have prepared suits your tastes as well. Would you like a glass of wine?" I ask, trying to keep the edge out of my voice.

"Yes, that sounds truly delightful," she replies with equal effort.

In the kitchen, I take another glass, and pour her some wine, and hand it to her. When we return to the dining area, I introduce everyone to each other. She soaks up the attention well, after I make the formal introductions.

"Everyone, I would like to thank all of you for coming. Dinner is ready to be served. Shall we take our seats and enjoy a meal together?" I ask.

At the far end of the table, Maria and Flint take the seats across from each other. Then Roslyn sits next to Flint, and Mrs. Wells next to Maria. I take my seat at the head of the table, with Cole to my left and Emma to my right.

Cole looks amazing in his black shirt and freshly starched denim. His face is freshly shaved, and I can smell the aroma of his cologne. If I'm not mistaken, his hair is trimmed as well. He is a treat for my eyes, as well as the rest of my senses.

Roslyn looks exquisite. Her gown is of a peach-colored fabric and has lace trim everywhere. It fits tight to her body, and the skirt has flounces of lace all the way to the bottom hem, which rests on the very floor she walks on. Her hair is in a tight bun, with tiny golden ringlets hanging to frame her face.

Emma wears a dress in a shade of pink. It contrasts wonderfully with her skin and dark hair, which is also curled, and her bangs are pinned back out of her eyes.

Mrs. Wells wears a dress a shade or two darker than mine. It is reserved and almost strict in fashion. She is gorgeous, nonetheless.

Maria has chosen a burgundy dress with small round buttons of pearl that ran from the nape of her neck down to her waistline. A string of small beads rests around her neck, and her hair is worn down, with one side swept back and held in place by a beautiful barrette.

In light that the candles and lamps are generating, everyone seems to glow, and time, for an instant, stands still. A feeling of ease comes over me at the sight of my guests sitting and visiting to enjoy each other's company. Smiles are given at will, and they all have gleams in their eyes.

"Let's serve up our plates and enjoy this meal that Tessa and her friend Maria has prepared," Mrs. Wells announces.

Everyone nods in agreement and places their napkins in their laps. The chicken and roasted potatoes are the first to go around, followed by the cob corn, and lastly, the rolls. The steam that rises from the main dish makes my stomach grumble. After we all have our portions on our plates, Emma once again says grace.

Passing the wine around, the women fill their glasses, while the men opt for whiskey. Emma has milk with her meal. As the food is being consumed, I steal a few glances at Cole, only to realize he has caught me doing so. I feel my face warm every time our eyes meet.

Flint and Maria engage in conversation at different times during the meal. Laughter and good spirits fill the room. Emma and I talked about what she has been up to at the store and with Mrs. Lacy. I observe her pass a potato or two under her chair, where the eager dog sits patiently, waiting for a crumb or two. I find it innocent and harmless, so I hold her secret to myself.

I pour another glass of wine to wash down the bit of food that remains on my plate. My arms are starting to feel loose, and I am having trouble cutting into a wedge of potato, even though it is cooked clean through. I am also glad to be seated; I am almost sure my legs are shaky as well. I hope the slight ringing in my ears will clear soon.

"Tessa, I was curious if you had given any thought to the new opening for the town's schoolteacher?" Mrs. Wells asks. Her speech is slow and hard for me to listen to; then again, it may be the wine.

"Yes, I have actually. I believe I am suitable enough," I reply as a piece of potato goes from my plate to the floor. Judging from the looks on their faces, I guess my guests have noticed my folly. When I bend in my chair to retrieve it, the dog swoops in and snatches it. As I sit back up, my eyes meet Maria's, and I see her mouth the words "I told you so."

Then Roslyn chimes in. "If you become the new schoolteacher, how would you manage it along with your responsibilities here?" she asks.

"I have been taking care of myself for quite some time now. I assure you I can handle it," I snip back.

"Besides, Tessa knows she has friends who live close by who could help if needed," Maria says in my defense.

"Tessa will do just fine; she may be the greatest teacher we have had yet," Mrs. Wells adds.

"What are your qualifications? Did you attend proper schooling that perhaps taught you how to teach young children?" Roslyn asks with thick sarcasm.

"I will have you know my mother was an excellent schoolteacher," I retort. "She taught me everything from grammar to etiquette. Perhaps it's you who should think back on your schooling for manners."

Whether it is the wine or the fact she truly gets on my nerves, I'm not sure. There is an awkward silence at the table, but only for a moment.

"Will you be my teacher, Ms. Tessa? I would like that very much," Emma blurts out with excitement.

"I promise to go right to town early Monday morning and go to the post office and take the job," I tell her.

"Then that means I can see you every day!" the little girl exclaims.

"Yes, and I could even walk you to the store to meet up with your papa," I comment.

The look on Roslyn's face is sullen, and I make a quick decision to be done with her attitude. Changing the subject, we all talk about the warm spring weather and the summer to come. Maria and Flint fill us in on how the foal is coming along and of their other plans for the ranch to thrive.

After dinner, we sit at the table for a spell, and Emma is exuberant about everyone trying her pie.

"Well then, I will clear the dinner plates and bring out all the wonderful desserts," I tell my guests.

"Tessa, do you need some help?" Maria asks.

Before I can answer, Cole excuses himself and stands. "No need, Maria. You enjoy your visit, and I will help Tessa clear the table," he says.

Stunned, I take an extra second to make sure my legs are up to the task of walking. My face feels hot, and I notice my friend has a large grin on hers. I pick up my plate and rest it on top of Emma's, then work my way around the table. Cole is doing the same on the other side; he works with such care the dishes are quiet, while mine are clanking up a storm. I damn my nerves for showing up right at the worst moment possible.

"I will bring dessert out as soon as I get these dishes to the basin," I announce as I walk to the kitchen. Cole follows closely.

In the kitchen I stack the dishes on the counter. My senses are well aware that Cole is in close proximity. I keep assuring myself that I look just fine. With my hands trembling and my nerves going haywire, I conclude I'm not very convincing, even to me.

"Tessa, being here for dinner tonight has been a great pleasure," Cole says. "The meal was well prepared and tasted good. I enjoyed seeing this side of you."

I turn around to thank him, only to find he has been standing right behind me the entire time. All I can manage is to stare into his eyes. My heart is pounding with such intensity I feel it knocking against my chest. My breathing is uneven, and I do believe it even stops a couple of times.

In his eyes I search for the answers to the questions I have asked him many times in my head. I want very badly to know what he is thinking.

"Thank you, I am very pleased you were able to attend tonight. It's good to see you outside of the store," I whisper.

The look in his eyes is more intense than before; I almost have to look away.

"You know, Tessa, I have been thinking a lot about your kitchen," he says, low and smooth.

Standing there before him, it only takes mere seconds to remember what took place in this very room the last time we both stood here alone. With that notion, I can't take the strength of his gaze any longer, so my eyes fall on his chest.

Gently he raises his hand to my chin and tilts my head back, and once again our eyes meet. I am holding back the urge to tell him everything, how I feel about him, the life I think we could have, and the way I yearn for him to have the same feelings toward me that I have for him. I hope he will go first, even if it isn't what I want to hear.

"Tessa, I have been thinking a lot lately. About what happened between us. I feel as if I need to explain."

"Cole, you don't owe me anything. I do not want to worry you," I lie.

Secretly I want to know exactly what is on his mind. Just a hint or a tidbit so I would know I'm not crazy. Some kind of proof that he at least thinks of me at some point throughout the day.

"Tessa, I told you that I would never be sorry for kissing you, and trust me, I'm not. It's just I don't know what to do. There are too many things that would get in the way." He stops.

Mulling over his words, I have to wonder what he is referring to. Things? I am lost.

"I am sorry, Cole, if I don't understand. What things are you talking about? Can you tell me more?" I plead.

"I…I can't. I don't know how to begin to tell you. It's too much to figure out. There's Roslyn and the store. I have to think about what's best for Emma. I just haven't been able to figure out how to make it all work," he stammers.

I feel like I have been punched in the gut. He doesn't want anything to do with me. I was right all along—I'm not good enough. Swallowing hard, the only thing I can offer is an apology. I speak bluntly.

"Cole, I am deeply sorry I caused you such worry and guilt. I can see you do regret what happened, even if only a little. I am a grown woman, and you do not have to protect my feelings by pretending. I know I don't have much to offer. I ask, though, if Emma and I can still remain close friends."

Feeling as though I am crumbling on the inside, I still look him square in the eyes. I'm not sure, but the expression in his features seems to be gone. Maybe he's suffering from shock over how well I have taken his rejection.

"That is not what I meant," he says. "It has nothing to do with what you think you lack. I want to take this chance with you, I just—"

"Cole," I interrupt. "Really, I am going to be fine. I am just relieved that you informed me before things got too far."

I turn to reach the pies and scoop them up to take to the waiting guests. I hear Cole call my name to come back, but I have to keep walking to save myself from further humiliation. As I place the pies on the table, I hope for my sake that no one notices I am a bit unnerved.

Cole appears shortly with the cake in hand, which he sets on the table as well. I busy myself with cutting the pie and serving it to those who want the treat. Cole has a request for the cake, and he serves it with kindness, as if he isn't bothered at all.

Back in my seat, I place a piece of pie on my plate and pour more wine into my glass. I drink half of it in one shot. Maria looks at me with great curiosity, but doesn't ask any questions. I'd bet my life she wants an explanation; however, that will have to come at a later time.

I engage in conversation as I eat my dessert. I act cheerful and even wear a smile, though I want to cry. Out of the corner of my eye, I can see Cole staring at me with fierce intensity. I notice that he forces a smile whenever someone offers a joke or talks of anything humorous.

After everyone has finished, compliments go around the table for all the efforts put into making the delicious food for this wonderful dinner. I lose count of how many times I fill my glass with wine; I don't care at this point in the evening. Cole still watches me, and I find that it no longer bothers me. My arms and legs feel heavy, and I even begin to notice how slow my speech is.

The influence of the wine has me giggling more than before, which feels nice, because just an hour or so ago, I could have given up. A little while later, Emma moves from her chair to the chaise lounge. The dog follows her, happy to have someone to cuddle up with. The two are really cute together.

With time passing into the late hours of the evening, Mrs. Wells declares she must be going home. Steadying myself, I get up to escort her to the door. Flint goes with her to help her into the buggy. Before she leaves the house, we exchange a hug and wish each other a good evening.

When Flint returns, it is he and Maria who next bid everyone a good evening. She and I agree to see each other in the next few days. I glance at my timepiece; it's nearly eleven o'clock. The evening went quickly, and I feel it was very successful.

Roslyn pipes up and admits she is tired and would like to go back to town. She thanks me for the invitation to dinner and commends me on how well I did. Cole walks over to where Emma is sleeping and pauses; he seems content to watch his daughter sleep.

"If you would rather not wake her, she may stay if you like," I offer.

Looking at me now, his face has lost the edge it held before.

"I will come and get her in the morning," he says. "It has gotten late, and I don't want to take her out into the night air."

"Honestly, I don't mind bringing her to town, if that works best for you," I tell him.

"No, no need. I will come around about midmorning. I will see the two of you then. Thank you again for dinner, we had a wonderful time."

"Anytime. I enjoyed the company as well; the pleasure was truly mine," I say.

Roslyn thanks me again as well. I don't know why she is being so kind. When she and I first met, I thought of her as evil and unkind. Tonight I feel as if she and Cole were not their normal selves. She acted interested in my well-being, and he was agitated and distant. After wishing both of them a safe trip home, I shut the door behind them.

I go to Emma and pick her up to take her to my room. That way she will have more room and will be familiar with her surroundings when she wakes. After I lay her down, the pup joins her on my bed, spinning circles until he gets comfortable.

I change into my nightclothes, then go extinguish the flames in the lamps and candles. I return to my bedroom to find the little girl sprawled out, taking up most of the bed. A smile touches my face as I bend and contort myself to fit into the free space left in my bed. I end up on my side, with my knees bent and my arms tucked up to my chest. I salvage some of the blanket and close my eyes. Hearing Emma breath is comforting.

I am tired from the events today and can't help but think about what happened between Cole and me. At least I know where I stand, and it feels better to know; however, at the same time I feel terrible.

At this point in my life, I am all right with being alone for the rest of it. Now that I know what to expect, I can plan for my future. I must accept a life of solitude. With that thought, I let out a heavy sigh and fall fast asleep.

CHAPTER THIRTEEN

The Race

As I place the biscuits in the oven, Emma still sleeps. I woke up early and decided to make some breakfast. Gravy with ground sausage is the topping for the biscuits. As usual the dog is waiting underfoot to see if anything is going to be dropped on the floor.

I pour another cup of coffee and sit down. Everything is tidy and restored to normal from last night's feast. Reflecting on last night's events, I curse myself for all the wine I drank. My head is throbbing a bit, but all in all, I feel pretty good.

I check the oven; the biscuits need a few more minutes. Going to my room, I peek in on Emma; her eyes are open when I walk in.

"Are you ready to eat? It's almost done," I say.

"Did my papa leave me here?" she asks.

She sounds worried, and I reassure her that he didn't just leave her. "No, it was late, and he didn't want to take you out into the night air," I say tenderly.

She bounces off the bed with energy as she speaks.

"Oh good, I was hoping he would leave me. I didn't want to deal with Auntie Roslyn. I'm glad he left me."

I chuckle a bit at her comment, just because she had me fooled for a minute. Here I thought she was worried, and it turns out she was exuberant about being left behind.

"Thank you, Ms. Tessa, for fixing me some breakfast. You are a really good cook," she says.

"You're welcome. I am glad to have your company this morning," I say.

I dish up our plates, and we sit at the table to enjoy our meal. She offers to help me with the chores. After eating, the two of us get to work.

Liquid Quiver

Emma does her best to feed Otis and Jed, then Maddie. By the time she is through, there is hay all in her hair and on her clothing. Her face holds a smile that warms my heart. I truly could spend every day with her doing just this. Our time together always seems joyful, and it's as if I have known the girl my whole lifetime.

We both have a lot in common even at my age. She enjoys gardening just as much as I do and baking goodies in the kitchen. I think of myself as plain and not of any great interest. At least that's what I have thought. And then I look at Emma. She is only five, but she is beautiful and fearless. Never afraid to speak of what's truly on her mind. I at times think we are different, but then again we make the perfect pair.

When we are finished in the barn, we hold hands and skip to the chicken coop. We gather the eggs and fill the feeder with grain, then giggle and chat on our way back to the house.

"Emma, your pa will be coming for you soon. Would you like me to make up a warm bath?" I ask.

"I'd like that very much, Ms. Tessa, just not too hot, OK?"

I busy myself with heating water while she plays with the dog. Before I empty the last of the water into the tub, I add a bit of rose oil to it. Once Emma is in the tub, I help her wash her hair. It is quite a chore to pick out all the hay in the tangled wet tresses. For the first time, I know what my mother went through countless times after I had spent a day with Pa at the livery.

Emma enjoys herself so much that I have to empty some of the water and reheat more twice before she is done. I wrap her in a towel and warm her by the fire.

"Look at my fingers and toes, Ms. Tessa. They are all wrinkly," she says, giggling.

"I see, now your skin looks like dried fruit—prunes to be sure," I tease.

She stands in the towel as I fetch her dress from the night before. I recall that I may have a dress my mama gave me that I wore when I was around Emma's age. A keepsake, I think she called it.

"Emma, come with me. I believe I may have something for you to wear," I tell her.

In my room, she climbs back on my bed as I rummage through one of my three trunks. In the very bottom, I find the cream-colored fabric I was looking for.

"Ah, here it is. Come, Emma; let's see if this will do."

The dress is just a bit long, but not by too much. The waist is larger too; luckily there is a ribbon that ties all the way around. For now it is suitable, and this way she doesn't have to wear the fancier gown from the night before.

"Was this your dress, Ms. Tessa? It sure is pretty," Emma says.

"Yes, my mama made it for me to wear on Sundays," I explain.

She walks to the mirror and checks her reflection, holding the skirt out, away from her sides, while turning in a circle. I do believe I did the same a time or two.

"Emma, let's brush the tangles out of your hair, and if you want, I can braid it," I tell her.

She skips over to my vanity and climbs in the chair. Working from the bottom to the top, I gently brush her hair. She thanks me when I am through, then bounds out to find the puppy. Taking the opportunity, I tidy up my own hair and check my reflection as well. There are slight dark rings under my eyes, so I dab a bit of powder on my face.

My hair is still in the twist, and I leave it at that. I change out of my nightdress and into a simple skirt and blouse. Remembering the night before, I think it's no wonder I am tired. Having the wine with Maria and then helping myself during and after dinner wasn't such a grand idea.

Out in the sitting area, Emma is petting the dog while he lies still on her lap. I sit next to her and pet him as well. Having her here is not only comforting, but I feel as though I have a friend to talk to.

"Is my papa going to be here soon?" she inquires.

"Yes, I do think so," I reply.

"I don't want to leave yet. Aunt Roslyn doesn't like me, and I don't like to be with her."

As I try to form the correct words in my head, I don't know if I should say anything. I try reassuring her. "Oh Emma, who wouldn't adore you? You are sweet and have a wonderful personality. Besides when she returns home, everything will be back to normal for you."

"I hope so, Ms. Tessa. I don't even want to go for a visit."

"No one said you have to. You don't have to go anywhere if you don't want to," I tell her.

During our conversation, my chest is tight and I am keenly aware of her concern that she is being forced to leave. Maybe while in town tomorrow, I will talk to Cole once again. He may think I am plumb crazy at this point, but I don't give a damn. My worry for Emma's safety is like an alarm going off tenfold for me to act on it.

A few minutes later, the dog lets out a soft growl. Standing at the window, I notice Cole is coming up the road. Emma and I begin to gather her things, and I can tell she doesn't want to go at all, which makes my heart ache even more.

We meet him in at the edge of the grass, where it meets the dirt. He dismounts, choosing to keep the reins in his hands, rather than tie the horse to the rail. By that action I know right away he isn't staying for long.

"Good morning, ladies," he says, tipping his hat.

Emma and I only nod at his greeting.

"Here are her things; she just had a bath this morning. The dress she has on, she can keep. I must thank you for letting her stay; we had a lovely time together." I tell him.

"I am glad you allowed her to stay, and last night's dinner was good," he says. Then he turns to Emma. "Are you ready, Emma? Aunt Roslyn is waiting back in town."

"I guess so," Emma says in a tiny voice as she looks at the ground.

Kneeling down, I look at her; she is close to tears.

"Oh, Emma, don't be upset. I promise you can return anytime you like. I will even come and get you if you want," I tell her softly.

She throws her arms around me and squeezes tight. Instinctively, I wrap mine around her small body and give a gentle squeeze back.

"You promise?" she asks.

"I promise," I say confidently.

When she releases me, she wears a halfhearted smile and turns to Cole. He scoops her up and places her on the back of his gelding, bids me a good day, then mounts up behind her. After a quick tip of his hat, he nudges the horse with his heels and rides away.

I stand there until they are completely gone from my sight. Letting out a loud sigh, I walk back to the house. Once I close the door behind me, a feeling of loneliness washes over me. The large house is empty once again, and it is quiet. The dog is still where he was before, and he watches me while his chin rests on his front paws.

"You miss her too, don't you?" I say aloud.

Judging by the back-and-forth motion of his tail, I have my answer.

There is still an hour or so before lunch, so I decide to get my gloves and go work in the garden. The sun is shining and I am thankful I placed the floppy straw hat on my head. The vegetables are beginning to poke through the soil, awaiting their time to stretch out their leaves and soak up the warmth from above.

Thinking back to the day Emma was here and helped me pull weeds makes me laugh. The image of her pinching her nose and making that face—I can't wait to see her in the morning. Just knowing that at the moment she might not be enjoying herself saddens me. I truly believe she deserves every ounce of happiness to be had.

After seeing to the job posting for a new teacher tomorrow, I may make a round to see how Mrs. Wells and Maria are doing. The more I think about taking the job, the more excited I become. I have always loved children and teaching them new things.

Deciding to take a break from the heat, I gather myself and my things. The basket of weeds I have collected will go to the chickens. The dog is walking close behind as we head back to the house. After removing my hat and shoes, I place my gloves on top of the small pile for future use. As I wash my hands, my mind reels with so many different thoughts, it makes me tired.

My insides feel upset, as if something is going to go terribly wrong; it just hasn't happened yet. After lunch, I retire to my room for a bit, tossing and turning for quite some time before falling asleep.

I don't dream; I just remember blackness. It was quiet, calm, and still. When I awake, there is a chill, and I think I can even feel a faint breeze. Breathing deeply, I swear I can smell sage mixed with a scent I am familiar with, but just can't place. I inhale again: that scent is of a fire. The kind of fire fueled by wood. Springing from my bed half-asleep, I am running as soon as my feet touch the floor.

Did I make a fire in my stove? Is it my house that's burning? The thought of a lamp still burning or a hot ember escaping the fireplace crosses my mind. I check every room and every lamp; I even check outside and in the barn. There is nothing. No fire anywhere. I can finally calm down.

I retrieve my wrap, then fill the heavy kettle with water to make some coffee. Sitting at the table, I ponder deeply what just took place and think maybe I have truly gone crazy. Maybe it is time for me to make that trip to Boston and see my parents. Getting away from here for a bit might do me some good.

Quickly that idea halts because of my lack of money. Tomorrow when I go for supplies, I will make sure to talk to Maria and Flint about getting my cattle to market. Only then will I have the means to live for the next year. I pray the beef prices are good this year.

If I can make it work, there will be plenty of time for me to make a trip to Boston. The teaching job will not begin until September, if I even get it. Getting my pencil and paper, I recheck my list of supplies. There are only a few staple goods I must pick up. I can feel my stomach working itself up again; I am nervous about seeing to the job in the morning.

What great fun it would be to inspire young minds and watch them grow throughout the year. Visions of their faces flash in my mind, and I already have a mental picture of how my room will look. My mama left a few of her things behind just in case I took the notion to teach; I must thank her when I see her.

After the evening chores, I busy myself with the rest of the mending. When I am done, I fold it nicely and place it in my saddlebags. In the morning all I will need do is saddle up and get on my way. Feeling ready for tomorrow, I take my hair out of the twisted fashion and take a bath. Relaxed and refreshed, I slip into my nightclothes and go straight to bed.

The next morning is chilly, and a slight fog hangs overhead. After rising especially early, I have already consumed more coffee than that of previous mornings. As I toss the bags onto Kate's back, I have a feeling in my gut that urges me to get going. I replace Kate's halter with the headstall, and we are on our way.

The mare must have picked up on my mood, because unlike times before, she, too, seems in a hurry. Arriving in town, I first go by the post office. Inside the small building, I ask the postmaster about the listing for the job.

"Yes, Tessa, let me get the form," the older gentleman replies.

"Thank you," I say as he passes me the paper.

After looking it over for a few minutes, I can't believe that not a single soul has signed up for it.

"Excuse me, are you sure this is the correct form for the position?" I ask.

"Why, yes it is. Is there something wrong?" he asks, his brows furrowed.

"No, I guess I am just shocked there are no names so far on the form. The position has been open for a month now," I say.

"Well, I am sure that there are a lot of women who want to take the job, it's just that most of them have young children at home to tend to. Honestly, Tessa, you may be doing them a favor by taking it. I'm sure they could use a break." He laughs.

Smiling back, I gladly sign my name next to the written numeral one. Thanking him again, I return the form and leave. I undo Kate's rope and I walk her toward Miller's store. As I go up the steps, I pull the small list from my pocket. The small bell tinkles as I walk through the door. I scan the inside.

"Good morning, Ms. Tessa," I hear Mason say as he stacks burlap bags filled with beans.

"Good morning, Mason. I have a small list for today."

"No problem. I can have this ready for you in just a few minutes," he tells me as I hand him the small piece of paper.

"There really is no hurry. I may walk to the hotel restaurant and have a cup of coffee," I say.

"OK, I will get started on it as soon as I finish restocking some things on the shelves," he says with a smile.

"Very well, Mason, I will see you in a while." I smile back at him.

I turn and go back outside, heading in the direction of the hotel. At the hotel, I choose a spot to sit, then hang my coat over the back of the chair. My seat has a view looking out of the window. I peer outside; the town is still sleepy, or it seems that way. It is earlier than usual for me to be here in town. How different it looks this early with the fog and the sounds of freight wagons being unloaded. It's as if the town has just opened its eyes from a long nap.

I order a breakfast of eggs and biscuits with my coffee. For some reason, I don't have the overwhelming feeling to hurry and get back.

With that, I'm not even worried about running into Cole. I only hope that Emma is doing fine. After a few minutes, my coffee and breakfast arrive. I thank the woman who brought it out, then begin to devour it. Skipping breakfast at home was probably not a good idea.

As I bring the coffee mug up to take a sip, I hear a voice calling my name. I look up and see Emma approaching my table.

"Good morning, Emma," I say. "How glad I am to see you! What are you doing out this time of morning?"

"Papa is at the store counting the crates that are being delivered, and Aunt Roslyn said I didn't have to go to Mrs. Lacy's, that she could take care of me before she leaves."

"Oh, I didn't know her stay was ending so quickly. Where is she anyway?" I ask.

"She is upstairs gathering her things. Her stage is supposed to come in the morning. I came down to wait for her so we could eat. What did you have?" she asks.

"Biscuits and eggs. Do you want to sit with me, Emma? You can take the chair across from me."

With that, she eagerly pulls the chair out and takes a seat. We chat about all sorts of things, and Dolly takes the seat next to Emma.

"Ms. Tessa, did you keep your promise?" Emma asks with a hopeful expression.

For a minute, I have to think to remember what she could possibly be talking about. "Of course, I always keep my promises. I signed my name on the list before taking my list to Mason," I reply, smiling.

Her face lights up, and she giggles with excitement.

"I can't wait for my first year of school!" she exclaims.

"Me either," I say back with equal excitement.

I take out my timepiece and glance at the face.

"Aw, do you have to go already, Ms. Tessa?" Emma asks.

"No, don't worry. I was noticing we have been chatting for close to twenty minutes now. Emma, you must be getting hungry. Let's get you some breakfast."

"I would like that very much. Can I have oatmeal? Aunt Roslyn won't let me put any sugar in it. She says it makes children uncontrollable."

"I'm not going to tell. How about you?" I whisper to her.

She shakes her head from side to side. When the woman comes to retrieve my plate, I order some oatmeal and toast for Emma. We continue to gab, as we have been doing, about the teaching position and how much fun we both thought it would be.

The oatmeal must be good; she eats it quickly while I drink another cup of coffee. She finishes the rest of her breakfast and drinks her milk.

"Did you get enough to eat?" I ask.

"Oh yes, Ms. Tessa, I did. Thank you," she replies.

There is no sign of Roslyn, even though it has been an hour. Who would let a child wander like this and not have any concern for their well-being? I drain the last of the brew in my mug and leave the money on the table for our meals.

"Well, Emma, I must be getting back to the store. Do you think that your aunt is going to come down?" I ask.

"I'm not sure. If I run up and ask, can I just go with you?" she says with a worried look.

"Of course. I will wait here for you to return."

She bounds up the stairs, and after a few moments she is back.

"She is not there. I couldn't find her anywhere," the little girl says.

I find that odd; why leave the little girl all alone? As I put on my coat, I reach out my hand. She takes it and smiles with Dolly in hand.

"Ready?" I ask.

"Ready," she repeats.

Exiting the hotel, we swing our hands to and fro and hum a song. I cherish the fact that she is comfortable with me and I with her.

When we enter the store, there are a few patrons checking items on the shelves. From the back of the store, I hear what sounds like two people squabbling. Listening closer, I think it sounds like Cole arguing with a woman. I look at Emma; she looks as confused as I am.

I begin to walk in the direction of the noise. Emma has a hold of my coat as she follows behind. When we turn the corner, Cole and Roslyn snap their heads in our direction.

"Emma! There you are. How dare you take off on me like that? You had me so worried, I was almost sick!" Roslyn cries.

At that moment I feel Emma's small hands clutch my coat even tighter. I don't know what that crazy woman is trying to pull, but it isn't going to work on me.

"I was just explaining to your pa that one minute you were there, and the next you were gone," she adds.

Cole looks angry and confused.

"Come, Emma Mae, we need to talk," he growls.

"Not without me you don't," I retort.

Roslyn's face goes a shade whiter than normal. I reach around my back and bring the little girl to my side. That bitch is lying and I am going to prove it.

Cole escorts us into his office and shuts the door. I have never seen Cole angry before; his eyes are sharp and his face is tight.

"I am not for sure what has gotten into you two females. All this fussin' and fightin' can drive a man insane. So the way I figure is, to let the two of you have your say-so. I have already been screamed at with Roslyn's version," he states firmly.

"Well then, I guess I better get to it," I say. I explain fully as complete rage boils just under my surface. "I came into town early this morning to take the teaching position. I then stopped here; Mason will know this because he took my list of supplies. Next I went to the hotel where I ate some breakfast. When I went to leave, I saw Emma, and she informed me that Mrs. Adams was coming down right behind her to eat as well. A half hour later, Mrs. Adams was a no-show, so I bought Emma something to eat. Just so we get this straight, it was a complete hour that both Emma and I waited. I sent her up to see what was taking so long, and she came right back down. Emma told me that the door to her aunt's room was locked, and she was nowhere to be found. Now here we are standing in front of you, being used by Roslyn, who clearly is trying to use us for causing uproar."

His stare, mixed with the silence in the room, sends a chill up my spine. My feet are firmly planted and my stance is rigid. I know exactly what happened and I'm not going to back down. It takes several minutes before he speaks, and I am truly interested in what he has to say.

"Do you think I am stupid, Tessa?" Cole asks.

Keeping my mouth firmly closed, all I do is mull over the question in silence.

"Maybe you do not believe this, but I can see right through Roslyn. My life has been complete hell since she arrived. Also I am very unsettled by the fact that my daughter was left alone at the hotel this morning. If it weren't for you, she still could be there alone at this moment. For that I am truly grateful. I as well think that she has something up her sleeve. I am just not sure what it is," he says.

"First, I guess I do owe you an apology," I say. "Though I never thought you were stupid, I didn't know if you could spot a liar, and a wicked one at that. She can fabricate quite the tale, spinning one thin, web-like lie and then another until she wraps everyone in it. I thought from the very beginning she had something in the works. What are we going to do?" I ask.

Watching his expression, I can see he is in deep thought. Then he says, "She leaves tomorrow on a stage to go back home. I plan on watching her close until then."

Suddenly there are sounds coming from outside; screams of men and women invade the small office. We run to the window to see what is going on. The scene is terrifying: men dropping everything they have been carrying and grabbing buckets and shovels. Stunned, I look at Cole, and we both know something is wrong.

Turning, I grab the hem of my skirt with one hand and Emma with the other.

"Run, Emma!" I scream. "Stay with me!"

Hurriedly, I run from the office back to the front of the store. Cole is right behind. As I stop to peer out the windows, he runs by me so fast that I feel the wooden floor give under his weight and then spring back.

Through the glass I can see a plume of smoke rising from a short distance away.

"Is there something wrong, Tessa?" Roslyn asks smoothly.

Her calm and cool demeanor makes me want to slap her face, and hard. How can she be so collected at a time like this? I can clearly hear the men outside shouting and feel the excitement in the air.

"I could take Emma off your hands if you prefer to run and help the men outside," she says in a silky, smooth voice.

Emma's hand tightens around mine; there is no way this wench is taking Emma anywhere.

"No. Emma will stay with me, and I will see to it that she is returned to Cole. Come on, Emma, let's go."

After leaving the store, we quickly walk in the direction of the confusion, being careful to stay out of the way.

"Can you see what's burning, Ms. Tessa?" I hear her ask.

"Not yet, just a little bit closer," I tell her.

As we walk on, we see men passing buckets down a line and more pitching dirt onto the fire with shovels. Many of them have soot and sweat smudged over their faces. Gasping, I recognize the building that's on fire—the new schoolhouse, now half burned.

"What is it, Ms. Tessa? What is it?" Emma asks.

Turning to look at her, I tell her it's the new schoolhouse that is ablaze.

"Oh, Ms. Tessa, now how are we supposed to go to school? You won't have any place to teach us," she says, her lower lip quivering.

I feel helpless standing there as we watch the structure burn to ashes. The smoke wafts with the breeze; it stings my eyes and catches in my throat. My stomach is queasy thinking about who could have done such a thing as this.

All Emma and I can do is watch as the inferno consumes the wooden skeleton until there will be nothing but embers left.

"Emma, I promise that I will do everything I can to have somewhere for us to go for schooling," I tell her.

She only nods her head in response, and I notice a tear running down her cheek.

A few hours later the blaze is reduced to a mere pile of smoking rubble.

Cole approaches us, wiping his face with his sleeve and looking tired. The bottom of his pants is slightly singed. His hair holds ash and soot, and he looks torn between anger and frustration.

"I am so sorry we could not save the schoolhouse. We will catch whoever did this," he says solemnly.

"The two of us are just glad that you are OK, Cole, along with the others," I say. "Don't feel as if you failed—it will work out in the end."

He exhales deeply and informs Emma and I that he needs to get back to the store. "Tessa, do you mind taking Emma to Mrs. Lacy's house? I thank you for what you did today."

"Yes, I will take her there, and she was no trouble whatsoever. After I make sure that she makes it there safely, I will return for my supplies. Then I must be going as well," I say.

Emma bids him good-bye, and we walk to Mrs. Lacy's house, where I tell her of the day's events. Shortly thereafter, I return to the store to get my things. After placing my items in my saddlebags, I tell Mason good-bye and walk out. Kate is patiently waiting, and I gently toss my saddlebags on her back.

The entire way home, all I can think about is the fire. I find it odd that the same day I sign up for the job, the fire burns the schoolhouse into a blackened scar that's now a blemish on the ground. Roslyn's cool and collected attitude was strange, and I have a feeling she knows something. I pegged her as the type to run around and act helplessly.

With Kate settled in her pasture, I hurry and do the chores. After pausing to start a kettle of water for coffee, I finish putting my supplies away. As the water heats, I change my clothes and wash my face and hands. Afterward, I sit in front of the fire with my coffee. The drink tastes wonderful. I'm not even sure why I'm so tired. For lack of a better reason, I blame it on the fire and my anxiety about the outcome.

I rise to my feet, and stoke the fire, deciding to retire early. It isn't dark out just yet, so I step out on the porch and check on things outside. Satisfied, I go inside, lock the door, and go to bed. Once I'm comfortable, sleep comes rapidly.

Suddenly, a loud banging noise breaks the silence in the late hours of the night. Being awakened by something so violently loud scares me straight into reality. When I don't hear it again, I think I imagined it, and I lie back down, only to hear it again—this time even louder and more forceful than the first time.

I reach under the mattress and pull the pistol from its resting place. I cock the hammer back and tiptoe to the front door with the gun by my side. My heart is pounding and I am shaking uncontrollably. With my back against the wall next to the door, my legs feel weak. The third time the pounding comes, I feel it through the wall each time the fist connects with the other side.

"You best state your business, or I will shoot right through the door!" I scream in hope that my warning will be enough to scare off whoever it is.

"Tessa! Tessa, it's me, Cole," I hear in reply.

"How do I know for sure?" I ask, trying not to sound frightened.

"Tessa, this is serious! Do you have Emma with you?" the same voice asks.

"I will open my door, and if you are not who you say you are, I will shoot you dead!" I retort.

As I open the door, I see Cole standing there with his hands up. Realizing it is him, I open the door the rest of the way.

"What the hell are you doing? And why would I have Emma?" I ask.

"It's a long story, but she wasn't there at Mrs. Lacy's. In fact her young daughter told me that a woman stopped by and picked her up. I thought maybe it was you," he explains.

"Then I remembered Mason telling me you had left alone this afternoon, and come to think of it, I haven't seen Roslyn since this morning. I stopped by Mrs. Lacy's after closing up the store and then helping with the schoolhouse. When I found out someone had picked her up, I thought it may have been you, so I came directly here. It didn't make much sense to me, why you would go home and then come back into town so late to get Emma," he adds.

All at once, fear for Emma and rage toward Roslyn come to the surface. What did she want from the child? I knew I had to help find Emma, no matter what it took. When I see Roslyn, I will slap that wench myself. I aim to find out what is going on and get Emma back home safely. I can't let Cole go alone, and there is no way I would stay behind and wait for word otherwise.

"Give me a few minutes to be saddled and ready. I'm going with you whether you like it or not," I warn him.

CHAPTER FOURTEEN
Taken

My body acts from memory as I get dressed to ride. I buckle the holster around my hips and shove the pistol into its place. The extra rounds that line the small of my back make me feel heavy. I throw a second coat over my arm and put my hat on top of my head. I turn on the heel of my boot and walk out of the room.

On the table are my saddlebags, which hold the few supplies I may need. I open the large pouch on the side and place another box of rounds inside. After fastening the bags shut, I scan the room one last time before I walk out. All the lamps are out, and both the fireplace and stove are cold. Carrying my things, I walk out into the blackness.

The chill in the air slaps my face and a shiver runs down my spine. Cole has Kate saddled, and as I walk to where they wait, I ask myself if I am ready for this. I toss my bedroll behind my saddle and secure it, along with my saddlebags. From the black that surrounds us, I hear Cole speak.

"You don't have to come with me, Tessa. I am sure that I will do fine on my own."

Turning to face him, I reply, "I know. I have to go to be sure Emma will be all right."

"It's my fault," he says. "I should have listened more to what you and Emma had been trying to tell me. I may never forgive myself."

Feeling my chest tighten, I reply, "Don't be so hard on yourself. No one could have known this was going to happen. Let's concentrate on finding her and getting her home safe."

Both of us stand there for several seconds in silence. I can see the anger and pain in his eyes and I want badly to touch his arm or his cheek and tell him that everything will be all right. Instead I stand there until he speaks. "We'd better get going and put some miles behind us."

Nodding my head, I turn and untie Kate, then step up into my stirrup and come to a rest in my seat. Sitting on the back of his gelding, Cole looks over his shoulder and asks if I am ready.

"Ready as I'll ever be," I reply.

As we urge our mounts forward, I flip the collar of my coat up and fasten the top button to keep the cold air out. I follow close behind him; the only way I can see is from the pale light of the full moon.

Thoughts are flooding my head at such a rapid pace that I feel faint. Where did Roslyn plan on taking Emma? Is Emma all right? I swear right then that even when we find Emma and she is in perfect condition, I am going to have it out with Roslyn, to make it clear she is no longer welcome anywhere around Emma, no matter what the cost—because I will pay it. As we continue to ride, neither of us says a word. I am curious if Cole is thinking the same thing.

***

As the sun hovers high above, I desperately want to stop and rest. We have been riding since last night and I feel as if I have no legs; at times my eyes have drifted shut. My bottom is sore, and it will be at least a few more hours until we arrive at the next town where the stage is due to stop. For Cole's sake, I won't say a word.

Relief comes about thirty minutes later when Cole suggests we rest the horses and get something to eat. We stop by a small creek and tie up the horses in the shade of a tree. Cole dismounts with ease, which leaves me to consider how I am going to get down. It has been years since I have ridden this much, and I don't want to make a fool of myself.

"Tessa, are you going to get down?" he asks.

"Yes, of course. I just need a minute," I tell him.

"Do you need help before I fill our canteens?"

"No, go ahead; filling the canteens is a wonderful idea," I reply with a smile.

I hand him my canteen, then wait until he turns his back before I attempt to dismount. Leaning forward over my saddle, I cup my hands around the horn and rest my chest on my hands. Then I wriggle both feet out of the stirrups. If I do this correctly, I should be able to lean to the left and slide right down to the ground. This is much easier said than done, especially when every muscle in your body is stiff and not cooperating.

I lift my head to make sure he isn't looking. The coast is clear. Tilting my body to my left, I begin to slide slowly from the saddle. When my left foot hits the ground, my leg buckles, and with a thud I am lying facedown in the prairie grass. Wincing in pain, I grab my stirrup and pull myself into a standing position. I worry that Cole will think I am weak. I loosen Kate's cinch to make her more comfortable while we rest. My next task is to make it to under the tree, where we are going to sit for a while.

It takes every ounce of willpower I have to make my body move in the direction I want to go. Once I make it, I slowly lower myself to the ground. Instead of sitting on my rump directly, I lean a little to the side to make it more comfortable. Cole is returning from the creek, and I am happy he doesn't see me land on my face. I put on a smile when he approaches.

"How are you holding up?" he inquires.

"Just fine, never better," I say, trying to be convincing. I can tell he doesn't believe me.

Taking a biscuit out of the cloth, I pair it with a bit of jerky, then hastily choke it down and chase it with water to make it easy. I would have gladly given up the food; for the minutes I waste on eating, I could be taking a nap. My body already feels stiff from sitting too long. The pace we have set isn't grueling, but it sure is no snail's pace.

When I am through with my meal, I tell Cole I am going to the creek to wash my face. Getting up proves to be challenging; I gasp short, quick breaths as my muscles tighten and fight against me. But stretching my legs feels nice; being in my saddle for so long really cramped them up. I kneel down at the bank of the creek and pool water in my hands to splash on my face. It is cool and soothing as it washes the dirt from my pores. I take out my handkerchief and pat my skin dry, then return it to my pocket. I stand back up and walk in the direction I came, taking my time so I don't have to get back in the saddle so soon.

Tired and sore, I keep reminding myself that I can do this, that I am going to make it. As I reach Cole and the horses, I debate heavily whether to sit down again; I am truly afraid I won't be able to get back up again. I walk past and go to Kate, where I check my tack and retighten her cinch.

"Tessa, in another hour or so we will reach the next town," Cole says. "There we can ask about Emma and Roslyn and pick up a few extra supplies. And if someone has seen them, I would like to push on," he adds.

Alarmed, I can only agree. I'm not about to tell him otherwise, and getting Emma back is just as important to me as it is to him. "Yes, that sounds like a plan. I think it's best we gain as much ground as possible."

I am alarmed by a few things: first that I am going to be made even more sore and stiff by moving on and hoping I could keep up; second, that I have never had to sleep out in the open alone—or with Cole Miller just a few feet away, for that matter.

***

With each stride the horses take, I can see the town coming closer. I stopped caring miles ago that my legs are completely numb and my backside feels as if I have had the worst paddling in my life. I want off my horse, and fast. On reaching the stage office, we stop our horses and dismount. I force my legs and arms to work with me, and I hold my breath every time my muscles pull and cramp in protest.

I nonchalantly loop Kate's rope over the rail; at this point I don't give a damn if she gets loose. I know she wouldn't go far; that mare has just had the longest ride of her life, and I'll bet she doesn't have the energy to even think of escaping.

While Cole goes inside to see if the gentleman has seen either Emma or Roslyn, I go to send Maria a telegram. It feels good to walk, even though my legs are wobbly and unsteady. A stiffness now takes hold of my back and shoulders. I spot the sign I am looking for, pause, and then go inside.

"Good afternoon, ma'am, how are you this fine day?" the man asks.

"I am just dandy. It's been a long trip. I would like to send a telegram or two if I may."

"Of course. Come right over here and pencil it down what it's to say and to whom I should send it to," he says.

With the pencil I write Maria's name on the form and proceed to compose the message. I ask her to check and feed the animals and to let Tigg out, that I had placed him in the barn. I also inform her that we may be a few more days, but I wasn't certain. At the end, I tell her thank you and that I hope to be back soon. I also note the direction we are traveling and tell her to send word there if she receives my message in a timely manner. I then start the other form. When I am through, I call for the man, and he appears at the counter.

"This one needs to be sent back to Munroe Junction, and this one needs to be sent to the town specified on the form, please," I tell him.

"I will send them right now, my dear," he replies.

I wait until he is finished, just to be sure he doesn't need anything else before I go. Then I say with a smile, "Thank you, sir. Have a good afternoon."

After leaving the telegraph office, I walk back to see if Cole has found anything out about Emma. I peer through the glass window of the stage office, but I don't see him inside. His gelding is still next to Kate, who has her eyes closed, blocking out the world around her. There is a crate nearby, and I decide to sit while I can.

When I notice Cole coming up the walk, he is carrying two burlap sacks, one thrown over each shoulder. I rise to my feet, curious about the contents of the bags and about what he knows.

"I found out that a woman with a young girl arrived here by stage just this morning," he says. "They just got underway a few hours ago. So the way I figure, if we press on until tonight, we will gain on the stage that holds Emma. It has to stop for dinner and will not proceed until the next morning," he adds.

Thinking this over, I swallow hard at the thought of riding all night. I won't have a backside left, or legs for that matter. I am beginning to feel hopeless. All I know is that I don't care if I lose my limbs or sanity trying to get her back; I'll do anything to see her safe again.

"All right, then. Let's get back on our horses and ride out," I say.

"First, Tessa, you need to tie this around the horn of your saddle," Cole says, shrugging one shoulder. The burlap hits the boardwalk with a thump.

"What's this?" I ask.

"I picked up a few extra supplies for the both of us, seeing as how we left in such a hurry to get started."

I bend over to pick up the sack, and as I tug to hoist it up, every muscle freezes at its heaviness.

"Here let me do it," he says.

"Thank you."

He easily picks it up and fixes it to my saddle. I wonder why it is so heavy, what could possibly be in there? Besides if we are riding straight through, why did he get two bags?

Before leaving town, we fill our canteens and water the horses. Cole's voice breaks into my thoughts. "Did you get your telegram sent all right?"

"Yes, thank you," I reply. "I let Maria know that I was OK and asked if she would check on things. When I return, she will probably see to it that I know what's exactly on her mind, with me taking off and all."

"I'm sure she will forgive you—aren't the two of you close friends?" he asks.

"Yes, the closest. Still, I hope she doesn't worry."

We mount back up and are soon on our way. The question lingers in my mind if I should tell him about the second telegram I sent. Quickly deciding against it, I promise to only tell him if it becomes absolutely necessary.

As we ride, I observe my surroundings. The horses make a swooshing sound as their legs pass through the lush grass. We even see a coyote or two, but they run out of sight as we intrude on their land.

I still wonder what is in the burlap sack. I toy with it enough to decide that there are potatoes or maybe onions in there. I hear a faint clinking sound come from Cole's sack when his horse takes to a trot.

"I must thank you, as well as repay you, for picking up my ration of supplies. I don't want you to think of me as a burden," I say aloud.

"You're no burden, Tessa. Besides I am enjoying the company," he replies.

I'm not sure what that means; he and I haven't really talked that much, and I for sure haven't done much of anything but tag along. I do wonder if I am slowing him down. I am left more confused about what he thinks, and his answers are never clear. Right then and there, I accept the fact that I may never know what he really thinks or is saying exactly. Rolling my eyes at his back, I brush it off.

***

It is almost dusk, and my stomach growls for the hundredth time. I try coughing or clearing my throat so Cole won't hear it and think we have to stop. After he asks if I am becoming ill, I quit so he doesn't think I am sick.

"Just a little farther, and we can stop to make camp and rest for the night," he tells me.

Camp? I thought we were riding straight through. My mind floods with questions and concerns. All of a sudden, I no longer worry about being attacked by the creatures of the night—that is second on my list. How am I to survive a night out here with Cole Miller? Maria is going to have my hide for sure!

We ride until we reach a small stream with magnificent trees all around and lush green grass. It is gorgeous. There is even a sea of wildflowers growing beneath the canopy of green, splashing color among the grass. The stream babbles, and crickets chirp in the background. It is the perfect meadow, the kind you want to lay down in and wait for the sun to rise and peek through the branches to caress your face.

Cole agrees to unsaddle the horses while I walk the perimeter to gather kindling for the fire. When I have an armful, I take it to camp and then go back out for more. My backside and legs are grateful to be out and about, not sitting in the saddle on the back of a horse.

The day is coming to an end, and as dusk approaches, the chill of evening returns to the air. I hope that the blanket I brought, paired with the fire, is enough to keep me warm for the night.

After finding plenty of kindling, I search for larger pieces to burn for the fire. From where I stand, I see that Cole has made a high line for the horses and has dragged two chunks of wood and placed them next to where the fire will be, to use as makeshift chairs.

Repeating my task several times, I produce enough firewood to get us through the night. I set to pulling grass where the fire will be and then put kindling on top of the dirt. I hope that Cole will soon come along and take over, because without newsprint, there won't be a fire if it is left to me.

Thankfully, he does come along. "Here, let me get that," he says. "If you'd like, could you fill our canteens?"

I sigh in relief that I am able to do something else.

"Oh, and in my sack there is a tin pot. Wash up some potatoes and bring back water to boil for dinner," he instructs.

"Sure, I'm better suited for that job," I say with a chuckle. "We would catch cold tonight; I cannot seem to make a fire without newsprint."

I walk to his horse, then reach inside the sack and retrieve the tin pot he mentioned, along with some of the potatoes. I pull the drawstring tight, then make my way to the stream with my items. Kneeling down at the edge of the water, I feel the coolness of the earth through the fabric of my pants. I take the handkerchief from my pocket, douse it in the clear, cool water, then wring it and wipe my face. With the falling temperature, my skin has instant goose bumps in protest as the cold rag touches my skin.

The vegetables sit in the pot, so I dunk the whole thing and wash each potato one by one. My mind is busy with thoughts. I hope Maria has gotten my telegram, as did another friend who isn't as far away now as she was a day ago. I dump out the water, refill the pot with fresh water, and fill the canteens before I go back.

"OK, I finished that. Is there anything else I can do?" I ask Cole.

"Nope, just set the potatoes over there, next to the fire. I am going to see if I can scare up a rabbit. I will finish tending to the horses and then go."

I walk to the fire and place my bounty outside the reach of the flames. Sitting down feels good, and I lean forward to stretch out my back. Cole gathers our saddlebags and places mine next to where I sit and then his where he has claimed his spot for the evening. He goes back and returns with our saddles, mine first, then his.

"Thank you, Cole, I really appreciate it," I tell him.

"Anytime," he replies.

I busy myself with laying out my bedroll and blanket. I'm proud of my work and smile at the fact that I did it myself.

"Are you going to be all right while I am gone?" he asks.

"Of course. I will keep the fire going and wait for you to get back."

"Don't go off without me. I won't be too long," he says.

As he walks out of sight, I peer in first one direction, then the next, all the while wondering, just where in hell am I supposed to go? I shake my head. I don't know where he comes up with such a foolish idea. Beyond the meadow is a vast emptiness; you can see for as far as you want. With the fire to my side, I feel its warmth on my face, which makes my eyes want to close. At one point I even shuffle away from the heat to keep my skin from feeling scorched. Being out here by the fire seems to relax my nerves and make everything better for the moment.

Hearing a twig snap, I look to my right. There is Cole with three rabbits in hand.

"Told you I would scare up a few of these," he says. "We can cook them over the fire and let the potatoes boil on the edge of the coals."

"I must say you are very impressive. I don't believe I could have done as well," I tell him, smiling.

We skin the game, and an hour after nightfall, the meat is roasting over the fire while the potatoes boil in their container. I can smell the mixed aroma that hovers over the fire. It brings back memories of when I was younger.

"What are you thinking about?" Cole asks.

"Just about when I was little and my pa and I went fishing; he and I cooked our catch over the fire."

"You looked lost in thought, so I was curious," he says.

"Memories, that's all."

"I'm sure it's ready—shall we eat?" he asks.

"Yes, I'm starved," I reply.

Using his leather glove, he tips the container to let the water escape. Then he reaches into his saddlebags and pulls two tin plates out and a pair of utensils. I am confused—I thought he hadn't planned on anyone going with him. Which makes me wonder why two of everything are packed in his saddlebags. He puts some of the meat on a plate and then dishes some potatoes next to it.

"Be careful, it's going to be hot," he warns.

I take the plate and cross my legs to fashion a table. The steam rises to meet my senses. I am so hungry, I probably could eat the food in an instant and not care if my mouth becomes scalded or not. I start by cutting the vegetables into more manageable pieces, blowing on them in hopes of cooling them faster.

I finish my meal before Cole does his, which may be a bit unladylike, but I don't care; I was starving. Eating in such a hurry leaves my stomach confused as to whether the food actually made it down; I feel as if I could eat more. I set my empty plate beside me, and eventually the warmth of the fire and the fact I have eaten make me feel more comfortable. The worries are subsiding, and I am finally relaxing.

"Tessa, if you hand your plate over, I will rinse it," he says.

I stretch out my arm and hand it to him. Normally I would do it myself, but the miles of riding have caught up with me. As he gets up, I promise him that I will take a turn next time—if we are out another night.

I fix my saddle and blankets and lie down. Watching the fire makes my mind go empty; I realize that for the first time the entire trip, I'm not thinking of anything. Sure I think about Emma and hope she is OK wherever she is. Being that she is out there and we are here makes me feel useless. I could saddle up and ride out into the dark and get even closer to her. Then again, if I did that, it could end badly and I wouldn't get to her at all. Weighing my options, I decide the best one is what I am doing now, resting up and being ready for whatever it takes to get her back.

Cole returns and takes his place by the fire. We make some small talk, and I feel my eyes getting heavy. Checking my timepiece, I see it is only a bit after seven. I haven't felt this tired so early in the evening for quite some time.

There is a definite chill in the air; I can feel it at my back. A quick shiver rattles my body, and I pull my blanket up even more. It is awful trying to get comfortable in all these clothes; my jacket is bulky and my pants are cold.

A coyote howls in the distance, and another chill runs up my spine. That sound is one I will never get used to or like. It makes me feel alone and vulnerable; there is an eeriness to it. I feel as if it is following me, as if I were its prey, taunting me with its solemn and creepy voice. I try to focus on the fire, my mind and body both weak and fighting sleep.

When the howl comes again, I reach down to my hip and unleash the pistol that lies waiting. I slowly bring it up to rest across my breast. With my thumb, I cock the hammer, hearing the distinct sound of the cylinder as it turns.

"Tessa, he won't even get close. We have a nice fire, and we have nothing of interest here for him," Cole tells me through the flames.

"I know that. It just makes me feel better," I retort.

He smiles and tells me to get some sleep, that tomorrow will be another day of hard riding. The last thing I remember before falling asleep is the thought of my backside being tenderized again and not having any feeling in my legs.

Waking up some time later, my teeth are chattering and my body is shivering. I pull my blanket away from my face to peer out of my cocoon. Cole is still awake and tending the fire. I don't know why I am so cold; I feel the heat from the fire, but the ground beneath me is freezing.

"You have been tossing and turning," Cole says. "I have your pistol—it fell from your blanket. Are you warm enough?"

"Y-yes, I am w-warm enough," I reply.

He takes his blanket and stands to hold it up to the fire, then he turns it around to evenly heat that side. He approaches me and lays it over the top of mine. The warmth seeps through, and my shivering ceases.

"Is that better?" he asks.

Nodding my head, I admit it is. My teeth are no longer chattering either.

"What about you?" I ask.

"Don't worry. I have my coat and a blanket from my horse. Now go back to sleep; it's late. I will watch and keep the fire going."

When I shut my eyes, sleep is easier to find this time.

The next morning, I realize I must have stayed warm throughout the night due to his extra blanket. When I awake, I'm surprised to see he has the horses ready. The fire is the last thing that needs tending to. Sitting up, I am embarrassed that I didn't wake up to help.

It is barely light out, and Cole isn't anywhere to be found. Hurriedly, I get up off the ground, groaning a time or two as I do so. These sore muscles and aches are going to be a challenge today.

I guess Cole is down at the stream, filling the canteens once more, so I roll my blankets and return them to the back of my saddle. The fire is almost out, so I kick dirt on it to finish it off.

Cole returns and bids me good morning, and I say the same to him. We clean up the meadow as best as we can, to make it appear as if we were never there, to leave no scars on this wonder of nature.

Liquid Quiver

Back on our horses, we lope toward the next town. I am anxious to know if Emma and Roslyn have been there and to know if I have word waiting for me. If so, I will have the answers I have been waiting for.

If we do not find Emma and Roslyn this time, then it will be a hard ride from here on out. Because in the town after this, people don't use horses to get where they are going; they ride steel.

CHAPTER FIFTEEN

Hide and Seek

The morning starts out brisk, but as it goes on, the sun makes it too warm for my heavy coat. I loop the reins around my saddle so I can squirm my way out of the coat. This time of year, spring can be irrational; one minute it's warm and dry, the next it's a downpour. Looking up at the sky, I see the clouds are getting darker the farther we ride. I lay my coat over my lap in case I need it all too soon.

"How are you holding up back there?" Cole asks.

"All right, I suppose. I'm a little hungry, but I can rummage through my stash," I reply. "Do you think we will run into that storm up ahead?"

"Let's hope not; it looks fierce," he says.

I calculate that it's a bit after noon, and if we do get caught in that storm, it isn't going to be pretty. Staring at the black mixed in with the darker blues, I see a flash that lasts only a mere second.

"Oh great," I groan under my breath. I gather my coat from my lap and put it back on. I only worry because if we are already in its path, then that means we have to face it. Where would we go?

"Come on, Tessa, let's pick up the pace. I have the feeling we are going to have to find shelter," Cole says with no hint of humor.

Kicking our horses with our heels, our pace quickens, and the grass beneath us becomes a blur. I am actually afraid of what is coming. The wind is picking up; tumbleweeds cross our path. The thunder is louder, too; each time it sounds, it rattles me to my very core and makes my heart beat faster. In the distance, a show of lights entertains our eyes. Lightning flashes and thunder booms as the clouds billow and move effortlessly across the horizon.

Liquid Quiver

All around us, the air feels charged with static, and the wind swirls around our bodies as our mounts cut through it. The trees are showing the undersides of their foliage, reminding me of the women who dance on the stage and wear fancy dresses and tall-heeled shoes. Even the horses feel it; I have to hold Kate back. Her ears are facing me in protest as if she wants to try and outrun it.

"Over here!" Cole shouts. I follow him, and we come to what I think is a rock wall. We ride up through some trees and find an opening that leads to a cave entrance big enough for the horses and us.

"Get down," Cole shouts. "We need to find some wood to start a fire. I will take the horses inside and then come out and help you."

Scrambling, I don't waste any time. I run as fast as I can, picking up anything that might burn. Just as he promised, Cole comes shortly to help. He grabs the bigger pieces of wood, while I take whatever.

We go back to the mouth of the cave and unload our bounty. When I pull sticks and twigs from my pockets, I hear a chuckle come from Cole.

"What?" I ask.

"Nothing," he replies.

"No, do tell what is so amusing to you," I retort.

"Nothing. Well, I find it interesting that you took the time to pick up the tiniest sliver of wood. That's all," he explains.

"Well! I will have you know that I was only doing as you instructed!" I say in disbelief. "And, Mr. Miller, I will have you know for a second time that I didn't come along to be laughed at!"

Standing in front of him with my hands on my hips, I glare my most serious glare and wait for him to say something. He is holding back laughter, and I think he has gone crazy.

"What on earth has gotten into you? Have you gone mad?" I demand. The horses are in out of the wind, but if we don't work together, there won't be a fire or supper. "I am going back out there to get some more wood. You get a fire started, OK?" I say sternly.

Spinning around, I don't wait for his answer. This is no time for him to go off the deep end; it makes me angry. When I step out of the cave, the wind is howling and gusting so hard it makes walking difficult.

My hair is being pulled out of its fashion and catching in my mouth and eyes. Going down the embankment, I take extra care not to fall. It is much darker, and I am glad that the rain has held off; the wood will still be dry for the fire.

Scouring around, I go this way and that. When I have an armful, I figure it's best to head back. Picking my way across the rocks, it is slow going. I don't want to chance tripping; picking up the wood a second time is not an option. My arms are getting tired and shaky, and I urge myself forward. It is taking me longer to get back, and fear creeps into my thoughts, and my stomach begins to flutter. The patch of trees I stand in don't look familiar.

"Don't panic; stay calm," I tell myself.

Just then a tremendous cracking sound comes from above. I jump, and some of the wood escapes my grasp. Cursing, I decide not to unload all the wood just for a few dropped pieces, so I leave what fell. After walking a little longer, I stop to see if I can make out where I am. I say a small prayer asking for help; in return I promise to cut back on my swearing.

It feels like hours as the minutes pass by, and I am close to giving up. I'm still not sure where I am going.

If by some chance Cole is yelling out for me and calling my name, it would fall on deaf ears. The whistle of the wind is the only thing screaming, and the rustling of the grass is all I can see. Another thunderous vibration and an ear-splitting crack come from the heavens, and at that moment, I regret going out in the open and getting myself lost.

The rain comes down with such a force that I can feel the droplets hit me through my coat. As it hits the earth, it makes a splatting sound. Even in the darkness, I can see the curtain of rain all around. In desperation, a tear runs down my cheek; I am lost and hopeless.

Then there it was—the smell of smoke. The kind only a campfire can create. Relieved, I follow the scent and eventually see the opening of the cave. It is lit up by flames that seem too large, but I don't care. It is a beacon for me to follow to return to where I need to go.

My coat keeps me mostly dry, but my legs and hair are soaked. Entering the cave, my body shakes and shivers. All the while my arms are locked around the wood.

"Tessa! There you are. I've been so worried. You're soaked clear through," he scolds. "I went out looking and screaming your name. I even fired a round or two. I didn't want to be gone long, in case you came back. I didn't want you to go looking for me," he explains.

Liquid Quiver

As if I don't feel foolish enough, he goes and talks to me as if I am a child. Being wet, cold, and hungry doesn't help matters, either. If I could talk through my clattering teeth, I perhaps would give him a piece of my mind. But all I can manage is to glare at him and hope he shuts up.

With my coat laden with rainwater, I am anxious to take it off and get into something dry, then warm up by the fire. Opening my arms, I let the wood fall to the ground. It echoes off the rock walls when it makes contact with the hard ground.

"There! There is the damn wood I went and gathered up. I want to sit by the fire after being out in that mess," I say angrily.

I go to my saddle and fetch the spare set of clothes I tucked away. In a dark corner, I change out of the sopping wet fabric in favor of the dry. Cole has his back turned to me the entire time. I watch him pour something into the tin pot as I finish buttoning my shirt.

I bring my wet clothes to the fire and lay them out on a rock to dry during the night. I am chilled to the bone; it feels as if I am never going to be warm again.

"I wasn't trying to sound upset with you," he says. "I was just worried, that's all. It should have been me out there not you. I'm sorry."

I think hard on what he said, but still offer no reply. I look away from him, to the fire. He sighs and continues to stir whatever is in the pot.

The storm outside is vicious; the tree branches whip back and forth. It is still early, but it is dark and gloomy out. Lightning flashes and thunder booms, filling our ears. My mood fits the events taking place outside; I feel as if the storm is agreeing with me.

I do feel childish for not talking, but I'm not sure I have anything nice to say. It's true I am grateful for having shelter; thanking Cole for that may be ideal. On second thought, seeing as how I went out for extra wood, I figure we are even.

Besides the sound of the fire, there is the sound of the metal spoon scraping the side of the tin pot time and time again. It smells good—whatever it is—beans maybe.

"Ready to eat?" he asks softly.

I nod my head. He dishes up a plate and hands it to me. He then tears off a piece of bread and places it next to the steaming food.

"Thank you," I say.

"You're welcome," he replies.

When the metal plate touches my lap, I think it is going to burn through my pants onto my legs. It feels good to have something warm; I can't tell if I am thawed out or not. To my surprise, the food is chili that he has been warming up. With the first bite, I scorch my tongue and don't care. I have felt hungrier on this trip than in my entire life. I would have never believed that spending so many hours in the saddle could work a person's body the way it does.

"There is plenty if you would like more," Cole says.

"All right, but I think you gave me enough this time around," I reply.

A bit later I use the last crumb of my bread to wipe my plate clean.

"That was good, Cole, thank you."

He only smiles back. He acts as if something is on his mind. I can't be sure what it is, so I try to make him feel at ease.

"She's OK, Cole. Emma is tough, and I'm sure that once the storm clears, we will catch up and get her back. You'll see."

"I know we will, and Emma is quite tough and stubborn," he replies. "Those qualities she got from her mother," he adds with a grin.

I grin back, and we hold each other's eyes for a moment. But the gaze is broken when I look to the fire. Rubbing my arms and legs, I still feel cold. Cole rises and takes our plates to the edge of the opening, rinsing them with the rainwater that is running off from above.

I reach for my blankets and make my bed. A sponge-like moss grows plentifully on the smooth rock floor. Once my bed is complete, it is actually cozy and even beautiful. I didn't realize that Mother Nature touches the inside of the earth as well. Running my palm across the moss is comforting; there is a bit of orange and yellow mixed in with the green.

Looking up at the cave walls, I see tiny vines that have even tinier flowers that are holding their faces open to catch whatever light there is. The leaves are dainty, and the vines have taken root in the smallest of crevices. The flames from the fire make our shadows dance within the cave.

"Lost in thought again?" Cole asks.

"Just taking a minute to appreciate what's around me," I say.

"Me too," he says in return.

I blush because I don't think we are talking about the same thing. I have learned not to get my hopes up; besides, he made it perfectly clear at the dinner that he wasn't interested. I have given up anyway—and good thing, too, after being laughed at earlier for being so precise. We would never get along, I think. Yep, I like my life the way it is. Dull, boring, and lonely.

The bad thing is, even I can tell I am lying. Every day I have longed for an adventure, or at least someone to talk to rather than the animals or myself. Maybe that isn't the life I am meant to have—at least it feels that way. Besides the friends and family I interact with, solitude was dealt into the cards I hold in life.

Now, feeling at my lowest and waddling in self-pity, I turn my thoughts to the journey ahead. Thinking about Emma's birthday cheers me up. I hope to ask Cole's permission to make her a cake and have her out. If not, maybe he will let me bring it to her.

I have no idea what to give her as a gift, but I'm sure I can come up with something. To see her smiling face is what I am aiming for. Roslyn has it coming, no matter what.

That turns my attention to the telegrams I sent out. I pray that I have two waiting my arrival in the next town. Savannah is my last hope. If she doesn't get the message I sent, then we have a long road ahead of us.

I bring my focus to the present and nervously fix the blanket I'm lying on. Glancing over, I see Cole's eyes fixed on me.

"What?" I ask cautiously.

"I really am sorry for earlier. I didn't mean to upset you. I wasn't laughing at you, either. Can I try to explain?" he asks.

It takes me several minutes to answer. I have no clue what he is going to say. However, my curiosity gets the best of me.

"Sure, I will listen to what you have to say," I tell him.

Straightening my back, I brace myself for the words to come. It feels like forever passes before he speaks.

"I...I don't know how to begin, Tessa. Please excuse me if I ramble. I wasn't making fun earlier, and I didn't mean to laugh. When you come into the store every Monday, I can't help but run and assist you. The way you talk, I always want to hear more," he says. "Do you understand?"

"Not really," I reply with an eyebrow raised. "Do you mean to tell me I talk a lot, and you see me each Monday to rush me out? I can't say that I understand."

"Let me start over. Uh, your quirks, I mean qualities, make you who you are. At times you seem frail, and other times you are fierce and unstoppable. I don't know how to take you; one minute I have you figured out, then the next, not so much," he explains.

"How about now?" I ask.

He sighs heavily and runs his fingers through his hair. "Never mind that I brought it up," he says.

"OK, never mind then," I reply.

The feeling that something didn't go well looms over me. If I thought I was confused before, I thought wrong. I talk about other things, such as what he is going to do when we return home with Emma. About his opinion on how the crops are going to do this year. Anything to ease the tension a bit. After a while we are both laughing, and it becomes easier to talk with him as the time passes.

Sometime later I ask if he wants me to take the evening watch. As usual, he declines and tells me to get some sleep.

"Are you sure?" I ask.

"Yes, Tessa, I'm sure. Do you want an extra blanket?"

"That would be very kind. My hair is still damp, and I think it would be a good idea," I tell him.

"Wouldn't want you to catch cold on this trip," he replies.

After lying down, I get comfortable and pull my blanket up to my chin. It is a bit chilly, but not too bad. Cole comes over and puts his coat over me, and the faint smell of his cologne lingers in the air surrounding me. I feel closer to him somehow, and I relax almost instantly. It is like a confirmation that he was really there, I wasn't dreaming or making it up in a fairy tale.

Closing my eyes, I try wishing my brain to transport me to the dream I've had where he and I are taking a walk and visiting getting to know one another. No such luck. I lie with my eyes closed, feeling as though he is watching me. I am too afraid to open my eyes to look.

"Goodnight, Tessa," he whispers.

"Goodnight, Cole," I reply softly.

For the first time ever, I think I sleep with a smile on my face the entire night. I now know what it's like to bid him a goodnight for real.

Liquid Quiver

I wake slowly to the smell of coffee and the clinking of metal cups. I see Cole tending the fire and pouring the dark brew.

"I hope I didn't wake you," he tells me.

"No, not at all. What time is it?"

"Late. Well, early, actually. It's about two."

"A.m.?" I fire back, surprised.

"Yes. I planned on letting you sleep for a while longer. The storm quit an hour or so ago, and I thought maybe we could get started," he explains.

"Of course. I feel refreshed, and I think we should have a bit of coffee and gather our things and get going," I tell him.

"Really? You're OK with that?" he asks.

"Yes, the sooner we get going, the better."

I get up and give him back his coat in exchange for a cup of coffee. Soon our horses are saddled and our things packed. I feel energized. The air is warm, and droplets of water are falling from the trees. Illuminated by the light of the full moon, the drops look like liquid silver dripping from a metal-worker's ladle.

As we ride, I can feel my horse sink into the soft earth with each step she takes. It must have rained quite a bit while I slept. The air is fresh with the smells of wet dirt and water. My heart beats fast with anticipation because somehow I just know we are going to find Emma. A smile crosses my lips, and a laugh leaves my mouth.

"What?"

"Today is the day, I just know it," I tell him.

"I sure hope it is," he says with enthusiasm.

Around eight or nine that same morning, we ride into town. We split up, going our separate ways: he to the stage office and I to the telegram office.

Swiftly I dismount and go inside, where I find two messages awaiting me. The first is from Maria, who lets me know that she will take care of everything and that I will be in big trouble when I get back if I don't fill her in on all that happened on my trip.

The second is from Savannah, who I knew lives in the next town and runs her own office. She is the doctor and at times is out on her calls, caring for expectant mothers. I met Savannah when my family lived in Boston.

She always had her doll wrapped with some kind of cloth, claiming it had an injury. It's no wonder she became a doctor.

Ripping the seal open, my hands are shaking. I read as fast as I can. She informs me that she is in town and will go forward with what I asked. Unless we find Emma before then.

Saying thank you to the clerk over my shoulder, I literally run out. I grab Kate's rope and lead her quickly to the stage office.

"Well?" I ask.

"The clerk said they were just here!" he exclaims, throwing his hands in the air. "They left and are headed to the next town as we speak."

"Let's go, Cole! We can do this; it's not too far from here. We can ride like the devil is on our heels."

In no time we are mounted and racing to beat the clock. I hope our horses will make it at such a rate. They had next to no rest, and we are riding at breakneck speed. I know I can trust Savannah to come through; she has to, for Emma's sake.

We slow the horses as we reach the edge of town.

"Cole, wait."

"What? Tessa, come on, they are just within reach," he scolds.

"I know. We can't risk being seen. I have a plan—do you trust me?" I ask.

I see the hesitation and then hear it in his voice. "Yes, I trust you," he replies.

"OK then, follow me."

Skirting the town, we go straight to the livery. Our horses are exhausted and a thick lather comes from under their saddles. A large bear of a man greets us at the entrance of the barn-style building.

"Afternoon, ma'am, sir. What can I do for you?"

"We will need to board our horses for the night," I say. "They are due for a rest. Hay and grain please."

"I sure can do. Say, you look familiar. Have we met?" he asks.

I look from him to Cole, whose face has curiosity written all over it.

"I got it! You're Eli Jackson's daughter," he replies, his voice booming.

"Yes, you are correct. I'm Tessa."

"Who is this with you?" he asks crossing his arms defensively.

"Oh, don't worry. This is a good friend of mine, Cole Miller," I reply.

He looks Cole over as if he were sizing him up, then makes a decision and throws his hand out toward Cole in an offering.

"Cole Miller, I'm Abe. I've known Tessa since she was this big," he says.

Cole takes his hand, and they firmly shake as if they were old acquaintances. "Nice to meet you, Abe."

"You don't worry 'bout them horses, you hear? Anything for Tessa and her friend," Abe tells him. Abe is a good family friend, and I can tell Cole wants an explanation.

"Listen, Abe," I plead, "I need a favor. We are here on important business. I don't want it out that we are here. I will fill you in later. Could you keep our horses out of sight?"

"You bet, and I won't tell," he says.

"Thank you, Abe." I stand on my tiptoes and place a kiss on his cheek. I assure him that we will be around, and if we need him, we will call on him.

Abe insists that since we want to stay inconspicuous, we stay with his family. He tells how his wife is an excellent cook, and his two young sons would love to have us.

We agree. Cole and I wait while he ties the horses inside. Then he takes us out through the back and shows us a door just down from the livery.

"Come on, you two, I will introduce you and then be on my way to take care of your mounts," he says. He leads us to the front of the house and shouts for his wife. "Ada! Ada, where are you?"

"Coming!" a small voice says.

When his wife comes around the corner, I see that her voice matches her size. She must be only an inch shy of five feet.

"Ada, this is Eli's daughter Tessa. She and her friend Cole will be staying with us for the night and for as long as they need," he says. She hugs us and welcomes us into her home.

"This is Alex; he is five. And this is Max, who is seven," she says proudly, pointing to her sons. "Come on, I will show you to your room. Clean up, because supper is almost ready."

We follow her to a room, which has only one bed, a washstand, and all the comforts of home.

"Thank you, this is more than we could ask for," I tell her.

"I'll take the floor, and you can have the bed," Cole says with a grin.

Hide and Seek

An hour later we are seated with Abe and his family for dinner. Roast and potatoes with fresh bread and salad litter the table. All of us visit and laugh, Cole however was quite. The only sound coming from him was the tapping of his fingers on the table. I could sense his nervousness. Alex and Max tell stories from their summers before and how they helped their dad at the livery, feeding the animals in the stable.

After the meal, I help Ada clean the kitchen, and Cole and Abe slip into the front room to have a drink.

"He sure is a handsome man," Ada says.

"Oh, um yes, he is so-so."

"When is the big day?" she asks.

"Big day?" I say quizzically.

"You two aren't engaged?"

"No, no. We are just friends and are here strictly on business."

"I see, my dear. You two are engaged but don't want anyone to know. Don't worry, I won't tell," she says with a wink.

Great, I think. I brush it off, figuring it could be worse. She means well, and it is improper for a single woman to be accompanied by a man—and a single one, for that matter. Better to be thought of as engaged than a hussy. I enjoy Ada's company; she is exuberant and charming.

When we are done, I am glad to call it a night, and go to bed. I am tired from all the excitement and want to be rested for tomorrow. I feel bad that Cole volunteered to take the floor, so I take the extra time to lay the blankets down, and I give him the plump pillow and me the flat one.

When I have it perfect for him, I crawl into bed. I feel a little guilty for turning in so early, but the past few days have worn me out. Abe's family is kind and generous, I think. Supper was excellent; it satisfied my appetite. I can't believe how fortunate I am to be once again sleeping in a bed.

Soon I am fast asleep. I dream of things that are random flashes of events, like a puzzle whose pieces were scattered into the wind: events such as the trip here, and of things that could happen, and then of the trip home.

Visions of tomorrow weave into my dream. It is going to be tricky, but with Savannah's help, I am certain it will work.

CHAPTER SIXTEEN
Doctor's Orders

I wake early to the sound of Abe getting ready to go to work at the livery. Hearing Ada tell him good-bye is my cue to rise from bed—I didn't want to interrupt their morning routine. I roll over to the edge of my bed and see Cole sleeping on the floor next to me. I take several minutes to admire him while he sleeps. There are so many things I want to know; I feel silly for some of the things I am so curious about: How does he like his pancakes? Toasted on the edges, or blackened on both sides? Would he prefer blueberry cobbler or peach?

For the moment I am completely mesmerized by his sleeping form. The way his hair is tousled from sleep makes his face seem softer. As his eyes move behind his lids, I wonder what he is dreaming. He even looks calmer somehow. Maybe while he slumbers he doesn't have a care in the world.

I try to think of ways to make him see that no matter what comes his way in life, I will be there. Yet I also try to ready myself for it to go all wrong. Even if it does, I think I will still try. Watching him sleep is indeed something I could do for hours on end. If I knew for sure that I wouldn't wake him, I would reach down and caress his face with my hand. I have admitted to only myself that my mind is frequently occupied by such thoughts.

At times I have felt ashamed because he is not mine, and I have no right to take liberties with such ideas and the thought that he ever could be. Often I have dreamed of a life with him, how it would be to make him breakfast and see him off to work. To mend his clothes and have him come home to a perfectly clean house. Emma and I could do so many things together after school—anything from horseback riding to making pies. If

I had the chance, I would take Emma to see my parents and show her what Boston is really like. My mother would show her everything in a day, taking her around to the bakeries and the doll shops.

I keep all of these thoughts and my emotions as my very own secret. I am too afraid to say what I feel for fear that someday I will have to face the fact that he may choose another. If that happened, I would have to watch as he and another lived a life that I had only dreamed of. I have wondered if he has such thoughts as I do, though, so I stand in the background waiting for something to happen. The only way I know how to describe what I am feeling is to say I would do anything for Cole and Emma, make sure they have nothing to worry about and see only happiness in their lives from here on out.

Finally I get out of bed, step over Cole, and walk into the kitchen, where Ada is working.

"Good morning," she says.

"Good morning."

"Would you like some coffee?"

"Yes, thank you," I reply.

She and I visit over our mugs of coffee about our daily lives and how Cole and I came to meet. I tell her of the misfortune with Emma and about our trip here. Ada tells me that she wouldn't know what to think if one of her children were to come up missing, only that she would never give up looking for them. Searching everywhere until they were found.

"I still think it's a beautiful thing, you know," she tells me.

"I don't understand."

"Your engagement. The two of you will do great things together."

"Oh, we are not engaged, really. We are both widowed and—"

"Dear, maybe you and your friend are not engaged, but I can see that he has feelings for you," she says.

I want to assure her that he doesn't see me in that way because it is next to impossible for him to see me that way.

"Ada, as much as I dream for that to be true, I think it is one-sided. I don't think he feels the same. It has been so long since I have let my heart feel anything, I think I have forgotten how," I say. "And besides, I don't see anything in his actions to tell me otherwise."

"In time, Tessa. I think you are looking too hard in the wrong direction. I can see it already. When he looks at you, his eyes warm and his face holds a smile." She grins. "And give him time, too; maybe he feels as you do—not sure how to say what he feels."

"Good morning, ladies," Cole says as he comes into the room.

My face warms at the thought that he might have heard what we were discussing. Ada acts like nothing happened and serves him coffee as well. He sits opposite us at the table, and I rise from my chair to fill my mug. When I am seated again, I almost can't look him in the eye.

"OK, before another minute is wasted on waiting for you to tell me I have to know what it is you are up to." he demands.

"Well, I sent a message to a friend of mine who lives here. She is the doctor, and her name is Savannah. We agreed that she would watch for passengers coming off the stage. If she saw Roslyn with Emma, she was going to quarantine them."

"For what?"

"Tuberculosis. We thought it would be reason enough to hold her up for a few days, giving you and I time to catch up," I tell him.

"I really wish that you would have told me, do you even understand my frustration? I worried the entire way here," he says with irritation in his voice.

"I'm sorry. I didn't know if she was going to be out on a house call or here in town. She is the only doctor and midwife in this area. I didn't want to disappoint you in case she never received word that you and I were looking for them. Then what?" I fire back.

Truthfully, I feel bad because I knew at some point she did get my telegram; but if I had told him and it didn't work out, I couldn't have watched him suffer.

"I wasn't trying to hurt or deceive you in any way. I prayed I would reach Savannah in time so we could get Emma back. If you are mad, then be mad and blame me for not telling you," I retort.

"All I was saying was that you could have told me," he says through clenched teeth.

"Like I said, I'm sorry," I reply, glaring at him.

For several minutes, we sit in silence. Ada kindly works around us as we have our spat. I don't like how I feel at the moment, as if I have let him down and can never make it up to him.

"What's the other half of your plan?" he asks.

"It was more like a thought, not really a plan. I doubt you are really interested," I spout out.

Shaking his head, he looks upset.

"The other half was to think of a way to get Emma away from Roslyn. If we catch her with Emma, we can get her back. But if Roslyn sees us first, she may try to run with her," I explain.

"Well, maybe we could sneak out word to Savannah and see if it will work," he says.

"I can send the boys to go fetch her," Ada remarks.

We turn our heads in her direction; the three of us look at each other and agree that would work.

"That is a great idea," Cole says. "We can have her make a house call, and no one would be the wiser that we are here."

"As soon as the boys have had breakfast, I will see to it they go right away."

Drinking the last of my coffee, I nod in agreement.

As the boys put their shoes on, we instruct them to tell no one about our presence. "OK, boys, be quick and go straight there and straight back," Ada says.

"All right, Mama," Alex says.

"Max, keep an eye out for your brother; don't get separated," she tells him, then kisses their foreheads before letting them out the door.

"Now we wait. The town isn't too busy today, and let's hope that the doctor doesn't have too many patients," Ada tells Cole and me.

After some time, I have to get up and do something. I help Ada clean and tidy up the house.

"Tessa, can you stop pacing?" Cole says. "I have watched you walk around this table a hundred times or so."

"I can't help it. It's been how long?" I ask.

"About an hour."

"That's it?"

"Yes. You should sit down. They will be back," he says.

"Fine." I take a seat at the table and begin to drum my fingers on the wood.

"Can't you sit still for just a minute?" Cole says.

"I'm trying to be patient. I can't help it."

"They will be here soon; just give them time."

After what seems like an eternity, I hear the door open. The boys have Savannah with them.

"Tessa! How have you been?" Savannah exclaims.

"I have been fine; you look great," I tell her. "This place must be treating you good."

"There is no shortage of babies; I have delivered both of Ada's boys, too," she replies.

We hug briefly, and Ada dismisses the boys outside so the adults can talk.

"Do you have Emma? If so how are we going to do this?" Cole asks.

"I have both your little girl and her abductor in quarantine for seven days. At least that is what she thinks," Savannah says.

"We need to somehow make sure we get Emma out and to safety, then deal with Roslyn," I say.

"I can call her into an examining room and keep her occupied so you two can get Emma. That seems pretty easy, I think," Savannah suggests.

"I think that would work," I say. "I can bring her here to keep her away from Roslyn, and besides she doesn't know where to come looking for her."

"All right then, but how are we going to get word to you and Cole that Roslyn is away from Emma?" Savannah asks.

"What if one of you stays behind and waits for her to come out, then follows her. While one of you goes and gets the little girl," Ada chimes in.

"I will follow Roslyn," I blurt out.

"And I will get Emma," Cole says.

"The boys and I will wait here in case you need help," Ada replies.

We all agree to the plan. Savannah leaves, and Cole and I get ready. He checks his pistol, then puts it back in the holster. I hope he won't have to use it. The plan is a simple one, and I say a quiet prayer while I get ready.

Cole and I head out and take our places, lying in wait. We are standing on the side of a building in the small alley, waiting to see Savannah come out with Roslyn. Cole asks me to check the time; he and I figure it has been longer than half an hour.

"Do you think there is something wrong?" I ask.

"I don't know; give it a few more minutes. If she doesn't come out by then, we may have to try something else," he says.

My head starts spinning, and I feel short of breath. What if something has gone terribly wrong, and Roslyn knows we are here?

"Tessa, quit tapping your foot. Are you getting nervous?"

"No, I just want this to be over already," I answer. "I want Emma safe again."

"As do I. Well, are you ready?" he asks.

"Yes, for anything. What are you going to do?"

"We can both go and bust down the door, or we can ask someone to deliver something to the room and report back to us what is going on in there," he says.

"I can go ask Ada while you wait here," I tell him.

He nods his head, and I quickly go and get her. When we return, Cole shakes his head no, answering the question I didn't have to ask.

"Ada, are you sure you want to do this?"

"Of course, Cole. Don't worry, I will be fine."

With that Ada walks from the alley and across the street to the hotel. All we can do is wait for her to come back. Seeing her outside so soon is a relief. But as she approaches, her face looks grim.

"What? What's wrong?" I ask right away.

"When the doctor opened the door, I wasn't allowed inside. I could see your little girl and her aunt. I also thought I heard a man's voice before I knocked, but there wasn't a man to be seen. The woman is refusing to come out of her room. She doesn't believe she has been exposed and wants to continue on her journey," Ada informs us. "I asked the doctor if there was anything needed by the sick, and she told me no, but to check back in."

Looking at Cole, I feel we need to do something—and quick. From there we will have to figure something out.

The three of us go to the hotel, and Ada leads the way to the room. She knocks on the door, and we wait for someone to answer.

Several minutes later, the door opens, and we hear Savannah's voice invite her in. Cole and I stay hidden in the hallway.

"What are we going to do?" I whisper.

"Let's give her a minute and see if Savannah is going to send her out with Emma."

As we wait outside the door, the sounds of "Camptown Races" being pounded out on the piano and loud patrons bellied up to the bar float up to the hallway we stand in. Suddenly, there is yelling coming from the other side of the wall.

"I told you, I do not feel ill!" she screams. "And neither does my daughter!"

Looking at each other, we both know it is Roslyn putting up the fight.

"You must understand it is for your own safety," Savannah replies.

"I will tell you that I am sick of this town and being treated this way. I need to catch the train to Boston."

"I am the doctor's assistant, and I assure you that she cares for the both of you," Ada says.

"Cole, let me go in there," I tell him.

"She will recognize you. You can't, Tessa."

"It's the only way. Once I have Emma in my arms, I will call to you. Deal?" I say. "It's just Roslyn, and I have Ada and Savannah—don't worry."

"All right, but at the first sign of trouble, you better call out. Do you understand? I can't believe I'm letting you do this."

"I promise," I say with a smile.

I walk up to the door and then take a deep breath, unsure of what is waiting for me on the other side. I knock lightly, then wait. As the door opens, Ada's face reveals the truth I don't want to see: instead of the soft features I am used to, her face is tight and rigid.

"Come in," she says, her voice trembling.

The door shuts behind me, and it is then I know why.

"You!" Roslyn yells. "Well, I expected to see you somewhere on this hellish trip. Just not so soon."

Glancing around the room, I see Ada and Savannah standing in one corner. I don't see Emma, and that makes my stomach tie up in knots.

"Where is she?" I demand.

"Who, Emma?"

"Of course Emma, who else would I mean?" I reply.

When she doesn't answer me, I take one step and then an icy and chilling voice stops me dead in my tracks. "Hold it. Right there," he says.

I turn to face the man of mystery and see a skeletal figure who has obviously made a life of drinking too much whiskey and rousing with women. His hand is over Emma's mouth. I can see that her cheeks are turning white from his grasp. Her eyes are red from tears, and her face holds fear.

"Let her go, or else," I tell him.

"Or what? You and your friends are going to do what? No chance you have, none at all," he replies.

"I think you would be surprised at what three women can do," I say, taking a step forward.

"Don't," he says, bringing a pistol from behind his back.

"That's what I thought. Nothing."

Ada and Savannah come to stand at my side.

"Look at that. Three whores are tryin' to take on ol' Pete," the man says. "Never thought I'd see the day." Tobacco juice runs from his lip.

I notice that Emma is winking at me. Pete begins to scream in pain. The louder he yells, the harder Emma bites down on his hand. Letting her go, he raises his hand to strike her. I run to grab her, and we both crash to the floor.

When the man places the pistol at my head I scream as loud as I can, "Cole!"

The hotel door splinters into thousands of pieces as Cole kicks it open, and it comes crashing down with a loud bang. Pete whips around, and I count two shots that ring out in the small room. Pete reaches for his chest. I can see blood starting to soak his shirt, as the rest of his life leaves his eyes. He crumples to his knees and then falls face first to the floor. His blood begins to pool under his body.

"Tessa! It's Cole, he's been shot!" I hear Ada yell.

Roslyn tries to escape the room, but before she can, Savannah's fist connects with her jaw, and Roslyn is knocked to the floor. Savannah then rushes to Cole, and Ada begins to tear the sheet on the bed to use for compresses.

"Ada, come and take Emma out this way. Go back home, and I will meet you there," I instruct.

"But my papa! I was only trying to help," Emma says through tears.

"You did just fine, and you were very brave. I need you to go with Ada right now, OK? I will come to you after we help your papa," I tell her.

"OK, Ms. Tessa, you promise?"

"I promise."

As the two of them leave the room, I rush to Cole's side where he is lying on the wooden floor. He turns his head to look at me. His eyes are glazed over and half closed.

"Cole, we have Emma back, and she is just fine. You're going to be all right, you hear? Stay with me, we have so much to be grateful for," I say to him.

A smile crosses his lips, and his eyes close the rest of the way.

"Tessa, we need to get him back to my office—now!" Savannah says. "The bullet is lodged in his shoulder, and he is bleeding badly."

I look at the hand I am using to apply pressure; it is covered in blood. I smell iron and salt in the room. I get to my feet, then step out of the room and holler for help. Within seconds I hear the sound of heavy boots coming up the stairs, and the music has come to a halt.

Four men appear at the door. I instruct three of them to carry Cole to the doctor's office, while the fourth makes sure Roslyn gets to the sheriff. I briefly explain why it is important she gets there and where I can be found if the sheriff has any questions for me.

I follow the men who carry Cole, holding back the urge to tell them to hurry faster. I look at my hands. They are covered in blood. Cole's blood. I can taste the bile building in my throat, and I feel sick. Holding the door open, I tell myself I have to be strong for Cole and Emma.

When they lay Cole on the table, he looks lifeless. Savannah and I thank them as they leave.

"Is there anything I can do?" I ask.

"Yes, you need to wash and either go sit in the waiting room or go back to Ada's," Savannah replies.

"What?"

"Really, Tessa. I need to work on him and fast. You may end up being in the way," she says. "Trust that I will do my best. I know how much he means to you. Go and get some rest. I will come see you when I am done."

I now know how Emma felt, but she is right; my meddling would be irritating. I would be more help to Emma right now than anything, by reassuring her that her pa would be just fine.

"All right, Savannah, I will do as you say. I will wait to hear from you. I am going to wash first, then leave you to your business. I will be glad to tend to Emma; I'm sure she is wondering what is going on."

"Tessa, I will be over as soon as I can. Just don't expect it to be right away," she says. "Go on—you and Emma have been through enough today."

After I leave her office, the whole way back to Ada's I contemplate what to tell Emma. My thoughts even wander past the point of where I want them to be. What if Cole doesn't make it? What would happen to Emma? These notions make my head light and my legs weak. I won't allow myself to think that way; being positive and praying is the only way to go about it. After Savannah tends to him, he will be in even better shape than before. As I enter Ada's house, she rushes me a cup of coffee.

"Thank you."

"You're welcome. I put a little something in it to calm your nerves," she replies.

As I bring the cup to my lips, I smell the distinct odor of alcohol. When I take a sip, I gladly welcome it.

"How is he?"

"She is working on him now. I'm sure he will be fine," I reply.

"Yes, Doctor Christensen is excellent at what she does," Ada says.

"Where is Emma?"

"She is in your bed, fast asleep. She ate more than the boys and wanted to go to bed," she explains. "Poor thing, I don't think she has had a wink the entire time."

"I am sure she has had a rough go of it," I tell her.

She and I sit in the kitchen for quite some time. It is beginning to get dark out, and I worry more and more about Cole. I keep picturing him lying there on the floor with a pool of blood underneath him. Shuddering, I clear my mind of it.

"You look tired. Why don't you go lie down?" Ada says. "If she comes by, I will come and wake you."

"OK, I am rather tired, and I would appreciate that. Thank you."

She smiles and nods her head as I leave the table.

Doctor's Orders

In my room I see Emma fast asleep on my bed. I don't know if it is the day's events or Ada's coffee that has made me tired so quickly. My eyes feel heavy. Crawling into the bed next to Emma is near impossible, so I grab the bedding Cole used the night before.

After spreading it on the floor, I lie down and get comfortable. Soon I am once again surrounded by his scent and the memory of our time in the cave. I can't help but feel saddened at his current condition. I have so much to tell him, to try and make him understand. Knowing that I am imperfect and plain makes it even harder to plead my case; hopefully he can see past that.

Inhaling deeply, I relax and let the smell of him ease my fears and chase away my worries. Ada assured me she would wake me if Savannah came. Now that Cole is in the care of my good friend and Emma is in the room with me, I'm not so worried. As my body relaxes, my mind pushes away all of the thoughts and troubles. Instead I think about all the memories from our past and the ones that led us here.

Just before the blackness of exhaustion takes my memories away, I indulge in thoughts of the future. I know they aren't real, but I still let myself be consumed by them. These are my most secretive of all, and I feel too foolish to reveal them to anyone. So as I drift off to sleep, I made a wish for the thousandth time that someday they will be real.

CHAPTER SEVENTEEN
Redemption

I halt in front of the door and stare at the pine box that leans against the building. The inside looks too small for a man of his height. Studying it, I don't like the feeling it gives me. Did he have any family? If so, did anyone tell them he was dead? My eyes begin to water, and I quickly escape into the building.

"You needed to speak with me, Sheriff?"

"Yes, I need to know in detail what happened," he replies.

"I will talk and let you know everything."

As I sit down, I can see Roslyn peering at me through the bars of her cell. For the first time since we met, she looks tattered. I can plainly see that her right eye was blackened by Savannah's fist, and without the mask of powder, there is bruising on the opposite side of her face as well. I ponder deeply how it could have happened. She finally turns away and lies down in her bunk.

"OK, ma'am, whenever you are ready."

For the next hour, I tell the sheriff everything I know, from the beginning. I recall every detail from Roslyn's arrival in Munroe Junction to how I have come to sit in front of him. I also speculate about the fire, putting two and two together. I am even more enraged than before to know that she had something to do with it.

"Thank you," the sheriff says. "If I need anything more, I will have my deputy come and get you."

I rise to my feet and shake his hand. "Anything I can do to help, I will," I tell him.

When I step outside, I don't even glance at the pine box. Just the thought of someone you love being put into one and placed under the earth is sickening. I feel like crying. I want to run away, far away, where no one can see or hear. Then when I reach such a place, I want to bury my face in my hands and weep until I run out of tears.

I know that being tired must have something to do with my feelings. But why can't my life be normal? No death or sickness and, dear Lord, no more kidnappings. Sometimes I feel as if I carry the world on my shoulders, and if I fall, who will be there to catch it?

Deciding to get some fresh air, I take a different way back to Ada's. I stop a few times to look into the windows of the businesses. I see the ready-made dresses and all the new and upcoming things. For its small size, the bakery holds many delicious-looking treats of all sorts. At this time of morning, there aren't many people out and about, which makes it easier to stop and observe all the items in the merchants' stores.

I think about all the things that happened this week and hope that nothing quite as tiresome and heart-wrenching as this takes place ever again.

My mind is weary from the worry, and now that Emma is safe, there is the issue of dealing with Roslyn. Heading home before she is dealt with is out of the question. I continue my slow pace, enjoying the time to myself. Having the option to think like this is nice, but it has its moments; not only do I think about the good things, but the bad also come to mind.

I am ready to get on with it, ready to put all this behind us and get back home and return to my daily routine. It would be the best for all of us. I never have understood how it could be that one person makes a bad choice, and it takes the innocent so long to recover from it.

I think about going to see Savannah, but I don't. I haven't seen her since I left her office. My heart and mind are fighting against each other. One tells me to go and see how Cole is doing, and the other tells me to wait.

Choosing to go back to Ada's, I walk in that direction. If she doesn't have much to do, then I may just lie down for a bit. The extra rest would be nice and would pass the time.

"Hello, Tessa. How did it go at the sheriff's office?" Ada asks.

"All right. I told him everything I know," I reply. "Do you mind if I lie down for a bit?" I ask.

"Not at all. Emma is playing with Alex and Max. She will be just fine," Ada says.

I thank her and go to my room. I lie down but can't get comfortable. I toss and turn, thinking about Roslyn and when I saw her in the jail. Something about the way she acted struck me as odd. The whole time I sat and explained to the sheriff what had happened, she stayed silent. I had her figured as someone who'd object in every way if something or someone did her wrong.

In the pit of my stomach is a feeling that persists until I make a decision. I get out of bed and go and find Ada.

"I need to go back to the sheriff's office. Could you spare a washcloth and soap?" I ask.

"Yes, of course, but what for?"

"I know it's crazy, but there is something I need to do," I tell her. "I will be back shortly."

I take the items she gives me and tuck them under my arm. Walking as fast as I can, I go back to talk to Roslyn.

When I step inside, the sheriff greets me. "Ms. Wells, did you forget to tell me something?"

"No, I was just wondering if I could take these items to Roslyn and maybe talk to her for a moment," I reply.

"Are you sure?" he asks, sounding surprised.

When I nod my head, he points in her general direction.

"Go ahead and go back. If she gives you any trouble, just holler."

"I will do."

Slowly I walk back and stop in front of her cell. She is lying on a cot with her back to me. Her hair is a mess and her clothes are in ruin. I slide a chair across the floor, and the sound of it scraping the wood announces my presence. She doesn't flinch or turn around to see who is with her in the room, so I begin to talk.

"I brought you a washcloth and some soap. It isn't much, but I thought you may want it," I tell her. "I'm only here out of concern for you. I left this morning, and when I tried to take a nap I couldn't sleep. You strike me as the type that would defend themselves and say what's on your mind, and this morning you were awful quiet."

I am still talking to her back with the feeling I am getting nowhere. I wrap the soap in the cloth and pass it through the bars. I feel sorry for her because the jail is no place for a woman of any kind. Half of me is glad she is getting what she deserves, and the other half knows something isn't right.

The room is so quiet, I can hear a buzzing-like noise in my ears. Looking around, I can tell that this is a place used more for the drunk and disorderly. A rancid odor of acid and liquor hangs in the air.

From the quiet, I finally hear her speak; her tone is dry. "You think you know me, but you don't. At one time I went from poor and used, to having a grand life. Now I am back to the lesser of the two," she says as she rolls over to face me.

Her skin bears the bruise on her right eye from Savannah knocking her to the floor, but the other numerous bruises I can't account for. She sits up, and I hand her the cloth and soap. She dips it in the cool water, then wrings it out and washes her face. When she unbuttons the front of her high-collared dress, exposing her neck and chest, I almost get sick.

"Good heavens, Roslyn. Who did this to you?" I ask.

Around her neck is bruising from someone's grasp. With a half-cocked smile and a wicked chuckle, she begins to tell her side of the story.

"At one time I was a lot like you, innocent and loving. I made the mistake of leaving home at a very early age, getting myself into a profession I am not proud of. Along came a man who loved me. Or so I thought. We had a great life until I finally realized he wasn't going to stop visiting the other whores," she confesses. "He found a new one and kicked me out into the cold. No home, and only so much money to live on. I had nowhere to go."

"I am sorry," I tell her.

"Don't be. It's the cards I have been dealt in this hand of life," she responds. "I found out that Emma is to receive a large inheritance due to a family member's passing. My plan was to figure out how to get her to come willingly to Boston and show I had custody to receive the money. I was going to bring her straight home, then return to mine, and no one would have been the wiser."

"So you never had rash thoughts about hurting her?" I inquire.

"Of course not. The day I met Pete was like meeting the devil himself. I did pay him to cause a distraction, but I called it off to return home alone. He found where I was staying and threatened me with my life."

"Why didn't you tell someone? Anyone? We would have helped you," I tell her.

"And you."

My stomach turns sour in an instant. Thinking back on the days before, I do recall seeing him more than I ever had before.

"Go on," I demand.

"The day of the fire, I tried to escape alone. I hoped he would forget the whole thing and about Emma. He held a gun to my back and told me to go up to Mrs. Lacy's door and fetch Emma. He had been following you and saw you drop her off there. He took out his anger on me by using his fists for standing in his way, protecting Emma. There was no way in hell I was going to let him hurt her. When I tried to send a telegram to tell you what was going on, I received this." She touches her neck.

I sit there mortified by her story. Roslyn continues to wash her face and neck while I search for something to say. Running her story through my mind a second time, I can't believe what I just heard. But my instincts tell me she was telling the truth.

"Why didn't you tell your side to the sheriff?"

"Who would have listened? Besides no one had asked. I am tired of pleading. I admit it was wrong of me to involve a child. I changed my mind and decided there was no way I could hurt my sister's little girl. But Pete decided he was going to do it with or without me. I had to go for Emma's sake," she replies.

"If it is just as you say, then you don't belong in here."

"I'm afraid it's my story over a dead man's," she tells me. "How is Cole? Is he going to be all right?"

"I don't know. I haven't seen or talked to Savannah since he was shot," I tell her.

"Please keep me informed. I have been praying for him."

With the new information, I am dumbfounded. I plan to go to the sheriff right away and tell him Roslyn's side of it. Even though at one point I was going to see to it myself she got everything she deserved for doing wrong, I'm not going to stand for wrong to rule over what was right.

"I will help you as much as I can. I just cannot promise anything," I say.

"Thank you, Tessa, but I worry that what has been done is final."

She pulls something from the breast of her clothing.

"Here, take this. It's all the proof I have. He took all my belongings from me."

I reach for the tattered piece of paper.

"All right, I need to get back. Rest assured I will return," I say.

I walk away from her cell and go straight to the sheriff's desk.

"Where is the sheriff?" I ask his deputy.

"He is at lunch. Is there something I can do for you?"

"Tell him I need to speak to him right away," I say. "Have him come and find me as soon as possible."

"Yes, ma'am. I will have him come to you as soon as he gets back," he replies.

When I leave, I decide to go directly to Savannah's office. She is my friend, so I hope she will forgive me for seeking her first. I rap lightly on the door and then go right in. The first thing I notice is the silence. I move slowly and try to be as quiet as I can.

"Savannah?" I whisper. "Are you here?"

I then see her emerge from a room in the back.

"Tessa, what are you doing here?"

"I couldn't help but wonder how Cole was doing?"

She has changed clothes, but I know she hasn't stopped caring for him. There are dark circles under her eyes, and her hair is unruly. I have a feeling he may not be doing so well.

"Tessa, I hate to upset you after the rough few days you have had. Come and sit down with me."

I follow her to a room with house-like furnishings, where we each take a seat in a chair around a table.

"What is it, Savannah? You can tell me," I blurt out.

"I removed the bullet that was lodged in his shoulder and cleaned the wound. The bad news is he is running a high fever, and I am doing my best to break it. If I can't, he may be worse off than I had expected."

I am sure the shock is evident on my face. Today is proving to be just as challenging as the rest.

"Do you think he is going to pull through this?" I ask. "Be truthful, I can handle it, Savannah."

"If I can't get his fever to break in the next day or two, then the outcome looks grim. Only time will tell," she answers.

"Can I see him?"

"Yes, of course. He is unconscious, but if you would like to talk to him, I'm sure it would be a comfort to him. Come with me."

Savannah takes me to the room where Cole is staying. It feels hot, and the air inside is thick. Cole is lying on his back with a blanket tucked under both arms. He has no shirt on, so the bandages and gauze are easily visible.

"I will give you some time alone," she says.

"Thank you," I tell her.

She exits the room, and I go to the chair by the bed. I have so many things to say, I try to narrow them down to the ones I think are most important.

"Cole, its Tessa. How are you?" I say quietly.

I feel stupid for asking, because I can plainly see that he is not doing so well. So I start over.

"Cole, its Tessa. I came by to let you know that Emma is doing just fine. She is playing with Alex and Max and having a good time with them. Can you hear me, Cole?"

As I look at him lying there, I figure I better get on with it and say what I feel, just in case this is my only chance. My chest hurts from all the emotions I have kept hidden behind a wall of uncertainty. Seeing him like this makes me feel useless. His forehead has beads of sweat across it, and his breathing is labored. Gently, I take his hand and place it in mine. It is hot, too hot.

"All right, Cole, it's just you and me here. There are so many things I need to tell you. I am going to start with what I have wanted to ask for the longest time. How do you like your pancakes? Golden brown, or blackened on both sides? You see, as simple of a question as it seems, I hope someday to find out. I don't know if I can stand it if another woman finds out before me. You see I don't really know how to explain it, but I am going to try. I come in on Mondays because I know for certain that you are there. I wait until it's you that can help me, even though I know your store like the back of my hand. And when you talk, I listen just so I can memorize the sound of your voice." I tell him.

I still feel odd, not knowing whether he can hear me. If he can't, then my heart can't be crushed later.

"You and Emma mean the world to me. To see the two of you happy is all that matters, even if it's not with me. You have to get better, do you hear?" I finish.

Squeezing his hand, I bring it to my lips and place a kiss on his palm, then return it to his side. I stand there and take one more look at him, then turn to leave. Then, grasping the doorknob, I pause and look back, figuring it is now or never.

"I love you, Cole Miller."

I leave the room and close the door quietly behind me. Savannah greets me in the waiting room.

"Are you all right?" she asks.

"Yes, I am fine. I would like to come back tomorrow if I can."

"Of course. If there any changes before then, I will come and get you immediately," she replies.

After giving her a hug, I leave her office. I feel better to have gotten some things off my chest; however, it is too bad that I waited so long. I may never receive an answer.

Later that afternoon, the sheriff comes by, and we have a long talk about Roslyn and what happened. He and I both agree that the intentions were wrong, but that she had no control over what Pete did.

"Before I left, she handed me this. It would be in her best interest if you could take a minute to look it over," I tell him.

He reads the crumpled piece of paper, and I wait for his response. I already have the penciled words memorized.

"Well, this clearly shows that she tried to get help. Do you mind if I talk to the little girl? I need something more than this," he says.

I go into the house and call Emma. She comes out and sits on my lap, and I introduce her to the sheriff and explain that he would like to ask her a few questions. When he is finished, she runs back inside to play with Alex and Max.

"What do you suggest we do?" he asks.

"Honestly, at first I wanted her to pay dearly for every mistake she has ever made. Now my feelings have changed. I would like to make a deal. I believe that a little compassion can go a long way."

He and I talk for quite some time about the idea I have come up with. After convincing him that Roslyn has never known forgiveness and second chances, he finally agrees to what I have in mind.

"Of course, you know I will have to talk this over with Cole and Emma first," I tell him. "He is still being treated at Doc Christensen's place. When I have word, I will let you know what we have come up with."

"Ma'am, I will wait to hear from you. However, she is going to stay in my jail. I don't care if it's two more days or two weeks until you come and see me," he answers. "And I got to hand it to you, I wouldn't have been that kind under any circumstances."

With his last statement, I second-guess myself. I watch him walk away until I can no longer see him. I still know I am doing the right thing. I sit on the porch for a long time, watching people go about their business and trying to figure out what each individual is up to. I also think long and hard about the turn my life has taken.

It has always been as if I were a step behind, either waiting for someone else to go first or waiting for my chance. At the end of this year's summer, I will see my twenty-fourth birthday. Already I am a widow with a beautiful house that hardly ever gets enjoyed.

Life is out there, and all I have to do is go get it. Pondering all of my decisions leads me to think I should change my hermit-like behavior and seek what I want and get it. Satisfied that I have talked myself into it, I have a smile on my face. I truly have so much to be thankful for.

"Tessa! Tessa!" I hear someone screaming from a distance.

Looking down the road, I see Savannah running in my direction. I swiftly get to my feet and run to meet her.

"What? What is it? Savannah tell me!" I say, my voice crackling.

"It's Cole, he may not make it."

CHAPTER EIGHTEEN
Shattered

I pour water into the basin and soak the washcloth for the hundredth time. Dabbing Cole's brow is an action I have repeated again and again. Today marks the second full turn of the clock that I have spent at his side. I have only left for short periods, to check on Emma and to bathe.

The room is hot and muggy even though the sun long since retired and the moon took its place. May is coming to an end, and June is about to begin. Cole's fever is taking its toll. His hair has been constantly soaked, as have his brow and skin. The once-soft flesh of his lips is parched and bright red.

Savannah and I change the linens on his bed twice a day and wash his body with cool water. She is doing her best at treating his wound; it is only time now that will tell.

When I sit in the chair next to his bed, I tell him how Emma is and what she is up to that day, or I tell him about the weather. If I run out of things to talk about, I work on my needlepoint or hum a song to him. Other times, I don't feel like talking at all, so I listen to the clock tick away the time. I think about everything from beginning to end, and also think of my future and that there is a chance Cole may not be in it.

I hear footsteps approach and look toward the door.

"Any change, Tessa?" Savannah asks.

"No. His fever is still high, and he comes in and out of consciousness," I tell her.

"I could take tonight, Tessa, to give you a break. You must be exhausted by now."

"I don't know, Savannah; honestly, I am afraid to leave him."

"I understand, but you need to take care of yourself. At least get something to eat," she says. "Take a break and then if you would like, come back."

"All right. Do you promise to come and get me if anything happens?" I ask.

"You know that I will," she tells me.

Smiling at her, I get out of my chair, and we close the door to his room. She and I talk quietly while walking toward the door.

"Tessa, I will be here for you. Anything you need, just ask. You're not alone in this; we are both fighting to keep him. Me as a doctor, and you because you care for him. Together we will overcome this and see him through."

"Thank you, Savannah, that means so much. I have complete faith in the both of us," I reply.

Leaving her to watch over Cole, I start toward Ada's house. Once inside I explain to Emma that her pa is still at the doctor's office and it may be another day until she can go and see him.

"Is my papa going with the angels, Ms. Tessa?" she asks.

Her question shocks me, and I struggle to come up with an answer.

"No, Emma, I don't believe so. The doctor is taking good care of him, and I think he will be all better soon," I say.

Emma just stares at her shoes and nods her head.

"Don't you worry, OK? Let me do that. Soon you, your papa, and I will be heading home. He just needs a little more time."

"All right, Ms. Tessa," she says as she walks away.

I wash my hands, and Ada brings me a plate of food and sets it on the table. "How is he really?" she inquires.

"He still has a high fever, and I don't know how long it will last or even if we can get it to break," I tell her quietly. I try taking a bite of food, which smells delicious but has no taste.

"Tessa, you need to eat. Even if you don't feel like it. I'm sure by now, with all that has been happening, that your food has no taste," she says.

"How did you know?"

She takes my hand and holds it tightly. Ada proceeds to tell me about when Abe fell deathly ill from some kind of infection he had gotten from cutting his hand at the livery. First, they cleaned the wound and thought nothing of it. Then a few days later, he became ill. She tells me how tiring it was to take care of him both day and night.

"What happened next?" I ask.

"A new doctor arrived in town—your friend Savannah. She helped me day and night. My body was tired, but I couldn't rest. I ate, but my food was bland. With her help, we saw him through it," Ada explains. "The day he came back to us was the day I found out I was carrying our first child. I trust her with our lives, so don't lose hope, Tessa."

"I don't plan on it. Thank you, Ada."

I am grateful that I have met her in my lifetime. She encourages me to be strong and to keep fighting for Cole.

I talk and play with Emma for a while, then change so I can go back to Savannah's. The moments have ticked by, and I didn't want to miss anything. If he opens his eyes, I want to be there. Tucking Emma into bed, I kiss her forehead.

"Where is Dolly?" I ask.

"That man took her away from me. I tried to ask for her back, but he threw her out."

"Oh, Emma, I am so sorry, I know how much she meant to you."

Emma nods and yawns.

"Tell my papa I love him, please."

"I promise to tell him," I assure her. "See you in the morning."

She closes her eyes, and I stay until she falls asleep. After making sure she is comfortable, I kiss her a second time and leave the room.

Ada sees me to the door and hands me a small basket. "Here is some food in case you get hungry. Go to him and be at his side, and if you haven't done so already, tell him what he means to you," she says kindly.

"I have told him, I but I don't know if it did any good."

"He is listening, trust me," she replies. "Maybe not with his ears, but with his heart."

We say our good-byes, and I thank her for not only the food, but the advice as well.

When I reach Savannah's I immediately go to Cole. "How is he? Any change?" I ask Savannah.

"His fever is still high; soon we will have to figure out how to get fluids down him. Let's hope that he wakes soon," she answers. "I am going to get you some blankets and a pillow and then retire for the evening."

Savannah comes back with an armful and sets them down in the rocking chair.

"Thank you."

"Anytime. My room is upstairs to the right. If anything happens, come and get me."

"All right. Goodnight, Savannah."

"Goodnight, Tessa."

I arrange the room to make a spot on the floor for me to sleep. I fold the largest blanket in half and lay it down first. The room is still warm from Cole's body, so I only lay down one smaller blanket for cover. The pillow is nice and plump, with a lot of feathers. Before I go to sleep, I stand at Cole's side and give him Emma's message.

"Cole, Emma wanted me to tell you that she loves you and that she hopes you feel better soon," I say. "In case you need me, I will be right here. I won't go anywhere, I promise."

With the cloth, I blot the sweat from his brow. I hear him groan but can't tell if it is from pain from the fever or relief from the cool cloth. If I could have, I would have traded places with him.

"You listen here, Cole Miller," I say. "Emma needs you. You are all that she has. I need you, as well. I need someone to help me when I come in to get supplies, someone to bring a smile to my face, and someone to dance with at the socials. Come back to us." I speak quietly so only he can hear.

I put the now-warm cloth back into the basin of cool water and stand to remove my shoes. My hair is set free from the tight wrap, and I go to where I will sleep. After turning the lamp down so it's glowing softly, I lie on my side. Inhaling a deep breath, I can feel sleep creeping up fast.

I don't remember how long it has been since I slept. I am definitely more at ease when Cole is near. When I close my eyes, the room feels as though it is spinning in the blackness. That feeling confirms my weariness. Before too long, my mind goes blank, and I fall hard into slumber.

I am awakened by a rustling sound. I sit up. Cole is thrashing around in his bed, and my first thought is that he is going mad with fever.

"Cole, Cole. I'm right here, you're safe," I say to coax him.

"Water, I need water," he chokes out.

I reach behind me for the pitcher and pour him a glass. He tries to reach for it, but his arms tremble with weakness.

"Hold on, let me help you."

I put my arm around his back and help him sit forward. After I place the glass to his lips, he drains it in no time flat.

"M-more please."

Cole drinks four more glasses and goes back to being unconscious in mere seconds. I am thankful that he has finally gotten some fluids in him; I take it as a good sign. I lie back down, figuring it is close to midnight. I hurry to get back to sleep so I can get some rest.

After the first time he asked for water, it seems I am getting up once or maybe even twice an hour to give him more. Instead of lying back down on the floor, I decide to get a blanket and sit in the chair next to the bed.

As his body fights the fever, he moves restlessly on the bed. His skin isn't as hot as before; I pray the water is helping. At last he lies still. I lean forward on the bed, rest my head on my arm, and close my eyes.

"She is at Ada's and doing just fine," I mumble in my sleep. "I'm waiting for you to come out of this. I wanted to be here."

Slowly I realize I am answering someone's questions. I fight hard to come out of the darkness and back to the world. I feel like I am trapped in a pitch-black room and screaming at myself to open my eyes. Popping my head up, I blink back the sleep, trying to make sure I wasn't dreaming.

"Cole?" I ask sleepily.

His eyes are only half open, but relief still washes through me. Immediately I place the inside of my arm to his forehead; he is cool to the touch.

"Tessa, why do you look so worried? And why are you checking my forehead?"

"Don't you remember anything?" I ask.

I watch as he tries to pull something, anything from his memory.

"Well, I remember you calling my name, then I kicked down the door. I remember shooting a man and feeling a sharp pain in my shoulder," he says.

"Is that it?"

"Yes, it's a little fuzzy after that. I can't believe that all took place yesterday."

"Yesterday? Cole, it wasn't yesterday," I say in disbelief.

"What day was it?"

"Friday."

"What's today?"

"Tuesday. Early," I tell him.

I see the irritation on his face. It makes me nervous. He just woke from an almost four-day fever and to have him mad already isn't good. He is quiet as he seems lost in thought. Cole examines the bandages on his left shoulder and sighs.

"So that's why you were so worried. Was it really that bad?" he asks.

"No," I lie. "You just had a high fever."

"You don't have to lie; I can see it in your face that it wasn't good," he says. "I don't remember much of anything, dammit."

"I'm sure in time that it will come back to you; we can ask Savannah about it."

"Yeah, I guess you're right. You look tired. Why don't you get some rest. I am fine now, and there is no reason for you to keep watch," he says.

"All right, I can't say no to that. But if you need anything, I will be right here." I point a finger down to the floor.

He smiles and shakes his head. "I will. Now get some sleep."

Snuggled in my spot on the floor, I am soon captured by sleep once again. I dream of things to come: the journey home and my life back in Munroe Junction. Now that I am certain that Cole is going to live, I allow myself to dream of everything my heart desires.

When I open my eyes, the sunshine fills the room with brightness. The air is cool and fresh; with Cole's fever banished, the room even feels lighter. I rise up slowly out of my bed and get to my feet.

"Good morning," I hear him say.

"Good morning," I respond. "What? Why the Cheshire grin on your face?"

He begins to laugh, and I shake my head, thinking I must have missed out on something. What could possibly be so damn funny? I've been asleep the entire time, so I am curious.

"Well, I am glad to know that your humor is returning, Cole Miller. Care to tell me what has gotten you to bray like an ass?" I ask with my hands perched on my hips.

When he is able to speak, he wipes the tears from his eyes.

"While you were sleeping, I overheard you talking to someone."

Great. "What was I saying?"

"I don't know," he replies.

Squinting my eyes, I dare him to give it up.

"I really don't know, Tessa, but what I do know is that you were tearing the hide off 'em." He bursts out laughing again.

I think that wasn't really so bad—at least I didn't blurt out mushy talk. For that I am relieved.

"I don't ever think I have seen you that upset. To tell you the truth, it was kind of cute," he says.

"You're impossible!" I retort.

Cole continues to snicker as I walk out. I look for Savannah to fill her in on how her patient is doing. I find her in the kitchen.

"Tessa, I was just pouring you a cup of coffee. How is Cole?"

My face holds no expression whatsoever.

"That good, huh?" she asks.

"Miraculous. I'd say he is on his way to a full recovery. By the way, do you have anything I could give him to put him back out?"

"Why? Is he in pain?" she asks, looking concerned.

"He may be in a minute," I reply.

"Tessa! How could you say such a thing?" Savannah scolds. "Besides he probably feels much better. Think of what he has been through. Here, drink this; it will help you perk up a bit."

She shoves a mug full of hot black brew in my direction, and I gladly accept. I stay behind in the kitchen while she goes to check on Cole. When Savannah returns, she gives him a clean bill of health.

"Why don't you go and clean up and return later, Tessa? You will feel much better."

"I guess you're right. OK, I will see you after a while. I may bring Emma to see him when I come."

"That would be just fine," she replies. "See you soon."

Nodding my head, I place the mug in the sink. I am looking forward to a hot bath and to washing my mangled hair. After saying good-bye to Savannah, I return to Ada's. Emma greets me as soon as I walk in. I tell everyone of the good news that Cole is going to be just fine.

Afterward, Ada and I sit at the table and talk over coffee.

"How are you holding up?" she asks. "I am sure you are drop-dead tired by now."

"I am tired for sure, but it's much more than that. I feel like a mirror that has been dropped," I tell her.

"How so?"

"With all that's going on, the decisions and trying to figure out what to do next, I feel broken, like my life has shattered and the pieces are scattered everywhere," I explain. "So much to tend to, I don't know if I can keep up."

"Well, I suggest that you start by choosing one piece of glass. Then, when you take care of it, pick up another. When you have gathered all the slivers, only then will you have a whole mirror again," she says.

I realize she is right. I don't know what I would do if she and I had never met. Ada is a calm and caring soul who possesses wisdom, and I have learned a lot from her already.

A couple of hours later, I find myself in a hot bath. My body aches from the lack of rest. As the water grows cold, I stand to reach my towel. Ada was kind enough to wash my other set of clothes. Putting them on feels nice after the hot water and soap, and I feel rejuvenated.

As I help Ada for most of the morning, she and I visit and laugh. Together we complete most of her housework and begin supper. I know she has become a lifelong friend.

"I would love for you and your family to come and visit us one day," I tell her.

"That would be wonderful. Then Emma and the boys could play out in the open."

We smile at the thought and continue working on the meal. I help her clean up, and she puts the ham and potato soup on to cook. The home-made rolls are set aside to rise.

It is early in the afternoon, and it is gorgeous outside. The sun is warm and carries a breeze that barely brushes my skin. Ada and I gather the kids and take them on a walk. After seeing all there is to see in town, we venture out of town, where there is more room for them to play. There are trees for Ada and I to sit under, and the kids choose to play on the open prairie. We watch and laugh as they romp around, pretending to be great men and, of course, one princess.

"Come on, kids, we need to get back," Ada calls out.

All three of the children protest, but we promise to bring them back out another day. On our return, I ask Emma to wash her hands and face because I promised her we would go see Cole. Before I left this morning, Savannah had told me to give her some time to change the bandages and linens.

I can barely contain Emma's excitement as we walk to Savannah's. When I open the door for her, she runs inside.

"Papa? Papa, where are you?" she asks.

When she hears him call back, she rushes in the direction of his voice. I enter the room just after she does. Emma didn't waste any time; she had already bounded onto the bed.

"Hey, sweetheart, I missed you."

"I missed you too, Papa," she says.

They hug, and I feel as if I am intruding.

Emma tells him of her many adventures with Alex and Max and about helping Ada.

"I am very proud of you for being a big help to her," Cole says.

That brings a huge smile to her face. Then she points to his bandage and asks, "Is that where you got shot, Papa?"

"I guess so, but I'm better now."

"Does it hurt?" She pokes the wound through the bandage.

Cole winces at the instant pain, and Emma apologizes. Cole dismisses it and shrugs his good shoulder.

"Will it hurt forever?"

"No, I don't think so," he says. "And if it does hurt, all I have to do is look at you."

"You will? Why?" Emma asks.

"Because looking at you makes everything better."

Emma throws her arms around Cole's neck, and I can hear her tell him how much she loves him and that she is glad he is OK. It is a tender moment between father and daughter.

Two hours later I ask Emma if she is ready to go back to Ada's for supper. Agreeing, she kisses her papa on the cheek and tells him good-bye. I turn to leave and hear him call my name.

"Yes, Cole?"

"I just want to say thank you."

"For what?' I ask.

"Everything, I don't remember much of anything after being shot or while laying here. I owe a great deal to you, Ada, and Savannah."

"You don't owe anything. As long as you get better, consider it paid in full," I say.

Smiling at him, I leave the room. I find Emma talking Savannah's ear off.

"All right, Emma, come on. Ada will be expecting us."

"Bye, Savannah," Emma calls over her shoulder.

I escort her back to Ada's, and we wash for supper. After supper and cleaning up, I fix Cole some of the soup to deliver to his room. I set the ceramic bowl with a lid into the basket and add a roll or two. I tell Ada where I am going, saying I will return shortly.

I think about talking to Cole about Roslyn and my idea while I am there. I decide to first feel out what kind of mood he is in before I attempt it; it may have to wait for another day.

When I walk into his room, he looks much better. His color is returning, and his eyes are clear and bright. I open the basket, take out the bowl, and hand it to him.

"Careful, it may still be hot. Here are some rolls."

He thanks me, then begins to eat. He has an appetite, and for that I am thankful. It means we will be on our way soon. I tap my finger on my knee as I sit there watching him eat.

"What's on your mind?" Cole asks.

"Well, I have something I want to run by you. But first you have to hear me out. Then decide if you would like to consider it."

He finishes his meal in silence. After placing the empty bowl on the nightstand, he crosses his arms. I know then that this won't be easy.

"Well, get on with it," he says impatiently. "Let's hear what you've got in mind this time."

Chapter Nineteen
Time Will Tell

It's midmorning on Friday, three days after Cole's fever broke. Cole, Roslyn, Emma, and I are standing in front of the livery stable saying our good-byes to Ada, Abe, and the boys.

"Come back and see us. Maybe we can come your way in the next few weeks," Ada tells us.

"We would love to have you," I say in return. "Thank you so much for everything you and your family have done for us."

"It was our pleasure. Anytime now, you hear?" Abe responds.

While Roslyn helps Emma into the wagon, I steady Cole as he climbs into the seat of the wagon. Abe helps me make sure that Kate and Cole's gelding are securely tied to the back, and then he helps me into the seat of the buckboard. He winks to me as he tells me good-bye.

Cole's arm is inside his shirt because of the sling Savannah made for him. Earlier, when I went to get Cole, she and I bid each other good-bye and promised that we wouldn't let so much time pass before we see each other again. I am not even sure how I am going to repay her.

With the reins in my hands, I urge the team to move on. Ada and Abe saw to it that we had many supplies for the trip home. With four of us and a wagon, the trip itself will take longer than before.

Truthfully, I don't care. I got what I had come for, and I met an incredible family in the process. Roslyn's nature, her personality and outlook on life, all have changed drastically. She has warmed up and is excited to live a normal life and to do for herself, rather than depend on others. I found out she is good at many things, such as sewing, baking, and playing the piano. It isn't going to be difficult to find her a place to apply her talents.

Liquid Quiver

We travel until dusk before we stop to make camp. The place we choose has a few trees and a small creek. I try to remember if Cole and I came across this place when we were traveling in the opposite direction. When I help Emma down from the wagon, she immediately starts to run around and explore her surroundings. Roslyn steps down and then helps me to help Cole down, since his left arm is of no use to him. I can only imagine what it is like for him to have no use of his arm—or a limited memory.

All of us work together to make camp. Roslyn wears a smile, and I notice that her face is softer; she looks her age, which is younger than I previously thought; she and I are only a year or so apart. I feel sympathy for her having been through all of the things she has experienced so far in her short life. In my heart I feel that showing her a bit of compassion was the right thing to do; she made a choice to better herself and her situation. For that I can't be happier for her. I want to see her succeed.

In my mind I can see her being more independent and flourishing in Munroe Junction. There are rooms available at the hotel, so at least for now I don't have to worry about where she will stay. Perhaps she can find work at the bakery or maybe at the new boutique being built in town. We decided that when we return, I will take her around and introduce her to everyone so she can feel more at ease.

Emma, Roslyn, and I gather enough wood while Cole busies himself building the fire. The three of us then go get items from the wagon for dinner. Potatoes and carrots go into the pot with an onion, cubed pork followed by a bit of pepper. I help Cole make a spit over the fire, and I hang the pot of food over the heat of the flames to cook.

As Cole tends to our meal, we work on making our beds around the fire. Truthfully, I am tired. The day has been long, and sitting in the wagon being bumped and tossed around made my body just as sore as if I had been riding. I help Emma with her bed, then make Cole's. I am amazed and secretly overjoyed because when I unfold his blankets, his scent wafts around me. It reminds me of the time we have spent together since starting this trip, the talks around the fire, and the meals we shared in each other's company.

"Cole, we girls are going to the creek to wash. I will bring back some water for you so you don't have to walk so far," I tell him.

"OK, Tessa, I will stay here and tend to the stew."

The three of us walk to the small creek to wash. I carry the empty bucket to fill and take back to Cole. Kneeling at the grassy edge of the water, we wash our hands and faces. I can't wait to get back and take a hot bath in my own home.

"Tessa, I want to thank you for all you have done for me. Without your help, I wouldn't be here. I owe you and promise to repay you when I can," Roslyn says kindly.

"You owe me nothing," I say. "I just want you to live a happy life and see what it is really like to live."

She smiles, and I feel it is genuine.

There are a few days left in May; June is fast approaching. Emma's birthday is coming up soon, and I still need to ask Cole if I can make her a cake and invite a few friends to share it.

I fill the bucket with water, and then we all walk back to camp. The aroma catches our senses, and my stomach growls. After setting the water next to Cole, I notice he is having trouble getting the buttons of his shirt undone so he can wash and tend to his left hand, which is tucked in his shirt. Watching him fumble, I can see that he is getting irritated, but is too stubborn to ask for help. I let him work at it for a few more minutes, and when he still can't get them undone, I step in.

"Would you like me to help you?" I ask.

He shoots a glance my way, and I can tell he doesn't like the idea of me interjecting, but I can't just sit there and let him keep growing more and more irritated.

"Fine. I think my button is stuck or something; it won't let loose," he says.

"I'm sure it is." I go to him and crouch down in front of him. "Let me see."

I reach for the buttons of his shirt and undo one after the other easily. As I open his shirt, the back of my hand grazes his skin, and I hear him suck in a breath of air.

"I'm sorry. I didn't mean to hurt you," I say apologetically.

"No, it didn't hurt."

I continue to part the fabric of his shirt to expose his hand, still hidden beneath. I'm not sure, but I think for a minute that he isn't breathing.

I look at his face; he is watching me intently as I make quick work of the buttons.

"There you go. You shouldn't have any more problems with those pesky buttons," I say. "Let me know when you are done if you would like help to refasten them."

He says nothing as I get up and wander back to the blankets that sit waiting for me by the fire. Roslyn is busy getting utensils ready for us to eat with, and Emma sits on her blankets, poking a stick in the fire. I watch as Cole washes his hands and wipes his face with his handkerchief.

Cole's beauty caught my eye a while back. His eyes enchant me with their dark qualities; I never know what is concealed behind them. His hair is equally dark, like a raven's, and when I took the time to examine it in the moonlight, it almost shone with a hint of blue.

"Tessa, I am through. Do you mind helping me to fasten my shirt?" he asks.

"Not at all."

Once again I approach him, line up the fabric of his shirt, and begin to button it up. My hands are a bit shaky this time, thinking he may be watching me closely. The heat burns in my cheeks, and I can't look him in the eyes.

"There you go, good as new," I tell him.

"Thank you. Your help is greatly appreciated."

His breathing is rapid, and I feel light-headed. The air around us is buzzing, and I hear it in my own ears. My nerves are on edge, as if I went beyond an invisible line that had been drawn. Leaving Cole's side, I feel dizzy when I stand. I plop down on my bed harder than I planned; my legs can't hold me up any longer.

"It's almost done," he tells us.

All of us sit in silence. I figure that exhaustion has caught up with everyone.

"Who's ready to eat?" Cole asks.

Three similar responses go his way. He first dishes up Emma, then Roslyn, and I follow. I hold his bowl as he takes some for himself. When he winces in pain, my heart aches. The four of us barely speak as we eat. When we are all done with the meal, I stand to claim the empty dishes so they can be washed.

"Sit back down, Tessa, I can do it. You have done enough today," Roslyn says to me.

"Are you sure? I don't mind."

"Yes, I'm sure."

Thankful, I take my seat. It is difficult enough to keep my eyes open, and my body is trying to force me into an early bedtime. My limbs are weak and tired; sleep won't be hard to come by tonight. Cole adds a few more logs to the fire, the heat and flames increase as the fire eats the dry wood. I take off my shoes and pistol and place them by my side. Emma is fast asleep and Roslyn soon follows.

"You should try to get some sleep, Tessa. Tomorrow is going to be another long day," Cole says quietly.

"What about you?" I ask.

"I'll be all right."

"It's your arm, isn't it? Is it keeping you up?" I inquire. "I can give you some of the medicine that Savannah sent along."

"No. If it's the same as what she had been giving me, that stuff is awful, and it makes me sleepy. I can deal with it."

"All right, but if you need anything, just call out and I will help you."

Smiling at me, he nods his head, and only then do I feel comfortable enough to close my eyes. Lying there, I listen to the crackle of the fire and the crickets. Soon sleep captures me, and I no longer hear anything.

When I open my eyes, it is hard to focus as I look around. Slowly the fire comes into view, and I smell coffee. The fire is low but warm, and Cole is still awake. Our eyes meet and hold each other's long enough for me to become self-conscious. I quickly drop my eyes to the fire as my cheeks heat up.

"It's too early for you to be up, Tessa. Why don't you go back to sleep? I promise I will leave you some coffee," he whispers with a grin.

Feeling more tired than I was before going to sleep, I don't argue with him. I pull my blanket up to my chin, settle in, and close my eyes again. I wonder what time it is, but quickly discard the idea of finding out. I must have only been half-asleep, because I remember telling myself I am still at camp, even though my mind tries to convince me I am at home in my garden.

Liquid Quiver

I am busy pulling weeds and gathering the vegetables. It is so real I can smell the earth and feel the plants in my hands. The day is nice and warm. Working in my garden always relaxes me. Out of the corner of my eye, I see Pete. Fear creeps up into my chest as I watch him come into full view. He holds someone hostage. That someone is me.

His filthy hand covers my mouth; I can taste it. I can't cry out. I see the fear in my own eyes; I try to speak through them, to scream for help. Watching myself in Pete's arms makes me sick. I can feel the emotions radiating toward me from my other self. His rotten breath tells me to do whatever he wants. Over and over, I yell for myself to wake up.

Jerking my body up, I arrive back at the fire. Cole is sitting upright, covered by his coat. His eyes are closed, and I am surprised my outburst didn't wake him. Taking a minute to study him, I wonder if my confession is swimming somewhere in his mind and if it is going to surface. A twinge of fear sits on my chest. What will happen if he remembers? Will he cast me aside because he doesn't feel the same for me? Angry with myself, I sigh heavily.

I was in the room when Savannah said that his memory of being shot and anything after may or may not come back. For his sake, I hope he never has to relive being shot. The pain and misery are bad enough. To add to that, the madness of the fever would be a gruesome thing to remember. It would be to my advantage if he doesn't remember anything I said; it may give me more time to figure him out. However, I am learning that figuring out Cole Miller is becoming next to impossible.

Still, I let myself admire him and how handsome he is. I know I would never be happy if Cole was nowhere in my life. Even if I have to settle for him just being there when I need supplies, any interaction with him would be better than none at all.

I'm startled when he opens his eyes and catches me staring at him. I am caught by surprise; I don't have a chance to close my eyes and pretend I am still sleeping.

"Tessa, why aren't you sleeping? Are you OK?" he asks just above a whisper.

"I'm all right. It's just hard to sleep. Sorry if I woke you."

I'm not sure why I apologized; I made no noise at all and was sure I hadn't woken him.

"Are you warm enough? I could stoke the fire. I have an extra blanket if you need it."

"No, really, I'm fine," I say to convince him.

The fire is plenty warm and the night is beautiful. The air is cool but not cold. The trees hover above us; with their branches stretched out over our camp, it is like they are protecting us from the outside world.

"How is your shoulder feeling? Are you still in great pain?" I ask to change the subject.

"It hurts; I'm not going to lie. The constant throbbing is what gets irritating. But I'll live," he replies with a half-cocked grin. "Since you're up, would you like me to make some coffee for you?"

"I would like that. I will go and get more water."

"No need. While you girls were sleeping, I went and got more. Just lay there and relax."

I watch him work to get the coffee started, amazed at how well he does with just one good arm. The lighter items he holds with his left, while the right does the work. Soon the pungent odor of coffee fills the air. We both wait patiently for it to be done as we sit on opposite sides of the fire. Staring blankly into the fire, I hear Cole say something, but it doesn't register, and I have to ask him to repeat it.

"I asked you if you were sure that you are all right. You look lost in thought and seem distant," he says.

I am not going to tell him that I was thinking about my dream and what it could possibly mean. We both know that Pete is dead and can no longer hurt anyone. But foremost, it is what his memory holds captive that weighs heavy on my mind.

"I was thinking about home, hoping that all is going well for Maria," I lie.

"I'm sure she is fine. Besides, Flint will help her if she needs it," he replies.

"I guess you're right."

"Coffee is done. I can't come to you—can you come to me?" he says.

I fling my blanket back and go to him. He pours my cup first and then his. He hands it up to me; I have to reach down to get it.

"You know, I won't bite. If you would like, you can sit here next to me," he says jokingly.

Liquid Quiver

A smile touches my face and I chuckle back. "Promise?" I ask.

He begins to say something but quickly hesitates. I think I have said something wrong when he drops his eyes and stares at the ground. My legs won't move my body to where I sat before, even though I am telling them to. When he looks at me again, his dark eyes are filled with sadness and concern.

"I wouldn't do anything to hurt you," he chokes out.

His eyes burn into my soul. Does he think he frightens me? Grief washes over me. I think about telling him everything—the way he makes me feel and how only the thought of losing him frightens me. But my fear keeps me from saying anything. Gathering my hem, I sit down next to him.

"I know that you would never harm me," I say. "Whatever gave you the idea I thought otherwise?"

"It's hard to explain; don't even know if I can," he says, looking into the darkness that surrounds us.

"Well, we have plenty of time and some great-tasting coffee. I will listen to whatever it is you need to say," I tell him reassuringly.

I take a sip of my coffee; suddenly it has no taste. I am curious but wary of what he is about to say. My heart thrums in my chest, and my ears are ringing. Does he remember what I said? I didn't think his memory would return so soon.

"Tessa, this is going to be hard for me to say to you."

Here it comes. My undoing is hanging on his words. He looks me straight in the eyes, and his seem blacker than before. Scary almost.

"As much as I don't want to say this, I have to. Tessa, you can't have anything to do with me. I don't want anything to do with you. This can never go any farther. When we get back, things will have to be different. I killed a man, Tessa, and he wasn't my first. Don't tell me that you don't fear me. I woke only because a memory had returned to me. It was the look on your face just before I shot Pete. Fear was etched on your face so deep, I will never forget it. Now that I have seen it, I can't have you around me, knowing that you fear me and that I can't be trusted with your life."

I know he isn't joking; his tone is serious and his face tense. I swallow hard, and it hits me what he is saying. He doesn't want me in his life. Not now, not ever. I feel my chest squeeze, and then my heart breaks into pieces. What is left crumbles and falls to the pit of my stomach. Tears sting the back of my eyes. I want to tell him that the fear I showed that day was only due to the thought of losing him. If I lose him, it will be like losing the hope of ever really living again. If he and Emma are not in my life, then I have nothing to look forward to.

I take a few minutes to reflect on what he has just said, then respond the best way I know how.

"If that's what you believe and there is no way I can change your mind, then you shall have just that," I retort.

My insides are churning and I think I'm going to vomit. I hold it down and try to wash the taste of bile from my mouth by drinking the cold black brew. We have a couple or three days' worth of travel left. I promise myself that I will stay as far from him as I can.

"Do you understand, Tessa, why it must be this way?"

Shooting him the most evil glare I can muster, I nod my head. I want to scream at him and make him feel what I am feeling that very moment: pain, confusion, and all-out anger. But with Emma and Roslyn here, I don't have that as an option.

"I have a favor to ask of you," I tell him.

"Anything for you," he replies.

"When and if you get your memory back, I would like it very much if you would wipe it clean of anything and everything that has to do with me. All of it." I stare at him with a vicious look. "You promise not to think of me, and in return I will no longer think of you. What's fair is fair." I finish, hoping my voice isn't faltering.

"What do you mean, Tessa? Is there more?" he asks quizzically.

"I guess you will never know seeing as how you are going to forget as soon as you remember," I spit back. "Like Savannah said, time will tell."

I get to my feet and dump the rest of my coffee onto the fire. It sizzles as it hits the hot coals. I am pissed. How dare he think that his words wouldn't hurt? Did he do it intentionally? I go back and forth, trying to decide whether he did it to push me away because he has no memory, or if he really meant it.

Regardless, he was going to get just what he wanted; maybe I don't know him as well as I thought. All I can hope for now is daybreak, which means we will be traveling and getting that much closer to home.

* * *

Liquid Quiver

Driving the team, I cluck at them to pick up their pace. Munroe Junction is coming into sight. Relief washes over me, because once we get to Cole's store, I can grab Kate and high-tail it home.

At the store, I halt the team at the rail and quickly get down from the wagon. I help Emma down. She is clearly happy to be home.

"Do you think, Ms. Tessa, that everyone has forgotten me?" the little girl asks.

"I don't think so, Emma. You are very hard to forget."

As soon as her feet hit the ground, she runs into the store. I tie the team and set out to untie Kate and get out of there. Roslyn approaches as I retrieve my things from the back of the wagon.

"Tessa, I know you are eager to be on your way. If you have a minute, I would like to treat you to some coffee or maybe tea," she offers. "My treat, of course."

"All right, but I can't stay long. I need to go."

She and I walk to the hotel and take a seat inside. A young woman greets us and takes our order.

"Tea, please," Roslyn says.

"Same for me," I say.

"I just wanted to tell you that I am grateful for all you have done. I know we got started on the wrong foot; I will not let you down. If we could start over, I feel we could be great friends if you will have me as one." Roslyn pauses only to thank the woman for our tea. "You have taught me a lot about compassion for yourself and others."

"I never believed for a minute that you could have done harm to your niece," I tell her. "I tried to see the good in you. And yes I do think we could be friends."

Smiling at each other, we finish our tea. I stand to excuse myself, and Roslyn places the money on the table.

"I will walk with you," she says.

That makes me feel a little better. This way, if I run into Cole, I won't be alone. When I get back to Kate, I reassure Roslyn that I will be back in a few days to introduce her to the locals and try to find her a place of employment. She plans to board at the hotel, so for now I don't have to worry where she is staying.

"OK, Roslyn, I will see you in a day or two. We will make a day of it. Maybe even have lunch. Thank you for the tea," I say as I loop Kate's reins around her neck.

"I will be looking forward to it."

With that I put my foot in the stirrup and swing up on Kate's back.

From behind me I hear Cole's voice. "Tessa, leaving without saying good-bye?"

Confused, I stare at him blankly. Did he forget that just days ago he told me that he didn't want anything to do with me? Why was he expecting me to make an effort to find him and bid him good-bye? I made an effort already on the return trip home. When he told me he didn't want anything to do with me, I hid my emotions so everything seemed normal. I am positive that Emma and Roslyn don't have a clue what went on.

As I gather my reins and turn Kate toward home, my reply comes with more anger than I want. "Good-bye, Cole."

Weary of the confrontation, I give him a smile that is plastered and fake, then kick Kate forward. I swear I can feel his dark eyes on my back, but I don't make a habit of looking back. The faster I get out of here, the better.

On the way home, I wonder if anything will look different. I know Maria can handle things, but when one is gone for two weeks, time has a way of changing things.

Finally back home, I am relieved and happy to back in my very own space. Looking around the outside, I can tell that Maria has already been here today. I sent her a telegram informing her of my return home.

I step down off Kate and loop her reins over the wooden rail. Stretching my frame, I reach to my saddle and untie her halter. After stripping her tack, I take it to the barn and get some grain for her. Otis, Jed, and Maddie greet me when I step inside. Tigg runs from Maddie's stall and greets me by jumping on my legs. It is comforting to know that at least my animals are happy for me to be home.

Tigg walks with me to deliver Kate's grain. All the while he looks at me and wags his tail. My nerves ease, and I can't wait until morning when my routine will be as it was before I left. Honestly, all the adventure I have experienced is enough for a long time. I am glad to get back to boring.

Liquid Quiver

Kate munches eagerly on her meal, while Tigg and I go survey the rest of the grounds. The garden has tiny green plants that have taken the place of the seeds I planted. I feel good because that means I will have fresh vegetables throughout the next few months and some stored in the cellar for winter. The grass that surrounds the house is getting greener, too, as are the fields.

"Come on, Tigg, let's go and put Kate away," I say to the hairy creature at my feet.

Sure enough, just the few minutes I was absent proved the mare loved her food. There isn't a crumb left in her bucket. I lead her over and walk her through her gate. When I release her, she gets off her feet and rolls in the grass, and when she stands back up, she takes off at a dead run, kicking up her heels. I'm not the only one glad to be home.

After securing the gate, I leave the halter there on the post. Kate will have a few days' rest before we have to go back to town to introduce Roslyn to the small town of Munroe Junction. My whole body is tired, and I want a hot bath. I check the mangers and then the chickens; they all have enough feed to last until morning.

As I go inside, Tigg races in on my heels. Directly he runs to my room, and I guess he will make himself at home on my bed. Everything is just as I left it, only dustier. Sighing heavily, I decide to put off the chores until tomorrow. I take some kindling to the fireplace and work on building a fire. There is no way a bath will feel welcome in a cold house. I can't wait until the mornings are decent, when I can open the windows to let the breeze invade my home.

The fire catches quickly, and I place more wood on it for it to grow even more. I fill my kettle with water to start some coffee, deciding I will have to wait for the fire to warm up the house. I work to bring the tub into the room. Once it is in place, I strip down to my underclothes. The doors are locked and I am enjoying the quiet.

I fill the tub to the brim, anxiously awaiting the moment I can get in. After checking that my curtains are fully closed, I go back to the tub and finish getting completely undressed. I feel the heat of the fire touch my naked body. It sends goose bumps along my flesh.

I test the water with my foot and step in. It is hot. I sink down into the tub, the water covering me fully, leaving only my head above it. I watch the surface as the steam rises and swirls out of sight. A tear escapes and runs down my cheek. My mind is weighing heavy on the things Cole said. I can't stop my mind from repeating everything from that night. Each time, his words sound louder and more hurtful.

Closing my eyes, I let the torturous thoughts consume my existence. I let my emotions take over and run with free will, and I begin to cry.

Chapter Twenty
Unfinished Business

I can't sleep that night, so I find myself waking up entirely too early. Not wanting to waste any of the sun-filled day, I dress and head to the barn. I fill the mangers, then take my stool and pail to Maddie's stall and proceed to milk her. She is patient, and for that I am glad, because the tiredness is already setting in. Tigg crawls into the corner and lies down in the straw.

All the while, I have many things on my mind—Cole being the first. My heart hurts in my chest, and the only idea I have is to distance myself from him, giving him a wide berth. Here on out it will be strictly business, no emotions. A clean slate.

Helping Roslyn is a whole different story. Worry is always seeping into my mind about getting her a job, but deep down I have faith in her. I really should stop in and visit Mrs. Wells; I'm sure she has heard what took place and is mortified about it. There are so many things to do, I feel over-whelmed. Tending the garden, house, and animals. At times I have thought about giving up and moving back to Boston to be with my parents.

Having Maria, Emma, and now Roslyn, though, makes it difficult to do just that. Also I love my home. It is the first real project I completed with someone I loved. There is too much blood, sweat, and tears invested in the land on which it stands for me to just wash my hands of it.

I haul the milk inside and finish by rinsing out the bucket I used. I decide to busy myself with housework. Humming as I work makes the task much less tedious. This time around, I greatly enjoy thumping the rugs outside with the broom. Striking them with so much force releases a lot of pent-up frustration.

Having finished the inside chores by early afternoon, I take my gloves and start my way to the garden. Since I've been home, the little dog has been my constant companion. The sun is warm on my face and the air fresh. The insects buzz about as the birds chirp to each other. I kneel down to be more comfortable and glove my hands. Plucking the weeds from the earth gives me time to think. This job isn't terribly difficult; it keeps my hands busy. When I have a pile of the unwanted vegetation, I walk it over to the coop so the chickens have something to do. On the third trip, I hear the faint sound of hooves.

Watching from my tiptoes, I see a figure appear. I can tell it's Maria. I wait for her at the rail.

"Tessa!" she calls from a distance.

I raise my hand and wave to her. I can't help but smile. Everything that happened on the trip has left me wanting to talk with her. Maria's opinion and thoughts would have done me a great service, but since I was alone, I did the best I could.

As she rides to where I stand, she barely stops her horse before she lunges out of her saddle to greet me. Flinging herself at me, she embraces me in a tight hug.

"I have missed you and was so worried. Don't you ever take off like that again," she tells me seriously.

"I'm sorry, truly I am. There was no time, and we had to leave in a hurry," I reply.

When she lets me go, we smile at each other, and then she ties up her horse. We both walk to the door, and I invite her in. Knowing that she and I are going to visit, I put some water on for coffee.

"Tessa, I have been to town. Are the rumors true?"

"Rumors. What rumors?" I ask, confused.

"There are rumors flying all around town about how it was Pete who started the fire and that it was Cole who killed him."

With just that one statement, all the memories come flooding back in an instant.

"Those aren't rumors; they are the truth," I tell her with a heavy sigh.

"Well, I am glad that you are home safe. If anything would have happened to you, Cole Miller would have had to deal with me," she says. "You are my very best of friends. Sisters, actually, the way I see it."

"I doubt that you will have to worry about him anymore."

Turning to look at Maria, I see one of her eyebrows is raised, and her mouth hangs slightly open.

"You must tell me everything—and I mean everything. Down to the smallest detail, and don't try to leave anything out," she warns.

I know right then that there is no way out of this one; I have to tell her everything. To relive all the emotions and details again for the hundredth time. The only difference this time is that I am actually telling someone about it, not keeping it all to myself. Good thing I milked Maddie this morning and bought plenty of coffee before I left.

Maria and I sit at the table as I begin to recount the whole thing from the start. I tell her every detail, from the first day of our trip. Her face changes with the many emotions she feels as I continue with my storytelling. Maria listens intently and barely speaks a word until I get to the part where I recount the gunshots that not only took Pete's life, but wounded Cole.

"What!" Maria yells. "He actually held a gun to your head? Tessa, it's no wonder that it wasn't Cole who brought you home in a box. Oh, to think of it. I can't bear to think of you as passed. I couldn't do without you," she gasps.

"I'm fine, really," I tell her.

My mouth is clamped shut to the confession of my recurring nightmare of Pete holding me hostage here at my own home.

"Good gracious, Tessa. All right, go on."

Resuming the story, I tell her of our stay at Ada's and Abe's and of the care that Savannah gave Cole while he was injured. I almost leave out the part of me making a fool of myself when I told Cole how I felt. If I were to leave anything out, I would reap a stern talking-to later. She is my best friend, so I tell her anyway.

"You actually said that?" she exclaims. "What did he say?"

"He had a fever, Maria, and I don't think he will ever recall my outright truth. Besides, he doesn't remember."

She looks at me like she has just figured out the biggest mystery of our time. Her eyes widen as she opens her mouth to say the obvious.

"Oh, now I see. You confessed your true feelings, and he has no memory of it, or so you think," she says with a sly grin. "Has he remembered anything so far? Tell me, Tessa, what ever will you do if he does?"

I'm not sure, but I think her snide tone is getting to me. Yet my heart still races at the thought of him remembering, because it is the only thing I haven't figured out yet. What am I going to do?

"I don't know, Maria. If Cole remembers and it turns out he had no feelings for me, then I will have to live the worst case of embarrassment for the rest of my life."

The truth of the matter hits hard just then. How could I have been so damn foolish? Wishing I could go back in time to change it, feeling childish and stupid, I look for wisdom from my dearest friend.

"What will I do, Maria?" I ask. "You have to help me. I may die from the shame alone."

"Oh, would you quit. Besides you won't die—you may just have to avoid him at all costs and slink around so you are never seen again," she replies, snickering.

"Thanks. I'm glad that not only do you not take this seriously, but that it humors you."

"Really, Tessa, it's not that bad. You are going to worry yourself sick about it."

I know she is right. I decide that what is done is done. I just have to convince myself that it is going to be all right.

I pour out the last of the coffee and start some more. She and I continue to talk about anything and everything. I tell Maria that I was going to ask Cole about having a party for Emma on her birthday, invite a few friends and bake a cake and all.

"I love parties! If he approves, you have to let me know right away, so I can have her a gift ready."

"Of course, you and Flint are both welcome," I say.

"Well hurry up and ask already."

I nod my head in silent agreement. My chest is beginning to flutter with hope, so I push back the excitement in case he refuses.

We talk until the light outside begins to diminish. After we say our good-byes, I walk with her to her horse. We promise each other that we will talk soon and seal the deal with a hug. Once she rides away, the feeling of loneliness returns.

The evening is actually warm enough that I don't need a coat. Even though it is still early in the evening, I complete the rest of the chores before I retire for the night.

Unfinished Business

The next morning is pleasant. So much so that I drink my coffee out on the porch, wearing just my nightdress. My ears are blessed with the sounds of songbirds and mourning doves. While I do the chores, I debate about going into town to see Roslyn today, or whether I go tomorrow. Not wanting her to think I have forgotten about her, I find my feet walking me toward Kate's pasture.

After I tie her securely to the rail, I go to the house and get ready. I brush my hair and braid it loosely over my shoulder. The pup is content to lie on my bed and take a nap; he doesn't even open his eyes to watch me go.

As I shut the door behind me, I can feel the nervousness starting to build in the pit of my stomach. Once on Kate's back and headed to town, I just want to get this over with, and fast.

I ride through town and stop Kate in front of the hotel. I dismount and look around cautiously to see if I have been noticed. I plan for this to go as quickly and smoothly as possible, to find Roslyn and show her around and then hightail it out of there as fast as I can.

In the hotel, I ask the clerk which room Roslyn is staying in. I thank him for the information and stride up the hall to find the room with a thirty-two painted on its door. I knock gently and wait for her to answer. After a few minutes, I try knocking again, only harder, which produces the same outcome. Since there is no answer, I will have to go looking for her—which means I will be seen by even more people than I had origi-nally planned.

"Great. Just what I wanted," I say to the door in front of me.

Back outside I look in both directions and scan the street, hoping to catch a glimpse of her. With no such luck, I start down the walk, peering into the windows as I stroll by. She is nowhere in sight. When I turn to look behind me, I am glad I started in the opposite direction of Miller's store.

After walking down one side of the street, I cross it and continue up the other. The new boutique is just a few doors away. Stopping in, I see that the building is freshly completed. There are many ready-made dresses, along with hats to match. Some are made of silk, and some are so gorgeous I hardly dare touch them.

"Can I help you?" a voice behind me says.

Turning around, I see Roslyn.

"Here you are. I have been looking for you," I say.

"Oh, I am sorry that I made you waste your time. I should have come to see you. I took it upon myself to get out in the world and explore a bit," she tells me. "You have done so much for me already."

"No time wasted," I reply. "It's good to see you out and about."

She seems content to belong somewhere and I am not going to dampen her mood by feeling sorry for myself.

"Goodness, Tessa, I am so happy. I have a real job, a purpose. This is my chance to start again," Roslyn says. "And I owe it all to you."

"Like I said before, you deserve to be just as happy as the rest of us."

Roslyn smiles a big, heartfelt smile, and I can tell this really is a new beginning for her. She is going to be just fine.

"Maybe this Sunday we could do lunch? I'm sorry to have to cancel for today; this is only my first day on the job," she says with a grin.

"Oh yes, some other time, then. I understand," I say. Bidding her a good day, I turn to leave.

As I cross the street a second time, my sights are set on Kate still tied to the rail at the hotel. I stare at the ground, only raising my head at the sound of someone calling my name. Focusing on the people coming in the opposite direction, I wait to hear it again.

"Ms. Tessa!"

Recognizing the tiny but clear voice, instant panic sweeps though me. I kneel to one knee as Emma throws herself into my arms.

"Where have you been, Ms. Tessa? I have waited and waited to see you again," the little girl tells me.

"Oh? Well, Emma, I have been busy tending to everything at home. All of the animals, and then there is the garden," I answer.

"Do you need any help? I could go home with you. Don't you remember how good I am at pulling all the weeds?"

I chuckle; I can't help but love her. "I don't think your papa would like that."

"But why not? Didn't you and I have fun last time?" she asks.

"Of course I did. It's just that he would miss you so much. Where is your papa anyway?"

"He was right behind me," she says as she looks over her shoulder.

I am trapped now. No way out. Quickly I look around, but don't see him.

"Hmm, Ms. Tessa, I don't know where he went. Could you help me find him?"

Torn between helping Emma find Cole and sacrificing what dignity I have left, I agree to help her. There is no way I could or would leave her here to fend for herself.

"All right, let's try to find your papa."

If I didn't know better, I'd have a slight notion that she is more excited than nervous. She grabs my hand and anxiously leads me along. Quite some time later, she and I have managed to search every business in town, including the boutique, twice.

"Emma, honey. We have checked everywhere but the store," I tell her. I'm tired to the bone.

"That's a good idea, Ms. Tessa!" she exclaims. "Let's try there."

I am confused as she drags me to the store.

"Emma, please, slow down. I feel as if I have run a race," I beg.

She only slows down when she and I cross the threshold of Miller's store. Immediately she beelines straight to Cole's side.

I freeze when he turns and his eyes meet mine. Turning away, I pretend to be interested in something on the shelf next to me.

"Tessa?" he says.

Looking his way, I scramble for the right words to say. "Cole? I didn't see you there," I lie.

Fibbing is a habit I seem to be turning to more and more, and I'm not sure I like it.

"Papa, I found Ms. Tessa," she tells her father.

"Where did you go, Emma? I only gave you permission to play outside the storefront."

I know that she went well beyond the storefront, but I keep the secret for only the two of us girls to know. Emma gives Cole a look of pure innocence, and the matter is soon dropped. Her actions do humor me. Because for one, she led me on a wild-goose chase. Secondly, I believe she knew where her papa was the entire time.

"Did you need to pick up any supplies?" Cole asks in my direction.

As I run through a list of items in my head, I can't think of anything I have to have at the moment. He begins to walk over to me, and I feel my hands getting clammy. He looks different. Not bad, just different. Ragged almost. His hair is tousled just a bit, and his face is unshaven, giving him a rugged appearance. Something close to dangerous. What I notice the most are his eyes. They are bloodshot and rimmed with red. It's as if he hasn't slept for days.

I start to wonder if, like me, he is having nightmares. It's the only thing I can think of to explain his roughness.

"Uh, no. I don't think I need anything right off hand," I say. "But I would like to ask you something."

I can hear the ticking from the clock overhead as he takes his time to answer. "Sure," he says.

Taken aback by my own boldness, my tongue is having a difficult time forming words. "I was just wondering, Emma's birthday is coming up soon, and I would like to make her a cake. Perhaps invite some people— you know, have a small party?" I blurt out.

An emotion I can't put my finger on washes over his face, something between anger and sorrow.

I go on like a babbling idiot. "If you object, it is OK. I...I just thought I would ask. I didn't mean to upset you."

Quickly, I turn on my heels and sprint toward the door.

"Tessa. Wait!"

This time I do. But before I turn around, I tell myself not to cry. Why does he regret me so much?

"What is it, Cole?" I say quietly.

"That would be very kind of you. Just promise me it will not be a big party. Something small will do fine."

"All right, you have a deal," I tell him.

He doesn't respond before he turns around and goes back inside. I am left there feeling happy, yet burdened by the fact that I may have upset him.

Since I am in town already, I spend the rest of the day going to see Mr. and Mrs. Wells, Maria, and Roslyn. I invite each of them to Emma's party. Mrs. Lacy, Emma's caregiver, will attend as well. Maria and I decide that she and I will decorate for the event.

When I return home, I do the chores and then write down what I will need for the party. Come Monday, I will pick up the supplies I need, and then some, for the party. As I go to bed, I feel excited to be planning such an event. Yet somewhere deep in my chest is a twinge of guilt because I can't figure out why I made Cole upset.

Not wanting to crush my good mood, I blow out the flame in my lamp and nestle in my bed. Quickly I fall asleep.

CHAPTER TWENTY-ONE
Surprise, Surprise

"I can't believe it, Tessa. The end of June is upon us," Maria says.

"Time flies these days; if you blink you are sure to miss something," I reply.

It is the eighteenth of June, and we only have two days until Emma's birthday party. Maria and I have been cutting out all the decorations from the paper I purchased. The whole house is covered in well wishes for the birthday girl.

Maria is the creative one of the two of us. She is able to make paper bouquets to go along with the real ones. I am so glad to have her help because without her, this place wouldn't look so good. Both of us enjoyed the time we have spent together as we worked and talked of all things from truth to gossip. As I always do, I make sure she can come early on Saturday to help keep my nerves from taking over.

"Tessa, how does this look? Do you think it's too much?" Maria asks.

Stepping down from the stool, I walk to where she stands. She has pink ribbons and bows hanging from the walls in the dining area and has made matching place settings for the table. The paper flowers are sprinkled over the surface of the table, making it look like a luxurious indoor garden. The scene really takes my breath away.

"Oh, Maria!" I gasp. "It's truly gorgeous."

"Thanks, it was nothing."

Amazed that my friend is able to do so much in such a short time, I feel like I am lacking.

"This is so exciting, Tessa, I can't wait!"

"I'm already getting nervous. What if my cake doesn't turn out? All those people will be disappointed. Perhaps they will think I am a complete failure." I tell toss my hands up in the air.

"There you go again, Tessa. I swear, you need to loosen up a little. Everything will be fine."

"I hope so, Maria. I don't want to make a fool of myself."

Shaking her head, she gathers her things.

"That's enough for today. I will see you soon. Saturday morning to be exact." She smiles.

"That's not soon enough—that's the day after tomorrow."

"Don't go and get all crazy on me until then."

I give her a quick hug, and she walks out the door.

I stand alone in the empty house until the pup comes to my feet, whining. "What? Is it past your dinnertime?" I ask him.

As soon as I ask, my stomach growls too. I didn't realize that the whole day went by, and Maria and I only snacked on crackers and cheese.

In the kitchen, I mix up batter for biscuits and line a pan with lard. Since it is getting late, biscuits and butter sounds good. Plus, with my stomach already nervous, something light will suit it better.

Turning my attention to the stove, I place my pan of dough into the heat to be baked golden brown. I quickly light some lamps and rush to change into my nightdress. My hair I let hang freely, completely without bindings.

After the biscuits have cooled a bit, I slather them with butter. I devour most of them, saving one or two for the dog. He doesn't mind eating what I eat; it shows by how fast he munches them down.

As I wipe up the crumbs and tidy up the kitchen, a faint knock catches my attention and stops me. The dog growls, and I am suddenly scared. Being in my nightclothes, I'm not even dressed to open the door.

Thinking it could just be my imagination, I pause to see if the noise comes again. To my discomfort, the soft rapping comes once more, and I jump clean out of my skin when Tigg runs to the door, barking and raising a ruckus, as if he knows I didn't latch the door. I pick up a cast-iron skillet from the counter and tiptoe toward the door.

The dog continues his mayhem as I approach the door slowly.

"Tigg, hush," I say, barely above a whisper.

Surprise, Surprise

I raise the skillet with both hands, just above my right shoulder. My entire body is shaking so hard I can't even ask who is there. Just as I reach the door, the familiar sound of the knob turning touches my ears. This is something straight out of my nightmares.

Quickly I squeeze my frame behind the door and wait for it to open. I wasn't going to die without a fight; maybe if I hit them hard enough, whoever found the bodies would know that I got them.

My palms are so sweaty I have to adjust my grip on the heavy pan several times. The door begins to creep open, and that's when I stop breathing. Standing as still as a statue, I wait for my chance.

The intruder steps once, then twice. He must be experienced at this because he stands just inside the door frame where I can't see him.

Hearing another boot step, I see the brim of a hat appear; he is obviously growing brave enough to step farther into my house. Feeling uneasy, I hold steady until the perfect moment. Finally the stranger comes forward and turns slightly, so I go for it.

I hear as whoever it is turns to shut the door.

I swing the iron skillet. I can see the murderer throw his hands up in defense. I'm confident that I hit my mark when I hear the loud pinging noise as the skillet connects with my target.

With relief, I see the body crumple to the floor. I quickly move to stand over him. I can't see his face because his hat now sits blocking my view. The form doesn't move, and a horrible feeling rises up from my insides. What if I really did kill him? Would I be sentenced and hung for my actions? Surely not—he came into my house!

I move around the body, kick his legs over, and shut the door. Keeping my weapon handy, I crouch down to remove the hat so I can investigate which unlawful villain I have captured.

When I see his face, I gasp and almost get sick on the very floor on which he lay. It is Cole Miller.

"Oh, shit!" I say aloud.

Dropping the skillet, I run to my room to pull my hair back and check my reflection. I look like some wild heathen from out in the sticks. Rushing back to where he is, I hurriedly look around for something, anything to make this better. So far I am failing.

Liquid Quiver

I go to the chair, grab a pillow, and put in on the floor. Then I unfold a blanket and put it down for him to rest on. I am almost positive that if I take hold of him by his wrists, I can drag him to his resting place.

I first check to make sure he is breathing. He is. After taking his arms and crossing them, I bear down and begin to pull. He groans a bit, and I immediately drop his arms, thinking he will wake. He doesn't. Eventually I get him dragged to where I placed the blanket.

I pull him alongside the makeshift bed, then move to his other side and roll him over to land on the blanket. He lands with a thud.

"Ouch. Sorry, Cole," I whisper.

I remove his boots and pick up his hat and place them neatly by the chaise lounge. I cover him up with a smaller blanket; it makes me feel better that at least I made him comfortable.

I glance around to make sure everything else looks normal. My skillet is still on the floor, screaming out, *She did it, she did it!* I jump to my feet, scoop it up, and hide it in kitchen.

Debating whether I should go to bed or sleep out here, I go fetch a pillow and quilt from my room. As I toss them on the lounge, I remember that his horse is still tied outside. I pull on my chore boots and a coat and run outside to put his horse in the barn. When I return, I shed the coat and boots, then take my place on the lounge and drift off to sleep.

* * *

Waking up early, I turn to spy on my patient. He has moved during the night even if it is just a little. His forehead just above his right eye has one hell of a goose egg.

"Oh my God. What did I do?" I say to myself. "What am I going to do?"

Regretting my actions, I feel absolutely awful. But then again, what was he doing here at that time of night? Why didn't he tell me who he was? As I think about it, I feel better, because at least I could say I was defending my home. However, Cole is going to end up hating me for sure. What I did is close to unforgivable.

As if on cue, he stirs and groans. Fear freezes me to the lounge, and I quit breathing again. When his eyes don't open, I let out a whoosh of air.

Surprise, Surprise

I get up slowly, tidy my bed, then move to the kitchen. I keep peeking in on him as the coffee is perking. I'm not sure whether waking him is a good idea; I don't know how to handle it if he is furious at what I did.

I pour a cup of coffee and sip it; it burns the roof of my mouth. Cursing soon follows. Then, putting my elbows on the counter, I lace my fingers together and bow my head.

"Dear Lord, please forgive me for pummeling Cole. I didn't mean it. Also, please make sure that given his condition of amnesia, that he doesn't remember a thing. Amen. Oh, P.S., I know I promised to cut down on my cursing; if you would just do me this favor, I will try much harder. Amen. Again."

Hearing Cole's voice, I go to the other room. His voice sounds groggy and broken.

"What happened? Where am I?" he asks.

"Cole, hey, how are you?" I ask hesitantly. "Beautiful morning isn't it?" I finish, hoping he doesn't realize it is still dark out.

"Tessa, what are you doing here?"

"Uh, well you are at my house, so what are you doing here?" I ask.

"What? How did I get here?"

"Don't you remember?" I ask.

"All I remember is I tied my horse and, well, that's it."

"Oh. You came by to see how the decorating was going, and then you went to leave and uh, you fell down the stairs," I fib.

"I did? Then how did I get in here?" he manages to ask.

"I dragged you in here."

"Really? Wow, my head is killing me." He winces as he prods the large bump protruding from his temple. "I must have hit hard. My ears are pounding."

"I'm sorry, is there anything I can do?"

"No, I'll just have to let it run its course. Although a cup of coffee does sound good right at the moment."

"Sure," I tell him and quickly get to my feet.

As I hand the coffee to him, I can tell he is suffering.

"If you would like, you could rest here for as long as you want. When you are ready, I will fetch your horse for you," I offer.

"For once, Tessa, I think I will take you up on that. I can't figure out how I could have been so clumsy. Truthfully, I am just really tired. Thank you."

"Then it's settled; you will rest while I busy myself with my chores," I say, smiling.

Cole finishes his coffee and I take his mug. He settles into his blankets and closes his eyes while I take his mug to the basin. Getting ready to do chores, I get dressed for the day and put my boots on again. It doesn't take long for slumber to find him; he is snoring before I reach the door.

Starting in the barn, I work slowly to give him time to rest. All the while I try to think of any reason for him to come by so late in the evening. My brain just can't come up with a logical explanation. I give up until I can ask him myself. On one hand, I feel lucky he went along with my story of him falling down the stairs. If he ever found out he came as close to his own death as one could by my hand, he would cast me aside for eternity.

Tending to his gelding gives me a relaxed feeling, almost as if I am supposed to be doing this. Then I feel foolish for letting myself believe that I could belong to him and take care of his needs. I will never understand why it is that when your heart guides your mind and sets itself on something, what your mind sees as impossible can't change your heart.

After dishing out the last ration of grain to the gelding, I go feed the chickens and gather eggs. It is light enough outside to see now, but the sun has yet to make an appearance. This kind of morning is the best—no wind, the entire prairie still and calm. The birds chirp while they hunt up bugs in the grass. The moisture that dampens the ground makes it smell as if it just rained.

I love mornings like this, feeling as though I am the only one in a perfect and serene world. A world where nothing bad would ever happen—only good—and where time didn't matter. Except for the guilt I carry for knocking Cole silly, I feel at peace. For once I feel that what I have done so far in this life actually matters. Living a perfect life no longer means everything to me. What matters is just to realize that living has its ups and downs, and how you handle each one is what means you are alive.

Using the bucket that held the corn for the chickens, I gather close to a dozen or so eggs. I walk to the house, where I take off my boots outside to make being quiet more feasible. Sneaking through the door, I see Cole is still sleeping. When I squint my eyes, I can see a gray ball of fur sleeping on the pillow above his head. Gently I walk across the floor and take the eggs into the kitchen; they will have to be washed later when Cole awakens and comes back to the land of the living.

As I serve up some coffee, I decide that pulling weeds is a good quiet chore. I gather my gloves and the hot drink and quietly go back outside. It is warm, with the sun's rays touching everything in sight. How gorgeous the world looks. The greens are green and the blues are blue. All the colors are magnified by ten with the morning rays shining down.

Kneeling at the spot where I left off weeding, I begin again. At this rate, I should have just raised a patch of weeds—then all I would have to do is water it. I sip from my mug one last time, then set it in the dirt next to me.

As I get to work on the pesky plants, I retreat into my thoughts about the party tomorrow and the guests. I wish that everything will go perfectly.

I am so lost in my thoughts that I jump when I hear a voice behind me.

"Tessa. Tessa, can you hear me?"

"Maria! What are you doing here? I didn't think I would see you until morning." I say, scared out of my wits.

"What has gotten into you? Is there something wrong?" she asks with concern.

"What would make you think that? No, nothing is wrong." I look to the house quickly, then back to Maria.

I know right away she has caught onto something, because she does the same and then looks back at me.

"Are you sure nothing is wrong?" she asks for a second time.

I stare at her blankly and can't figure out how to answer.

"Tessa Ann! What have you been up to?" Maria spouts as she begins marching to the house.

"Maria! Wait! I'll tell you, I swear!"

I run after her and stop her just at the bottom of the steps. She narrows her eyes at me and taps her finger on the railing.

"Well, let's have it."

"All right, but we have to go to the window," I tell her.

"What? Why?"

"You'll see—you do want to see, don't you?"

"Of course."

"Well then, come on," I say with frustration.

What will my friend think of me? Not only do I have to worry about what Cole thinks, but now Maria just got added to the list. She is going to think I really am crazy, and apparently I am doing a good job proving her right.

"Tessa, what are we doing?" she asks when we reach the window. "This is crazy."

"I know! As if I didn't think that already. Go ahead, peek in."

"Why are we peeking into your own window?"

"Just go on and do it, you'll see," I tell her under my breath.

Maria rolls her eyes at me and sighs. When she realizes what she is seeing, her jaw drops and she slowly turns and looks at me.

"What the hell?"

"It's not like that," I reassure her.

"You have a man on your floor," she quips back.

"Shh, don't yell. I don't want to wake him up. Come on, let's go to the barn and I will tell you everything."

Before she can protest, I grab her by the arm and haul her off the front of the walk so we can talk in private.

After I explain everything to Maria, she begins to laugh so hard, I think she is going to pass out, or wet herself.

"What? Why are you laughing?" I ask. How dare she laugh so much at the situation I have gotten myself into? It doesn't help that she has tears running down her cheeks.

When she catches her breath, she wipes her face and composes herself before she is finally able to speak again. "Oh, Tessa. I'm sorry. Whew! It's been so long since I have had a laugh like that."

"Thanks a lot; I'm glad I could help. Now tell me what is so funny?!"

"I saw Cole in town after I left here yesterday. He asked if we were in town together. When I told him I was alone, he said he may come to see you. Judging by the fact that he is out cold on your floor, I'm guessing he didn't get to tell you."

"Tell me what?" I ask.

Her face turns serious and she takes a deep breath. "I don't know—he came here to tell you."

Surprise, Surprise

"You are confusing me, Maria."

"Tessa, all I know is he said that he remembered something," she finally says.

I feel my face drain of all color. I am light-headed and weak. All I know is that whatever Cole remembered, I may have just erased from his memory completely.

CHAPTER TWENTY-TWO
Make a Wish

It is Saturday morning and already has been a busy start to the day. Awake before the stars disappeared from the night sky, I am a mixed bag of emotions: sheer excitement for Emma's birthday party and nervousness about everything going just right.

Thanks to Maria, we were able to saddle Cole's horse and help him on it to get him on his way home. I don't think I could have helped him mount up by myself, either; it took everything she and I had to get him up there. My cheeks turned a shade of red when he stumbled and my hand caught him on his backside. Just thinking about it makes my face warm and the room become stuffy.

Scolding myself, I try to remain on task to complete the homemade candy for the guests to take home as a "thank you" for coming. Maria should be here in a couple of hours, so she and I can finish up the rest of the decorations, cake, and punch. There is plenty of coffee for my morning; I knew beforehand I would need it.

I assess everything I have done already. The table looks like something straight out of a fairy tale. I don't know how Maria does it, but I am grateful for her talents. The plates and cups I set out this morning, and my kitchen is tidy and ready for making the cake. Tigg is sleeping on the lounge; I don't think he likes getting up so early this morning.

"Come on, boy, time for chores."

He stretches and jumps from the lounge, then he stretches again before he comes the rest of the way to greet me.

I rush through my chores, then hurry back inside to take a bath. After filling the tub, I sit in the hot water for quite some time. I secretly hope the lavender oil will soak all my worries away, and that, when I toss the water, my worries will go with it. When I get out of the tub, I wrap myself in a towel and empty the tub. Then I go to my room to get dressed.

I want to look special today, because to me a birthday is a reason to celebrate. Especially when it is the birthday of a young girl like Emma. The dress I choose is one of my favorites. Not overly formal, it is just the right one: cream-colored, with ivory buttons. Lace dons the collar only down to the top of my bust. The sleeves are fitted, as is the waist, and the skirt falls loosely, with many layers of soft, light fabric that sits just above the floor, giving the impression I am gliding instead of walking. I put my hair up and let soft ringlets fall around my face and cascade down my back. I apply a peach-colored powder to my eyelids and then darken my lashes. Sheer pink lip color is last.

Feeling as ready as I can be, I step out of my room and go to the kitchen, where I put on my apron. After tying the strings, I move about the house and open a few windows to not only let in fresh air, but to help with the heat from the stove as I bake the cake.

In the kitchen I take my bowl and measure the flour to begin the batter. Singing to myself as I work helps me calm down. I mix the ingredients, pour the thick mixture into the pan, and place it inside the oven. Using a second bowl, I begin to work on the icing. I add a few drops of red food coloring to make the icing pink.

I hear a knock and holler for Maria to come in. She is gorgeous. She wears a lavender dress, and her hair is French braided—stunning.

"How are you doing, Tessa?" she asks. "You're not nervous, are you?"

"Not now, because you are here." I smile as she makes her way into the kitchen after placing Emma's gift in the dining room, where I had placed a small table to hold the gifts.

"So you need help?" she asks.

"I think I got it, but if you could check all the decorations to be sure they are still in place."

"Of course."

When the icing is done, there is an hour or so before everyone else is due to arrive. Perfect timing for the cake to cool and the icing to set.

After cleaning up my mess and while waiting for the cake to be done, I go check with Maria.

"Everything is in place, Tessa," she says.

"Oh good! Now all we have to do is finish the cake and wait for everyone to arrive," I say.

We talk in the kitchen as she prepares the punch. I take the cake out of the oven and place it on the counter. The whole house smells of vanilla and sugar. As the cake cools, we set the table with the remaining utensils that will be needed.

The time for the party to begin is growing closer. Mrs. Wells arrives and informs us that Mr. Wells is once again away on business. Roslyn, Flint, and Mrs. Lacy show up shortly after. They sit in the dining room and visit with each other. They talk about how they are doing in their lives.

As I ice the cake, I grow nervous because Cole and Emma are over twenty minutes late.

"How are you holding up in here, Tessa?" Maria asks.

"I'm OK. I hope they make it here soon."

"Don't worry, they will be here," Maria assures me. "Let me know when you are done with the cake, and I will help you bring it to the table."

I mouth the words "thank you" to her as I finish icing the cake. I place the knife in the basin. Everything is perfect. The gift table is stacked with Emma's presents, and I couldn't have made a better cake.

I take off my apron and join the others to visit. Everyone compliments Maria and me on all the hard work we did on the decorations. I try to remain calm, but my mind worries about where Cole and Emma could be.

When I have almost given up, I hear the horses nicker at another horse approaching. I stand to greet them at the door.

Opening the door, I see Emma running in my direction while Cole tends to the horse.

"Ms. Tessa, I'm here. You didn't start without me did you?"

"Gracious no, we couldn't start without you," I tell her.

Emma's dress is a light blue and makes her look as if an angel delivered her straight from heaven. A wide black ribbon goes around her waist to make a beautiful bow at her back. The headband she wears keeps her dark curls out of her face, and her petite shoes are also glossy black.

I glance toward Cole; he hasn't even looked our way. His pants are freshly ironed and fit him nicely. The shirt he chose is the blackest of black, and his hat matches the shirt. I take note that he is the only one dressed in attire of that shade. He works slowly at securing his horse and making his way inside.

"Are all of those for me?" Emma asks when she sees the table of presents.

"Yes, sweetie, those are all yours," I tell her.

She walks over and checks all the packages on the small table. All the guests greet her, and she goes to sit on Maria's lap. I am still standing at the door, patiently waiting for Cole with a smile on my face to welcome him.

He finally makes his way to the porch. His eyes are trained on the ground, and when he reaches me, he lifts his gaze. I immediately notice there is something on his mind. His dark eyes are rimmed in red and look a bit swollen. I don't dare ask what is wrong; I just smile and welcome him as if I don't notice a thing.

"Cole, it's good to see you."

"It's good to see you too, Tessa," he replies, only for my ears to hear.

The goose egg on his temple has gone down considerably, I am happy to see. When he enters the room, Flint stands to shake his hand, and both men continue to stand as they talk. We all visit and drink punch. As the women and I visit, sharing gossip, I steal glances in Cole's direction.

Emma can't contain her excitement any longer, so we decide it is time for her to open her gifts and then blow the candles out on her cake. We form a circle around the gift table; Emma is now the center of attention.

"Which one do I open first?"

"Whichever one you want to open first, sweetie," Roslyn says.

Emma looks over the table and chooses a small box. Tearing the paper off, she finds a book of her favorite child's fairy tale.

"Thank you, Mrs. Lacy."

"You are welcome, Emma. The one you and I read every day is getting worn out. I thought you would like a copy for your very own."

Emma smiles and gently places the book on the floor next to her. The next gift she chooses is a large package, and it is soft. Ripping the paper off, she finds a hand-sewn blanket made with a star pattern in green and pink.

"Thank you, Maria," she says with a wide smile.

"You're welcome, Emma. It was my pleasure to make it for you," Maria says.

Next she goes to a small crate sitting on the floor by the table. On the side black letters form the word "Fragile."

"You might need a bit of help with that one," Mrs. Wells chimes in.

Flint moves to help Emma with the crate. He pulls his knife from his pocket and carefully slides the blade under the wooden lid. When he finally wedges the lid from the box, he helps her lift it off. Her eyes widen with surprise as she reaches inside and takes out a small cup made of china.

"Look. Now I can have a real tea party, Papa!" she says with enthusiasm.

Stealing a quick look in Cole's direction, I find that he is looking back in mine.

"Papa, look, it has flowers on it," she tells him.

"It's beautiful, Emma, just like you," he says.

The little girl places the cup back into the crate and asks Flint if he would put the lid back on to keep it safe.

She takes the next-to-last gift, which is wrapped in paper from the new boutique. Inside it, she finds a new dress.

"It's for when you get to go to school," Roslyn explains.

"Thank you, Aunt Roslyn. It's pretty."

I think Roslyn is close to crying. It is these kinds of events in life that she missed out on. I am so glad she has found happiness.

Emma takes the final gift and removes the paper. A stuffed bear waits for someone to play with. She turns my way and thanks me.

"Now I have someone to make tea for!" she shouts.

Everyone laughs, and we help her collect her things and place them safely on the lounge until she is ready to leave.

As they take seats at the table, all the guests admire Maria's work on the paper flowers and bouquets. Emma sits her stuffed animal in her chair so it can sit with her.

"Mr. Bear, it's time for cake," she tells it.

Maria and I both go to the kitchen to prepare the cake. I place six candles in the top. The two-tiered cake looks delicious, almost too good to eat. Everyone is in awe of our creation when we place it on the table.

As I light the candles, we sing to Emma and tell her to make a wish. Inhaling deeply, she closes her eyes and extinguishes the flames with one breath. We clap and cheer for her as she giggles and smiles. Then Maria and I slice the cake and pass the slices around the table.

Liquid Quiver

The party lasts well into the afternoon. When it is over, we help put the gifts into Roslyn's buggy. She assures us that she will drop them off at Cole's on her way back to the hotel. The visiting continues outside and breaks up little by little as each person leaves. Maria stays behind to help me clean up. We wave to Emma as she rides away with Cole.

The two of us turn to go inside. I feel giddy, as does Maria, because the party went off without a hitch. In the kitchen, we stack plates to wash, talking and laughing while we work.

Suddenly we hear, "Ms. Tessa? Are you here?"

We look at each other, confused as to where the small voice is coming from. Drying our hands on our aprons, we go to the entryway.

"Emma. Is everything all right?" I ask.

"Yep. Me and Mr. Bear came back with Papa," she explains.

Both Maria and I stuff ourselves into the door frame and see Cole pacing repeatedly back and forth, from the edge of the grass then back to his horse.

"Go and see what he wants, Tessa," Maria says with urgency. She puts her hand into my back and shoves me out the door. I hear it slam behind me.

Having no choice, I steady myself and walk down the steps. I look over my shoulder and see Maria's face glued to the window as she watches me go.

I can't tell if Cole is angry, so I approach him cautiously. But then again, if he remembers that I clocked him with a skillet, I couldn't blame him if he is mad. I have to face him sooner or later. I guess sooner comes first.

"Cole. Is everything OK?" I ask weakly.

Now he is circling me, and I feel like a meal for a hungry predator. He doesn't answer me right away. I stand there wringing my hands, almost to the point of bolting.

"Tessa. I have been thinking, and everything's not OK," he says.

"All right. Do you wish to talk about it?"

"I will only talk about it on one condition: you do not interrupt," he says.

"OK, I won't," I respond.

It is suddenly hard to breathe, and surely it's warmer out than it was a few seconds ago. My mouth has gone dry, as if I have swallowed cotton.

"Tessa, I can't do this anymore. Seeing you as often as I do drives a stake right through my chest. So deep it hurts." He walks to me and looks me directly in the eyes.

"I remember, Tessa."

"You do?" I choke out.

"Uh-huh, and you're interrupting."

I feel my composure starting to crack. I open my mouth to save my own hide and explain why I hit him. He stops me short by putting his finger to my lips.

"I remember almost everything. It took me a while, but I did. Not allowing myself to believe it, I didn't see it or think it could be true." He speaks in a whisper seething with sarcasm and accusation.

Growing more and more irritated with him because he won't get to the point, I have had enough. If he is playing with me like a cat with a mouse, I'll give him what he wants: a full confession. Slapping his hand away from my face, I bring hell on him.

"Fine!" I yell. "I did it. Is that what you wanted to hear?"

My hands are clenched into fists by my sides.

"You are the one who sneaked into my house, so I beat you down with my skillet. Serves you right if you ask me," I finish.

He takes a minute to think about what I just admitted. Curiosity flashes across his face. "I thought I fell down your stairs," he says in all seriousness. "What are you talking about?"

"What are *you* talking about?" I demand.

"Enough of this nonsense," he tells me as he stomps toward me so fast that I almost back up. But I stand my ground.

He cups my face with his hands, and I can feel the back of my eyes starting to sting.

"Tessa, I have something to say. I came by the night before to tell you what it is I need to say," he says softly.

"Say what it is." My voice wavers. "Tell me," I plead.

"Golden brown," he answers.

"What?" I asked surprised.

Liquid Quiver

"Come on, Tessa. If I can remember, so can you."

Thinking back I can't place where he would have gotten such a thing as that. When it finally hits me, our eyes lock, and I know he can see into my very soul. I can't help but cry. With his thumb, he wipes away the tear that escapes down my cheek.

"I love you too, Tessa, I always have. And I like my pancakes golden brown."

Tonya S. Murray was born and raised in a small town in southern Texas. On her fifth birthday she received her first horse, named Tiny. When she wasn't in school she rode from sun up to sun down. Riding her trusted mount she fought off Indians and slayed a dragon or two. Tiny was both her friend and mentor.

She now lives in another small town in Eastern Washington where her and her family still enjoys horses. For eight hours a day and rotating weekends, she lives and works at a fish hatchery. In her spare time you will find her reading, writing and listening to music.

Sometimes when she rides her buckskin mare, she allows herself to become the girl she once was. Picking up right where she left off, letting herself dream and imagine all things possible.

Made in the USA
Charleston, SC
22 October 2015